D1288074

Tribe of Star Bear

Sept 19/98

For Michelle;

With Much Love,

Namaste,

Victoria

XO

For Simcha

Tribe of Star Bear

by

Victoria Mihalyi

BOREALIS
BOOK PUBLISHERS

1998

Canadian Cataloguing in Publication Data

Mihalyi, Victoria
    Tribe of Star Bear

ISBN 0-88887-830-3 (bound) – ISBN 0-88887-832-X (pbk.)

I. Title

PS8576.I29535T74 1998   JC813'.54   C98-900544-3
PZ7.M44TR 1998

Cover by Bull's Eye Design, Ottawa, Canada. Author's photo by Bear Studios, New Market, Canada; phoot of bear on cover by Art Wolfe, Seattle, U.S.A.

Printed and bound in Canada on acid free paper.

Borealis Press
9Ashburn Drive
Nepean, Ontario K2E 6N4
Canada

Thank You to Glenn Clever, Karin English,
Amber Matthews, Rosie Mihalyi, Farley Mowat,
Josephine Newman, Veronica Schami,
Jim Strecker, and Frank Tierney.

Special thanks to Lynne Thomas,
my mentor and beloved friend.

And to my husband, Max Miller—it would not have
been possible without you—thank you Sweetheart

When the Earth has been ravaged
And the animals are dying
A tribe of people
From all races, creeds, and colors
Will put their faith in deeds
Not words
To make the land green again.
They shall be known as the
Warriors of the Rainbow,
Protectors of the Earth.

— Hopi Indian Prophecy

Chapters

1

The Gathering

Oooo Berry
Best Berry
Blue Berry
Bear Berry
Ooooooo Berry

sang Bohadea. It wasn't a *real* bearsong. It was just a silly ditty that Bohadea had made up as she lay sprawled out in the middle of the blueberry patch. The morning sun glinted off her glossy black coat. Her ears twitched at the buzz of a gnat. Her muzzle, normally the color of maple sugar, was stained blue with berry juice. Blueberry leaves and bits of twig clung to her fur, and part of a squashed berry was stuck on the end of her nose.

Oooo Berry
Best Berry
Blue ...

Bohadea suddenly lifted her nose and sniffed at the air. "Hmmph," she snorted curiously. It was an unfamiliar scent. Odd and vaguely unpleasant but it didn't have the smell of danger on it. She shook her huge head and lumbered to her feet. *What to do? What to do?* Eat more berries, she decided.

It was time to move on to a fresh patch anyhow. She padded off a few paces in the direction of the rising sun and chose a clump of bushes that seemed to sag under the weight of their fat gleaming berries. Bohadea took an entire branch into her mouth. "Mmmm," she sighed, her eyes half-closed with pleasure. A tiny gust of wind ruffled her fur. Leaves shivered in the breeze. And there was that smell again! Stronger than last time.

Bohadea poked her nose high up in the air and followed the strange scent to the edge of the blueberry patch where a deer trail began. Everybody used the trail: rabbits, wolves, chipmunks, raccoons, bears; but it was called a deer trail because the deer were the ones who took the trouble to keep it tidy. They clipped and pruned and trimmed things on a regular basis.

Raccoons, on the other hand, were natural-born slobs. They mocked the deer, calling them "neat-nuts" and "tidy-toes," and they pranced around with their faces all puckered up and their tails stuck straight up in the air doing deer impressions. The deer just turned up their noses and ignored the raccoons. Or they had, until the night of the last full moon. On that particular night, the raccoons had held a wild noisy party right on the open trail, and left behind a mess of peach pits, corn husks, and apple cores for the deer to clean up. The deer were furious and filed an official complaint with the Forest Council. It was open hostilities now.

But all seemed peaceful this morning. Trees as old as the legend of Star Bear rose up to touch the sky. Snowberries crept around logs, orange and purple mushrooms capped the green moss, and bunchberries glistened like rubies scattered across the forest floor. The only thing that tainted the day was that funny smell.

It grew stronger as Bohadea set off along the deer trail. She wound her way through the old pine stands, past the cedar grove, across the stream, and finally clambered up onto Lookout Rock. Whatever made the smell was very nearby and Bohadea was not foolish enough to stumble onto some strange creature from Far Away without getting a peak at it first. She nestled into the hazel thicket, then carefully and very quietly nosed her way forward. Without rustling a single leaf, she parted the branches and peered out onto the clearing beneath.

Shining Star Bear! breathed Bohadea.

There in the grass, curled up in a tight ball, was a little creature no bigger than a cub with a thick mane of long golden fur at the top of its head and a bald little heart-shaped face. Its body and limbs were covered with a strange brightly colored pelt in shades of heather and fireweed. Bohadea's heart went out to the odd little animal. It reminded her of a lost bear cub—although it was much too skinny for a cub—and Bohadea wondered if it had lost its mother and couldn't find any food by itself.

Part of her wanted to dash straight into the clearing to rescue the small creature. But she knew better than that. One must never disturb the young of another. After all, the thing's mother could be lurking nearby, and who knows how big she might be. But then again, if this little one had such a strong scent, wouldn't its mother's smell be even stronger? Yet, there was no scent of anyone other than the cub about. Bohadea decided to risk it.

She climbed back down Lookout Rock and picked her way quietly around to the edge of the clearing. Again she parted the branches, peered out, then sniffed the air one last time to make sure there was no mother about.

Bohadea stepped softly into the clearing and over to the little heather-pink cub. She nosed it once under the chin, and gently touched the hind leg. It stirred and grunted softly, as a waking cub will do, and then its eyes blinked open.

"Aaaa," screeched the cub, scrambling up onto its behind.

"Aaaa," cried Bohadea, jumping back in fright.

"Oh," gasped the cub, its eyes as wide and blue as a summer's sky.

Bohadea had never seen eyes that color before, not on any other forest creature, not ever, and it made her forget to be frightened. "The sky's in your eyes!" she exclaimed.

The poor cub just stared at her, not saying a word, but sliding a little further backwards on its rump.

"Where on earth did you get blue eyes from?" asked Bohadea.

"From my mother," said the cub shakily. "Almost everybody on her side of the family has blue eyes."

Bohadea looked about with alarm. "Your mother? Did she bring you here?"

The cub blinked at Bohadea, its lip began to quiver, it sniffed, and then burst into tears. "I don't know where my mother is," it cried, "we set up camp on the pebbles by the lake and I just went off to find some pinenuts so we could make a pesto sauce for dinner, and before I knew what had happened, I was lost. I walked around till it got dark and then I just fell asleep here."

"Oh my," said Bohadea. "I knew it! I had a feeling you were lost."

"Tchip, tchip, tchip," came a sound from above. They both looked up into the arms of an old oak tree that over-hung the clearing, and there sat a squirrel with a big bushy tail and a thick fluffy coat the color of red chestnuts.

"Oh. Hello, Olli," called Bohadea.

"Good morning, Bohadea Bear," the squirrel called back politely. "I was up on Lookout Rock collecting some hazelnuts, when I saw you down there." He peered curiously over her shoulder at the little creature on the grass. "Who is that?" he chattered. "Who is it? Who? Who? Who?"

"Um … that's my new cub!" Bohadea blurted out.

"Tcheee," scoffed the squirrel. "I didn't fall out of an acorn shell yesterday, you know. I can see what it is. That's no bear cub. That," he pronounced, "is a human."

"A human?" repeated Bohadea, somewhat taken aback. She swung her great head around just in time to see the little human clamber straight up onto its hind legs and dust itself off with its forepaws. "I've heard about them," she said with awe in her voice, "but I've never seen one before. Are you sure it's a human?"

"Sure I'm sure," squeaked Olli. "My cousin who came to live here from Far Away told me all about them. He said they always carry around a special kind of nut that has two nuts inside every shell. He says, if you sit up straight, stare them right in the eye, and think nut-thoughts, they'll hand one over." Having said this, Olli sat up very straight on the branch and glared down at the little human, staring it straight in the eye.

Bohadea looked from Olli to the human and back to Olli again. "Nothing's happening," she said. "It's not doing anything, it's just standing there. Are you sure you got the story right?"

"You two are being very rude," said the human.

"Tchip," said Olli. Bohadea raised her eyebrows in surprise. The human balled up her forepaws and plunked them down on her hips. "Where I come from," she said, "you don't talk about people who are standing right there, like they weren't even in the room with you."

"Room," chirped Olli. "Room. Room. Room. What's a room?"

"Oh, a clearing then. Just say it's a forest clearing like this one. And everybody's in it together. And anyway, the point is, if you have any questions, you can ask me. You don't have to talk about me like I wasn't here."

Olli and Bohadea looked at each other, then they looked back at the human, neither one saying a single thing.

The little human sighed. "First off," she said, "I am a girl. I am not an *it*. I am a *she*. And I will thank you *not* to refer to me as an *it* any more." She paused. The squirrel and the bear blinked at her. "And the squirrel's right," she said, "I am a human. And the nut you were talking about is a peanut."

"Told you so. Told you so," squeaked Olli.

"A lost human," said Bohadea.

"Yeah, a lost one," said the girl, sadly.

"By what name do they call you?" asked Bohadea.

"Amber," said the girl. "My name is Amber."

"Amburrr," said Bohadea. "I am known as Bohadea."

"Ollidollinderi. Ollidollinderi," shouted Olli, jumping up and down on the oak branch, making the leaves dance in the sunlight. "I am Ollidollinderi. But the bears all call me Olli, so I guess you can too. Got any peanuts?"

"No, I'm afraid I don't, Olli. I have nothing at all to eat. In fact, I'm pretty hungry myself."

"Yes. I knew it," said Bohadea. "I had a feeling. Much too skinny. Just like a bag of sticks."

"I'll show you where the hazelnuts are," Olli volunteered. He rushed back along the oak branch, down the trunk, and scurried across the clearing to where Amber stood. "Come on, come on, let's go," he peeped, hopping up and down.

"If I was at camp I would've had pancakes for breakfast," said Amber wistfully.

"No pancake bushes here," said Olli impatiently. He dashed around Amber in excited little circles. "No pancakes. Just hazelnuts. Lots of hazelnuts." And off he went racing toward Lookout Rock.

"Come along, then," said Bohadea, lumbering after Olli. "We'll get some nuts first, and then I'll show you my blueberry patch. We can eat there till the sun reaches the treetops, and then I'll make you up a nice batch of spearmint mash, and we'll dig up some lovely fat grubs to go with it, and then …"

"I don't think I'd like grubs very much," interrupted Amber. She was trying not to be impolite, but her nose still wrinkled up with disgust.

"Hurry up, hurry up," called Olli. He had run straight up the face of Lookout Rock and was already perched at the edge of the hazel thicket.

"We've got to get some healthy food into you," said Bohadea. And she led Amber around to the far side of Lookout Rock, which was a lot easier for non-squirrels to climb.

"I think I'd rather have berries than grubs," said Amber.

"Hmm," said Bohadea with disapproval. "Well, I guess we could go down to the bramble patch by the bog then. And maybe on the way back we'll visit the beehive for some honey. You do like honey, don't you?"

"Yeah," nodded Amber. "But I'd like to get back to camp. Maybe you guys could help me find my way back. My parents will be so worried by now."

"Oh dear," grunted Bohadea. She nudged aside a log, clearing the path to the top for Amber, and then shouldered her way into the hazel thicket.

"Tcheeez," complained Olli, "what took you so long?" He already had a neat little pile of empty nutshells stacked beside him.

"Amburrr wants us to help her find her den-place," said Bohadea doubtfully.

"I don't know where it is," said Olli. His cheeks were lumpy and his words smudged together because of all the nuts he had stuffed into his mouth.

"Me neither," said Bohadea. "But I think she must have come from Far Away." Bohadea plucked a nut and crunched it open between her teeth.

"Lake Wakimika," said Amber. "We made camp on the beach there."

"Never heard of it," said Olli.

"Me neither," said Bohadea. "Sounds like Far Away to me."

"Ohhh," groaned Amber. She flopped down cross-legged on a grassy spot between the bushes and let her head drop into her hands. A mane of honey-gold hair slipped down over her face. "I'll never get back!" she cried unhappily.

"Don't be sad," Bohadea pleaded. "We'll figure something out." She quickly broke off a hazel branch laden with clumps of brown nuts and dropped it in Amber's lap. "The nuts will make you feel better. Eat some nuts, and then we'll decide what to do."

Amber picked up the branch and yanked a couple of the nuts loose. "I don't have a nutcracker," she said glumly." I can't eat nuts without a nutcracker."

"What's wrong with your teeth?" asked Olli, sitting up high on his haunches and looking at her oddly.

"Nothing's wrong with my teeth," said Amber. "I just can't crack nuts with them, that's all."

"Then what good are they?" asked Olli as he skillfully split open another hazelnut. "You may as well be a big dumb old bird if you can't crack nuts with your teeth."

"Now, Olli," said Bohadea crossly, "maybe the young ones of her kind can't crack nuts till they're full grown. Why, I remember how my sister Potelia's cubs had to have everything done for them when they were her size."

"My uncle Mike can get a beer cap off the bottle with his teeth," said Amber proudly. "But I don't think even he could crack open hard nuts like these ones."

"I'll crack them for you Amburrr," Bohadea offered kindly. She nuzzled Amber under the chin, then pulled the branch back toward her and began to take the nuts into her mouth one at a time, cracking the shells open, and spitting the fat round nutmeats into Amber's lap.

Amber didn't want to eat them at first, on account of the bear spit, but her stomach was growling so hungrily that she popped one into her mouth anyway. And then another, and another. They were the most delicious nuts she'd ever tasted.

"After we've had our nuts," said Bohadea—she cracked open another and dropped it into Amber's hand—"I think we'd better stop by Hog's Hollow so you can roll in some mud and get that smell off you."

"Good idea," chirped Olli. "Stinky, winky," he giggled, rushing up the trunk of a nearby tree to pelt Amber with nutshells.

"I do not smell!" said Amber, tossing her hair back angrily. "I might have a few leaves and things stuck in my hair, but I had a bath in the lake yesterday afternoon." She pulled at a coil of wavy hair, plucked out a dried leaf, then sniffed the hair. "See! You can still smell the Pearly Peach shampoo." She stretched her hair out toward them, offering the perfumed scent as proof.

"Pee-U," shrieked Olli, scrambling back down the trunk and rushing past Amber to steal one of the nuts from her lap. "Purrly Wurrly Stinkeroni. Stinky. Stinky. Stinky," he sang.

"Stupid squirrel," grumbled Amber, fluffing her hair up, then smoothing it down over her shoulders.

"Oh dear me," clucked the bear. "I shouldn't have mentioned it. I shouldn't have—"

Just then an enormous shadow passed overhead and Bohadea's words were drowned out by the powerful wing-beats of a most magnificent bird.

"EAGLE!" shrieked Olli, and overcome by the fright of it, he leapt straight into the big front pocket of Amber's heather-pink jumper, where he curled up in a ball with his eyes squeezed tightly shut and his paws clamped down over his ears.

Amber's hands flew up to her cheeks. Her eyes widened to two blue circles, and her mouth made a pink round O. She had never seen an eagle before. Never would she have guessed that any bird could be as huge and splen-did as this one was.

The eagle glided downward, his wings spread so wide that they blocked out the sunlight. Long sharp talons pushed forward like the landing gear of an airplane, and he touched down on the splintered rim of a tall and jagged tree trunk. The top of that tree had broken off a long time ago and nothing else of it remained but a few moss-covered logs scattered here and there around the hazel thicket.

The eagle shrugged his shoulders, fluffed up his feath-ers, and then folded back his great wings. Amber couldn't keep herself from staring. He was so beautiful. His eyes were a deep rich brown and shiny as marbles. His feathers were like autumn oak leaves, the tips dusted gold with sun-light. He wore a mantle like a lion's mane of pure copper about this head, and on his legs was an elegant ruffle of feathers. A patch of pale yellow crowned his sharp black beak, a beak that to Amber looked powerful enough to crush a tin of peeled tomatoes.

"'Morning, Bohadea," the eagle said to the bear. Amber could feel Olli shivering in her pocket.

"Good morning, Almedon," sang Bohadea, clearly delighted by the eagle's unexpected visit. "What brings you to these parts on such a lovely morning?"

"A disaster brings me," said the eagle solemnly.

"Oh dear me," gasped Bohadea. "Have those silly raccoons gone and upset the deer again?"

"It's not that simple," said Almedon, his voice full of gloom. He swiveled his head in a half circle, and stared straight at Amber, who caught her breath as a silvery third eyelid flicked down over the eagle's eyes. And then he turned back to Bohadea.

"What are you doing with that strange creature?" he asked the bear. "Are you having her for lunch?"

"I suppose so. The poor thing is lost and I don't think we'll be able to find her den before lunch, so I was planning on taking her back to my blueberry patch for a nice berry picnic."

"You plan to fatten her up before you eat her?"

"Oh, good gracious, no," gasped Bohadea. "Amburrr is my friend. I don't eat my friends."

"Perfectly good meat going to waste then," grumbled Almedon. "I don't see what good she is if you aren't going to eat her."

"You eagle types are all alike," scolded Bohadea. "You think that everybody in this forest was put here for you to eat."

"Yeah," squeaked Olli from inside Amber's pocket. "Eagle, schmeagle."

Almedon's head swiveled around toward Amber again. She clapped her hands over her pocket to stifle Olli. "Yes, well," said the eagle, "there isn't going to be a forest for much longer. That is why I have come."

"Whatever are you talking about?" asked Bohadea. "Of course there will be a forest. There has always been a forest, and there will be a forest until the end of the world."

"Then that is the news I have come to bring you," said Almedon from his perch atop the broken tree trunk. "The end of the world is coming."

"Oh pooh," said Bohadea. "Wherever did you hear such rubbish?"

"It's not something I heard, Bohadea," said Almedon gravely. "I saw it!"

"What did you see?"

"RUMBLERS," he said, that one fateful word rolling across the hazel thicket like a huge black thundercloud. A chill ran up Amber's spine and she felt Olli scrambling inside her pocket to dig himself in even deeper.

"Rumblers?" repeated Bohadea. "You mean the Rumblers from the Star Bear Legends?"

"The same," said Almedon.

"But those are just stories. The Rumblers aren't real!"

"The Rumblers are real," said Almedon. "I have flown from the shores of Porcupine Lake to the Cliffs of Pointy Noggins, and I can tell you Bohadea, as I have told the others: Rumblers are eating up the forest. They are destroying every living thing!"

"Even bears?" asked Bohadea in disbelief.

"Even bears," said Almedon. "Every one of them is as big as twenty bears put together. And when they leave a place there is nothing left. *Nothing!* Just tree stumps and black earth for as far as an eagle's eye can see."

"Oh my stars," moaned Bohadea. "We must do something at once." She began to pace back and forth mumbling to herself: "… birds can drop acorns on them, gophers can dig trap holes, raccoons can sneak up at night and pour tree sap on them.…"

"Exactly what is a Rumbler?" asked Amber rising to her feet and stepping closer to the tall stump where Almedon was perched.

"Don't get too close to the eagle," hissed Olli from her pocket. "Don't get too close."

Almedon turned his head slowly, like a grand old man accustomed to being treated as a king. He narrowed his eyes to two dark slits and studied the girl for a moment. The silver eyelid flickered once and he opened his eyes wide again. "Peculiar creature," he said to no one in particular. "Most peculiar."

"I am a human," said Amber. "And not at all peculiar. I'm a regular kid."

"I don't like humans," said Almedon, and he turned his head away to look out over the clearing.

"Well, I've never met any other eagles, but if they're all like *you*, then I don't like eagles either."

"Oh please don't argue," cried Bohadea. "The Rumblers are coming and we must figure out what to do."

"Maybe I could help if I knew what they were," said Amber.

"Monsters," whispered Olli, poking his head out over the top of her pocket. "Horrible monsters with big shiny teeth." Almedon stirred at the sound of the squirrel's voice, but Olli was too quick and ducked back down into Amber's pocket before Almedon's head was even halfway around.

"According to bear legend," said Bohadea solemnly, "a long time ago there was a forest creature known as a Saroo. The Saroos lived in grassy circles in the forest, like fairy-people, and made magic with willow sticks and colored stones.

"The Saroos arranged everything in circles. Their paths were circles, their dens were circles, their magic stones were put in circles. Until one day a wandering Saroo brought back some smooth oddly cut, red crystals. They looked so strange and unusual that he decided to put them into a strange and unusual pattern. He arranged them in the shape of a square.

"When the other Saroos saw this strange new shape, they too began arranging their stones into squares. And before you knew it, everything was being arranged into squares. And this is when they began to have problems, because the forest was filled with all kinds of natural circle shapes: tree trunks and beach pebbles and rain puddles all made circle shapes; the moon and the sun and even the clouds made circle shapes. But no where in the forest could the Saroos find a natural square shape; and fitting all their square shapes into a round forest became more trouble than it was worth."

"So they went back to making circles?" asked Amber.

"No." Bohadea shook her huge head. "That seems like the sensible thing to do. Especially considering that they couldn't squeeze one single drop of magic out of all their squares put together. But still the Saroos didn't go back to making circles. Instead, they left the forest to go in search of a more geometrically shaped place where they could live in their squares."

"My bedroom is square-shaped," said Amber. "But our tent was one of those big round ones. I wish I knew where that tent was right now," she sighed.

Almedon swiveled his head smoothly around to face Amber. His eyes flicked over her sternly. "Be still," he commanded. Then he turned to Bohadea. "Get on with it Bohadea. Time is short."

Amber wondered if all eagles were as bossy as this one. He reminded her of Mr. Boswick, the old man at the convenience store back home who snapped at the kids like a nasty old mud turtle.

"Well," sniffed Bohadea, "to make a long story short, the Saroos found a trail studded with those strange blood-red crystals that had formed the very first square. Taking this as a good omen, they followed the crystal trail out of the forest to the ends of the earth. And there, at last, they found the biggest, flattest, most perfect square any Saroo had ever set eyes upon. And to their great delight, they discovered that this perfect square was made entirely of the strange smooth red crystals they so treasured.

"At first, the Saroos only took little bits of the fine red crystal to make their square-shaped decorations with. But soon they branched out into rectangles and boxes, and they began to build their dens of red crystal. They needed more and more and more of the red stones and began to dig it from a square-shaped hole right in the very center of the great smooth crystal desert.

"Their dens became bigger and taller and wider and the hole from which they dug the red crystal became deeper and deeper and deeper. They built a whole city of red crystal and still they wanted more and more of the precious stones.

"The legend says that many wise bears have made the dangerous journey to warn the Saroos to stop digging up the red stones, because," and here Bohadea paused dramatically, "because that great crystal square is the only door on earth that leads straight into the Pit of Darkness where the Rumblers dwell. The Rumblers were sealed down there by Star Bear, a long, long time ago, when the moon was young, and forest people were still just a twinkle of lights.

"But Star Bear predicted that one day the Saroos would dig to the very bottom of the hole, and when the last red crystal had been plucked from its floor, there would be a great crack of thunder, the floor would turn to dust, and from the Pit of Darkness the Rumblers would come, led by Dreeg, King of the Rumblers.

"Giants, they are, with teeth and claws sharp as spikes, and eyes big as cabbages that shine red in the dark. And they have no heart or soul like bears, just a big empty pit in their middle. All they want to do is fill that pit. But it can never get full. So if they are set loose, they will eat and eat and eat until everything in the world is gone."

Amber's eyes were wide as saucers. Olli stood on tip-toe in her pocket, his little brown nose poking out over the top, his tiny fingers clutching at the pink cotton pocket edge, his black eyes bulging with fright (even though he already knew the entire story by heart, for it was not just a bear legend, but a squirrel legend, too).

"That can't be true," said Amber, shaking her head. "I've never heard of such a thing."

Almedon swung his head toward her. Olli ducked. "What you have *heard* is of no consequence to anyone. Do you deny the evidence of an eagle's eye?" he boomed.

"Well, no … not really," shrugged Amber. "It just seems so … unreal."

"What you think makes no difference at all," said Almedon. "The Rumblers will eat you just as soon as they will eat a bear or a tree or a bug." His silvery eyelids flickered. "Or for that matter, the squirrel you're hiding in your pelt-pocket," he said.

"Tchuk, tchuk, tchuk," squeaked Olli. "I'm a cracked nut now," he wailed, trying to fling himself head first through the bottom of Amber's pocket.

Amber cupped both her hands over Olli's hiding place. "This squirrel is my friend," she warned the eagle, with a frown. "If you try to hurt him, you'll have to get by me first."

Almedon laughed a deep gravelly eagle laugh. "Bohadea," he chuckled, "your human friend is a brave one."

"I mean it," Amber said angrily.

"I will not harm your squirrel, Human," said Almedon. "You are both friends of Bohadea. I will not harm either of you."

"Good," snapped Amber.

"Enough of this bickering," scolded Bohadea. "We have Rumblers to think about. Almedon? Does the Forest Council know about this yet?"

Almedon lowered his head, the sun danced across the feathered mantle at the back of his neck and glinted off the curve of his beak. Finally he spoke: "They knew of the coming of the Rumblers before yesterday's dusk," he said grimly. "Lone Hawk of Two Tip Hill landed in the Council clearing only a few wingbeats after I did, and together we told of what we had seen. But they wanted to see for themselves and we could not dissuade them. The head wolf led the whole Council right up to the Rumblers. They were going to negotiate." Almedon sadly shook his head. "There is a Forest Council no more."

Bohadea slumped down onto her rump. "Someone must be left," she said, her voice quivering like a raindrop on a willow leaf.

"Lone Hawk and I are all that remain," said Almedon. "Some were eaten right away. The others were taken prisoner. I rode the wind up beneath the clouds and followed them along their path of destruction to a great hole. I don't think it was the Pit where the Rumbler King lives. Just some kind of way station where they take the prisoners.

I waited all night. I waited past dawn. But they never came out again, and it became too dangerous to wait any longer with all the Rumblers about."

An eerie silence settled in the hazel thicket. No one moved. No one even seemed to breathe, and then Bohadea spoke softly: "It's just as Star Bear predicted it would be," she said. "In the winter times, when we were all snug in our den, my mother used to recite the Star Bear Legends to me and my sister, Potelia. And she sang us all the Mystical Bear Songs. There was one in particular, I remember every word. It tells of how the forest people would defeat the Rumblers."

"Song of the Warriors," nodded Almedon wisely. "It is part of eagle tradition, too."

"Will you sing it for us?" Amber asked Bohadea.

"Yes. Sing, sing, sing," squealed Olli.

"Oh, I couldn't," said Bohadea shyly. "It can only be done when there are other bears present. Otherwise who would beat out the stick rhythms? I must have music if I am to sing."

"Shell music?" asked Olli eagerly. "I can play the shells. Why those ones right there are perfect," he pointed out a pair of fine half rounds of hazelnut shell that lay on the ground.

Seeing that Olli was not yet brave enough to retrieve the shells for himself, Amber stooped over to pick them up. Poor Olli nearly fell right out of her pocket when she leaned forward, and would have, too, if he hadn't latched himself onto a pawful of Amber's hair.

"Tchip, tchip," he scolded her. "Tchip, tchip, tchip."

She handed him the nutshells and he snatched them away with a frown. But one beat of the shells and Olli was happy again. *Da-da, de-da-da, de-da-da-da-dum,* he tapped out with the shells.

"It's not right," said Bohadea shaking her head. "More bearish. It needs to be more bearish."

DA-DA, DE-DA-DA, DE-DA-DA-DA-DUM, tapped Olli.

"Still not right," Bohadea shook her head. "Like this!" She took two hazel sticks into her paws and struck them together: *Pa-Pum, Pa-Pum, Pa-Pum, Pa-Pum.*

"I can do that. I can do that," cried Olli. And he did, repeating perfectly the rhythm Bohadea had just played.

Amber reached for a pair of sticks, this time bending at the knees so as not to disturb Olli. And following the squirrel's lead, she rapped the sticks together, beating out the tune of Bohadea's bearsong.

Almedon blinked and shifted uneasily, but a moment later Amber could hear a clacking sound coming from the tall jagged tree trunk where Almedon sat, and she could see that his beak was moving in time to the beat.

Bohadea tapped her foot, cleared her throat, and began:

> Of earth and air
> Of squirrel and bear
> Of fur and feather
> And pelt of heather
> A tribe will bravely come.
>
> Wisdom they'll seek
> At Half Moon Peak
> By whisker of cat
> Through cave of bat
> To the beat of Istarna's drum.
>
> With fear they'll walk
> By Weeping Rock
> With grit and wit

Down into the Pit
To battle the Rumbler King.

A twinkle of light
Will pierce the night
The tribe will rise
To the Rumbler's demise
And all the forest will sing.

"That was fun," laughed Amber. "I like that song."

"But don't you see?" cried Bohadea springing onto her hind legs. "Of earth and air," she hollered, pointing first to Amber and then to Almedon.

"Of squirrel and bear," she cried, now pointing at Olli and then poking her paw back at herself.

"Of fur and feather and pelt of heather," she recited the words, with both paws thumping at the air for emphasis.

"Pelt of heather," she repeated more quietly, gesturing at the front of Amber's pink jumper. Bohadea dropped back down onto her forepaws, her head nodding in agreement with herself. "We are the Tribe of Star Bear," she said matter-of-factly.

"Absurd!" exclaimed Almedon. "You are twisting the legend all out of proportion. In the first place, the coming of a Warrior Tribe to defeat the Rumblers was foretold by the Great Sun Eagle and not some old Star Bear. And there is certainly no mention of any foolish humans among the warriors. Much less a squirrel," he harrumphed.

"The Rumbler legend lives among all the forest people, Almedon," said Bohadea crossly. "But it was Star Bear who sealed the Rumblers into the Pit of Darkness in the first place. It was *she* who foretold of their coming back up onto the Earth. And your Great Sun Eagle did nothing but translate it into Eaglese."

"Hmmph," sniffed Almedon.

"Go ahead Almedon," challenged Bohadea, "recite the first verse of the Sun Eagle version."

"Well," said Almedon, clearing his throat, "it doesn't say anything about there being any squirrels involved, that's for certain."

"What does it say, exactly?" asked Bohadea.

"It says: *'Great majestic bird of the air,*
Most humble friend of the bear …'"

"Ah-huh," shouted Bohadea. "There you have it, Almedon: 'Most humble friend of the bear.' That's it. That's the squirrel."

Almedon frowned.

"Humble, bumble," grumbled Olli, peering out over the edge of Amber's pocket.

"We must go to Half Moon Peak. We must find Istarna," said Bohadea. "At once."

"Who is Istarna?" asked Amber.

"Istarna," said Bohadea with great respect, "is the oldest and the wisest bear in all the forest. She is so old, they say that her fur has gone completely white. And Istarna is the last living descendant of Star Bear. Star Bear was her great great great great great … well, I don't know exactly how many greats, but Star Bear was the grandmother of all the bears that came before Istarna. She will know how to stop the Rumblers."

"Waste of time," grumbled Almedon. "If you want to know how to fight a great battle, you must speak with a great warrior, not some dotty old great-grandmother of a bear."

Bohadea stuck her nose in the air and snorted noisily. "Istarna is not anybody's grandmother," she snuffled at Almedon. "She is a great-*granddaughter.* A great great great great … well I don't know how many greats, but a lot of them … Istarna is a great-granddaughter of Star Bear.

And since we are the Tribe of Star Bear, we must find her, just like the legend says we must."

"To the beat of Istarna's drum," chanted Olli, clacking his nutshells together.

Amber tapped her sticks in time.

Bohadea picked up the rhythm and began to sing the second verse again:

> Wisdom they'll seek
> At Half Moon Peak
> By whisker of cat
> Through cave of bat
> To the beat of Istarna's drum.

Amber stopped playing her sticks and let them fall to the ground. Nervously, she gathered up a dusty blonde curl and twisted it around her finger. Without looking Bohadea in the eye, she said: "I was just thinking ..." Then she glanced timidly at Almedon. "Maybe, before you leave, Mr. Almedon, you could fly up over Lake Wakimika and look for my campsite. I really have to get back there. I ... I don't really belong here."

"There's no time," said Almedon gruffly. "The fate of the forest is at stake."

"I'm sure Almedon will be happy to look for your den-place as soon as the Rumblers have been sealed back into the Pit of Darkness," said Bohadea kindly. "But your place is here, with the tribe. You're one of us now."

"Oh," breathed Amber unhappily. "My parents will be so worried."

"Don't worry, Amburrr," Bohadea padded over to the girl and gently brushed up alongside her, as she would do to an anxious cub. "We'll get this Rumbler business all sorted out, and then we'll *all* help you find your den-place." With her eyes she flicked a warning in Almedon's direction. And Almedon, who was just about to say something not very helpful, clamped his beak shut and preened one of the feathers on his chest.

Amber let her hand drop to Bohadea's back, and absently stroked the thick soft fur there. She sighed. "Well, I guess we'd better think up a plan then. These Rumbler things sound pretty mean."

2

The Journey Begins

Almedon was very still while the others gathered a few nuts to take along on their journey. He didn't turn his head, but his eyes kept sliding from Olli to Amber, Amber to Olli, and back again. He couldn't get over it. A half-grown human and a fur-brained squirrel among the Warrior Tribe? Eagles and hawks and wolves were warriors. A bear, perhaps. Maybe even a marten or a weasel. But a human and a squirrel? Truth was, Almedon did not believe for one moment that this sorry lot had anything at all to do with the Warrior Tribe. The little band of stragglers bumping about the hazel thicket was most surely *not* the legendary Tribe that would rise from the forest to defeat the Rumblers.

The squirrel, Almedon noticed, had become much bolder now. He sat perched on the girl's shoulder and only hopped back into her pocket when he noticed the eagle staring at him. It made Almedon's mouth water and his talons itch to see a squirrel flitting about in the open like that, but he had given his word and he must now do his very best not to think of Olli as lunch.

"We'd better go now," announced Bohadea. "We'll find Istarna at Half Moon Peak and she'll give us the magic we need to stop the Rumblers."

"Hmmph," snorted Almedon. "Half Moon Peak, indeed! There is no such place as Half Moon Peak. It's a legend! A name from a bearsong."

Amber and Olli looked expectantly at Bohadea.

"Half Moon Peak is real!" insisted the bear. "Istarna lives there and that's where we're going." Bohadea set her jaw in a hard, stubborn line.

"Then, in which direction is Half Moon Peak?" the eagle demanded.

Bohadea blinked uncertainly, then reared up onto her hind legs, and with absolute conviction, pointed in the direction of her blueberry patch. "That way," she said.

Almedon lowered his head and a spark of green fire flashed across his dark eyes. "You have no idea at all, do you?" he said. "You don't know where Half Moon Peak is, and neither does anyone else, because there is NO SUCH PLACE!"

"If we go that way," Bohadea pointed again in the direction of the blueberry patch, but with far less conviction this time, "I'm sure we'll find it." *By whisker of cat, through cave of bat, to the beat of Istarna's drum,* the words of Star Bear played in her head. "We just have to find a cat, some bats, and listen for a drum, and then we'll have found Half Moon Peak."

"Only place around here with bat caves are the Cliffs of Pointy Noggins," growled Almedon.

"That's it!" Bohadea seized on his words. "Pointy Noggins is thataway," she swept a paw excitedly, gesturing to a place beyond the blueberry patch. "Half Moon Peak is at the Cliffs of Pointy Noggins."

Almedon thumped one foot in exasperation. "Don't think I don't know that you're just making this up as you go along," he scoffed at the bear.

"Where would you have us go instead, Sir?" Amber asked the eagle in a small steady voice.

He swiveled his head angrily toward the girl. *Where? Where?* He wasn't sure where. In the general direction of the Rumblers front lines, he supposed. Which was not all that far away from the Cliffs of Pointy Noggins. And what if there was some truth in the old Star Bear legend? It was, after all, a part of the Sun Eagle legends too. "All right, Bohadea," he said to the bear, "we will go to the Cliffs of Pointy Noggins. But if we find no Half Moon Peak there, then we do it my way. Agreed?"

"Agreed," nodded the bear.

"Agreed," echoed Olli.

"Follow the Big Cone Trail," said Almedon. "I'll scout up to Bear Tooth Rise. If there's any trouble, I'll be back to warn you. If it's all clear, I'll meet you there."

Bohadea nodded once, then led her little tribe from the hazel thicket. Almedon sailed up to an oak perched atop Lookout Rock and watched until they had turned onto the trail. Then he flapped his mighty wings and lifted off into the clear blue sky. He circled above the treetops for a while, watching for flashes of bear fur and the bright heather-pink pelt of the human, as they passed between the trees.

He hit a warm patch of air and rode the upward current. It carried him in slow sweeping circles: up and up he went, his sharp eyes following Amber and Bohadea until they were nothing but tiny specks that finally faded into the green of the forest. It was times like this that Almedon loved best: the world stretched out below him, the sun riding on his back and the wind curling beneath his wings. But things were different today. Today he could see an ugly black smudge on the horizon, a dead place where the Rumblers had eaten a hole into the forest. And the smudge was bigger now than it had been the last time he looked.

The tip of one wing swept upward as Almedon glided into a turn. He flapped his wings once, twice, then settled himself on course above Big Cone Trail. From this height, the trail was only a faint brownish thread weaving its way through the forest. But Almedon knew every dip and turn of the forest as well as he knew the patterns of his own feathers.

A gust of wind swept the eagle further upward and a bit off course. He lifted over the hump of air and then swooped earthward. As soon as he had a clear enough view of the trail below him, he leveled off and set himself a slow easy pace.

There were a lot of forest people cutting across Big Cone Trail, Almedon noticed. Many of them, like the deer, were moving fast. Not as fast as they would go if there was a forest fire, but a lot faster than usual. They were panicky. His eyes flicked back to the ugly black smudge on the horizon.

The Rumblers are coming!

Bohadea stopped short as a small clan of deer broke cover in front of them. The deer leapt across the narrow pathway and crashed through the undergrowth on the other side without as much as a sideways glance.

"That's the third bunch of deer we've seen rushing by," frowned Amber.

"The Rumblers are coming!" shrilled a trio of chickadees. The little birds flitted nervously above the trail, then streaked off after the deer.

"Rumblers on the march!" came a husky voice from above. "Buttercup Gully! Gone! Ruined! Destroyed!" A rustle of blue black feathers set a bough of pine needles swaying above their heads. A large crow opened and closed her wings to steady herself.

Bohadea poked her nose up at the crow and squinted: "Is it true? Did the Rumblers really destroy Buttercup Gully?"

"'Course it's true" squawked the crow, pitching so far forward she nearly toppled off her perch. "They ate my tree! Nest and all."

"Ate her tree!" Olli exclaimed with horror. "Tchip."

"Oh dear!" fretted the bear. "We've got to find Half Moon Peak. Do you know the way to Half Moon Peak?" she asked the crow.

"Nope," said the crow. "Gotta go. *Caw! Caw!*" She spread her wings and flapped off noisily, heading in the same direction as the deer and the chickadees.

"We'd better hurry," muttered the bear, padding off along the trail.

Amber sighed. She stood there for a moment, not moving, just watching as the bear waggled away. She looked back over her shoulder. The trail twisted and turned behind her. In some places it was overgrown with prickly thickets. Amber didn't think she'd be able to find her way back to the clearing from here.

"Let's go," chirped Olli. His little claws nipped at her shoulder. "Go. Go. Go."

"Okay, I'm going," she said in a huff. Amber hurried off after the bear. She knew she was going deeper into the forest. Farther from camp. Farther from her parents who would be frantic with worry by now. But what else could she do? There was no point in wandering around on her own.

Amber wondered if her father had paddled their canoe back to the forest rangers' office to report her missing. He probably had, she decided. By now there would be a search underway with helicopters and speedboats and everything. All she had to do was wait for a plane to come by, and she would be rescued. They would find her. It was just a matter of time. She stepped more lightly, skipping a little ahead of Bohadea, then suddenly froze solid in her tracks. "Oh, oh," she said under her breath.

"Oh, oh," sang Olli. For there in front of them stood four skunks. All four tails swished straight up in the air as the skunks spun around: one, two, three, four. Their rear ends were aimed straight at Amber and Olli.

"On your mark," said one skunk.

"Get set," said another.

"Hold your fire," called Bohadea.

"What for?" the third skunk demanded.

"We mean you no harm," said Bohadea.

"Are you sure?" asked the fourth skunk.

"Of course I'm sure," said Bohadea.

"Do you surrender then?" asked the first skunk.

"If you insist," said Bohadea.

"Say it!" demanded the skunk.

"Okay," shrugged Bohadea. "We surrender."

"All right, boys," said the largest skunk, as she lowered her tail and spun around. "Lower tails and about face." The smaller skunks followed suit, lowering their tails and turning around with precision timing.

"I am Mizz Fuzzlewink," sniffed the largest skunk. "And these are my boys: Tinkalouie, Lolimink, and Pinklenot," she said proudly. Each boy bobbed his head politely as his name was mentioned.

"How do you do, Mizz Fuzzlewink," said Bohadea. "I'm sorry if we alarmed you. I know everyone's a bit on edge today with all this Rumbler business. We're in something of a rush ourselves. We're looking for a place called Half Moon Peak. Have you heard of it?"

"Can't say that I have," said Mizz Fuzzlewink. "Although it sounds familiar. Do they have good grubs there?"

"I don't know," shrugged Bohadea. "Well! If you'll excuse us, we'll be getting along. We have a long journey ahead."

"Let 'em pass, boys," ordered Mizz Fuzzlewink. Tinkalouie, Lolimink, and Pinklenot shuffled off to the side, tails slightly cocked and heads tilted at a saucy angle.

Bohadea and Amber gave them a wide berth as they moved past. Amber kept her eyes on the three boys and her back to the bush as she skirted along the edge of the path.

"Make tracks," whispered Olli. "You can't trust skunks."

Bohadea picked up the pace as they hurried along Big Cone Trail, pausing only briefly now and again to ask the forest folk they encountered if they had heard of Half Moon Peak. No one had, and Bohadea was beginning to wonder: Was there really such a place as Half Moon Peak? Or was it just a myth? Was she on a mission from Star Bear? Or just chasing after the words of a bearsong? Or worse, suffering from delusions of grandeur, thinking that she was THE bear from the Tribe of Star Bear.

"Look!" shouted Olli. He bopped up and down on Amber's shoulder, pointing down the path. "Crazy raccoon, running in circles up ahead!" he announced.

"What's wrong with him?" frowned Amber.

The raccoon was not quite running. It was more like hopping—in erratic little circles, snorting and shaking his head and stopping every few seconds to shake out a paw.

Bohadea tiptoed in carefully and sniffed at him. "Not sick," she shook her head. "What's wrong with you?" she demanded loudly.

The raccoon had been so intent on his weird little dance that he hadn't seen them approaching. "Yikes," he yelped, jumping straight up in the air and landing on all fours. "Ouch!" He quickly pulled up one of his front paws and shook it out. He spit and cursed. "What's wrong with you people? Sneakin' up on a guy like that. Look at that!" he stuck his paw under Bohadea's nose. "You made it worse!"

"I don't see anything," said Bohadea. "What's wrong with it?"

"Don't see anything! How can you not see it? It's as big as a muddy old tree trunk." The raccoon poked his paw closer to her nose.

Bohadea squinted harder, but she honestly couldn't see a thing. She cast a glance at Amber, her eyebrows raised in a question.

Amber crouched down and leaned in closer to the raccoon. "Do you mind if I have a look?" she asked him.

"Go ahead," snorted the raccoon. "Have yourself a muddy good look. I'm doomed! How can I run away from the Rumblers with only three good legs?"

Amber gently took his paw into her hand, and although the raccoon carried on moaning and complaining, he didn't resist her. "OWWW," he hollered, as her finger brushed up against a thorn stuck in the soft velvety flesh of his paw. "Aw, geez, you're killin' me!" he wailed.

Amber pinched the thorn between her fingers and swiftly pulled it out. "There!" she said. She held the thorn aloft.

"I'll take that!" hollered Olli. "Here, gimme it. Gimme it. That'll make an excellent tool. Good for scraping stuff out of things." Amber handed him the thorn and Olli dove down into her pocket to stash it.

The raccoon soberly examined his paw. He shook it out, stretched his fingers, then tentatively set his foot down on the ground. Slowly he shifted his weight onto the injured paw. "Hmm, not bad," he said. He took a few steps this way and a few steps that way. "It works!" he announced. "The muddy thing works!"

The raccoon cast a sideways glance up at Amber. "I ain't got nothin' to give you right now on account of my being on the run, but once these Rumblers have been bumped off, you come on over to Sneezeweed Grove and ask for Corny-Q. I've got connections. Corny-Q can get you any kinda apple you want. As much as you can eat.

And guaranteed there won't be no peelers comin' after you once you're too stuffed to run."

"That's very kind of you," said Amber. "I do love apples. But we really must be going now. We're on our way to Half Moon Peak to find Istarna."

"Half Moon Peak, eh? Well you keep an eye out for that rogue cat, Pudd Wudd Princeling."

"Pudd Wudd Princeling!" shouted Bohadea. *"By whisker of cat!* That must be him!"

"It wouldn't surprise me none if you folks were headin' out to Half Moon Peak to settle some kinda score with this Pudd Wudd fella," said Corny-Q. "I had a run in with him myself last summer. I caught this vole, you see, fair and square. I was just about to sit down to my dinner, when this big yeller cat darts in outta nowhere and tries to scoop that muddy vole right out from under me."

"By whisker of cat, through cave of bat, to the beat of Istarna's drum," whispered Bohadea. Then her eyes snapped wide open: "Where is Half Moon Peak?" she asked the raccoon. "Can you tell us how to get there?"

"Thought you said you were goin' there to settle up with that cat?" said Corny-Q, looking somewhat perplexed. "How can you be goin' someplace if you don't know where it is?"

"We are going there!" exclaimed Bohadea. "We just aren't sure where it is, exactly. Can you tell us the way?"

"Go to the Cliffs of Pointy Noggins. It's thereabouts," said the raccoon, vaguely waving one paw. "Never actually seen Half Moon Peak myself. Just got the buzz that it's Pudd Wudd's hangout."

"The Rumblers are coming!" squawked a blackbird from a nearby treetop.

"Muddy Rumblers," muttered Corny-Q. "Gotta keep movin'. Rumblers are comin'." He waddled off into the bush.

"At least we're on the right track," nodded Bohadea, as the tip of Corny-Q's ringed tail disappeared into the undergrowth. She sniffed carefully at the air, then moved on, deep in thought.

Amber followed, humming softly to herself. Olli was nose-first down in Amber's pocket. His bushy red tail waved back and forth, tickling Amber's neck and the bottom of her chin.

"What are you doing down there, Olli," she peered down at him.

He popped out, blinked up at her, and then dove back down. "Oh, just organizing some of my stuff," came his muffled voice. The thorn had not been the only thing he had collected along their journey.

"I hope you're not stashing a whole bunch of junk in there. It's still my pocket you know."

"JUNK!" squealed Olli, flipping right back up. "I'll have you know that I've got some very valuable stuff in here."

"Like what?"

"Like this, for example." Olli tumbled down inside and then popped up with the two half shells he'd used for making bearsong music. He zipped down and up again. "Or this," he grinned, holding up a big hunk of orange fungus.

Amber had no idea what use a squirrel might have for such an odd thing, but Olli seemed so pleased with it, that all she could do was smile back at him. The squirrel climbed out of her pocket and she boosted him up onto her shoulder.

Olli *never* could have imagined that he would be riding around the forest like this, on the top end of a human. What would his brothers and sisters say if they could see him now? He sure wished they *could* see him.

And what would his friends think when they found out that Olli knew an eagle? They'd be so impressed, they'd treat him like a king. His tail began swishing with excitement. "I am King of the Squirrels," he sang, his voice as loud and bushy as an opera singer's. Smack went his tail, right across Amber's cheek.

"Olli," she complained, sweeping his tail away with her hand.

Olli wiggled his rump, fluffed up his whiskers, and sat straight up on his haunches. "I am King of the Squirrels," he sang again, his two front paws stretched out in front of him in a kingly gesture. "King, oh King, of the—"

"Hey, you noisy fuzzhead," screamed a squirrel from high up in the trees. "Shaddup! Shadiddy, shadiddy upiddy duppiddy!" It was not the voice of any squirrel that Olli knew.

"Tchurr," growled Olli, dropping back down onto his front paws and looking up into the forest canopy. "Tchurr," he growled again.

"Tchuk," came the voice from up above. "Tchuk! Who goes there? This is the Kingdom of Tumbling Puffball, you noisy fuzzhead. Who goes there, yelling about being the King? Who? Who? Who?"

Olli leapt from Amber's shoulder onto a low-hanging pine branch and scurried up its trunk, spiraling around so he could see what was above him from all different angles.

"Hey," Amber called after him. "Olli? Where are you going?"

But Olli had one thing on his mind: he wanted to get a good look at this Kingdom-of-Puffball dude.

"Tchurr," the voice rattled out a warning from above.

"Tchurr," Olli returned the challenge. He was getting closer now and could make out a blur of reddish fur up near the canopy. He stopped and squinted through the haze of green. It was one of his people all right. A red squirrel.

"Stay right where you are, fuzzhead," the voice shouted down. "You're trespassing."

"Says who?" called Olli.

"Says Tullywanooli," shouted the squirrel. "Who are you?"

"Ollidollinderi."

Tullywanooli crept a bit closer to Olli, then sat right up tall and stared hard. He twiddled his fingers, but didn't say a word.

Olli thought he was a rather weedy little fellow for someone with such a big mouth. "I didn't mean to trespass," he said, feeling kind of sorry for the nervous squirrel. "It's just that I've never heard of the Kingdom of Tumbling Puffball before and I was wondering what it was all about."

Tullywanooli stopped wiggling his fingers around. "Oh nothin'," he said, looking sideways, and up and down, and anyplace other than at Olli. "That's just what I call my tree. You see, when me and my brothers were babies we kept falling out of the nest. It runs in the family, you know. All my relatives are prone to falling out of their nests. So the neighbors started calling us the Tumbling Puffballs and it stuck." He blinked at Olli. "You don't wanna fight, do you?"

"Not really."

"You're not planning to steal my tree are you?"

"No. I have my own tree back home."

Both squirrels sat staring at each other for a moment and then Tullywanooli spoke up again: "I saw you riding that strange animal that was following the bear."

"That's my human," said Olli proudly. "Her name is Amber."

Tullywanooli tilted his head and examined Olli out of the corner of his eye. "You're not a real king, are you?" he asked.

"Naw, I was just singing a song." Olli shrugged and shuffled back toward the tree trunk. "Anyhow, I gotta go now," he said. "Gotta go catch up with my friends."

"But don't you wanna come see the Kingdom of Tumbling Puffball? I thought you would wanna see my tree. At least to see my tree."

Olli blinked uncertainly, but Tullywanooli's nose twitched in such a forlorn way that he turned himself right around. "I guess I could come and see your tree," he shrugged again. Tullywanooli led the way back to a very fine, very grand old beech tree. He leapt onto a sturdy branch and Olli followed him to a cluster of twigs and leaves tucked into a crook between the branch and the tree's trunk.

"It's beautiful," said Olli, nodding his head with approval. "Why, you can sit here and eat beechnuts right off your front porch."

"That's right," smiled Tullywanooli. "I think this is the finest house in the whole forest." His tail twitched and he frowned. "That's why I'm staying here to guard it," he said. "Those Rumblers better watch out." Tullywanooli balled up his little fists, hopped about, and punched wildly at the air. "I'll show them. They've got no business stealing other people's homes. I'll give it to them good, those lousy no-good monsters."

"But they're so big," said Olli. "Big enough to eat a whole tree in one gulp."

Tullywanooli seemed to crumple up like a balloon with all the air let out of it. "Well, I don't care," he said. "I don't care how big they are. We can't *all* run away. Somebody's gotta stay and fight for our homes."

"I'm not running," said Olli. "Me and my friends are going to find Istarna, the Wise Old Bear of the forest. She has strong magic. She'll know how to stop the Rumblers. Why don't you come with us? We can all fight the Rumblers together."

"No!" said Tullywanooli. "It's kind of you to offer. But this is my family's home. I fell out of this tree. My mother fell out of this tree. My grandmother fell out of this tree. Tumbling Puffballs have been falling out of this tree for generations. And I will stay here to defend it."

Olli nodded his head. He touched his nose to the tip of Tullywanooli's nose and then turned to leave.

"There's a short cut through the treetops," Tullywanooli called after him. "It'll take you way past the next bend in Big Cone Trail. Just follow that long skinny sunbeam that cuts through the tops."

"Thanks," said Olli with a last wave of his tail. He leapt into the tree that bordered the Kingdom of Tumbling Puffball and followed the sunbeam's trail. Sweet-smelling leaves brushed at Olli's face and bits of shaggy bark poked at his toes. Bugs scurried up the tree trunks and along the branches carrying important messages back and forth. Olli was tempted to stop and watch a while, as he often did on such lovely sunny days, but he had his own important business and couldn't waste time.

The Rumblers are coming!

He only briefly paused at a fork in an oak tree, overcome by the rich scent of acorns. He quickly picked six of the fattest acorns he could find and jammed the whole half dozen into his mouth—three tucked into one cheek, three tucked into the other cheek—then bounded off, following the flicker of sunbeam as it danced through the treetops.

Olli settled himself in a towering old hemlock that sat at the very edge of Big Cone Trail. From there he could see all the way to the cedar grove and to the bend beyond it. And it was not very long after that he saw flashes of heather pink between the trees. Next came Bohadea's nose bobbing around the corner. At first, Olli wanted to shout out a greeting, but his mouth was too stuffed with acorns, so he waited until they were directly beneath him, shifted his weight from one foot to the other, then took aim and leapt right onto Amber's shoulder.

"Yeoww," yelped Amber as she jumped with fright. "Oh, Olli," she scolded. "Don't sneak up on me like that. You scared me."

Olli smiled sheepishly, dove into her jumper pocket, dumped in the acorns, and then scrambled out again.

"Any news of the Rumblers up in the treetops?" Bohadea asked the squirrel.

"They're getting closer," said Olli, his whiskers twitching.

"We heard a raven say they were headed for Mosquito Marsh," said Amber.

"My mother took me and Potelia to Mosquito Marsh many times when we were little," said Bohadea. "We knew a beaver family that lived out that way: Soaker and Bucky Toppler and their three kits. I hope they're all right." She chattered on, telling tales of her cubhood: games of Splash with the Toppler kits, how she and Potelia thought that dragonflies were bear fairies, and stories of a heron called Salty, who would trick the young cubs into collecting the strange water bugs he liked to eat.

The forest climbed steadily toward Bear Tooth Rise. The trees thinned out, straggling toward a distant rim of tall fir trees. Near the middle stood the skeleton of an ancient pine that had died but not yet fallen. On a crooked branch near the top perched the golden silhouette of an eagle.

Amber glanced up at the sky. Oh, if only a rescue plane would come, she thought. If she were rescued, then she would save Olli and Bohadea, and Almedon, too. She would make sure that they all got into that rescue plane together.

3

Into the Night

It was a raggedy band of travelers that finally reached the outskirts of the Cliffs of Pointy Noggins. Even Almedon looked a little unsteady perched on an outcropping of rock. Bohadea and Amber were sprawled out on the moss-covered rocks beneath, and Olli was curled up like a teddy bear in the crook of Amber's arm.

"Are you sure, Almedon?" asked Bohadea wearily. "Are you sure you don't see anything that looks like it could be Half Moon Peak? Anything at all?"

Almedon shook his head, ruffling the feathers of his mane. He didn't like to disappoint Bohadea, but he hadn't really expected to find Half Moon Peak. He still considered it a make-believe place. The eagle shifted uneasily on the jagged point of his rock. A vision flashed through his mind of the massacre he and Lone Hawk of Two Tip Hill had witnessed. The screams. The smell of so much blood in the air.

He needed to tell Bohadea that he would be leaving the group. He needed to go and find some *real* warriors who would fight the Rumblers with claws and beaks, with sticks and rocks ... *with fur and feather and pelt of heather* ... oh, *fibbertigibbet,* grumbled Almedon to himself. Those were the words from the bearsong.

"I just don't understand it," Bohadea was saying. "We should have seen something by now."

"Maybe we came at it from the wrong direction," offered Amber. "You know how sometimes you can't see a thing because something else is in the way. That could be the problem. Maybe if we walked around a bit more …" her voice trailed off.

"It will be dark in a few minutes," said Bohadea glumly, her nose pointing upward to a yellow moon already hanging low in a deep purple sky.

"A half moon," said Amber, her face turned up to the darkening sky. Little specks of moonlight were reflected in her eyes. "A perfect half moon."

"Half moon," repeated Olli, snuggling deeper into the crook of Amber's arm.

Bohadea blinked up at the half moon. A full half moon. That must mean something, she thought. It must! Half Moon Peak was probably some kind of a riddle. Star Bear loved riddles. They were sprinkled all through the Star Bear Legends. If only she could figure it out.

Almedon was looking curiously up at the moon too. There was something about that moon. It had a bluish tinge to it. And something about the cliffs. Something … but he couldn't quite put his talon on it. He shook the thought from his mind. No sense in clogging up his head with any more foolishness. Somebody had to take charge of the sensible things.

"I will take the first watch," said Almedon. "We must have a night watch. The Rumblers are getting closer."

"Yes," said Bohadea. "Good idea. We'll get some sleep and then we can start looking for Half Moon Peak again, first thing in the morning."

"I'll take the second watch," offered Amber.

"I'll take the third, then," said Bohadea.

"Guess I'll go fourth," said Olli reluctantly. He was afraid of the dark and didn't like the idea of being up in the middle of the night all by himself.

"I'll wake you when the moon stands over the top of Hognose Cliff," Almedon told Amber, gesturing toward a plump snouty hilltop with his beak. "You wake Bohadea when the moon stands right above us. And Bohadea, you wake the squirrel when …" Almedon hesitated. *The squirrel?* He was going to trust their lives to a squirrel? Ridiculous! "Bohadea," he said, "you will wake me when your watch is finished."

"What about Olli?" asked Bohadea. "He should have a turn too. It's only fair."

"Squirrels … need more sleep than most people," ventured Almedon.

"True," piped Olli eagerly. "Squirrels need more sleep. I get very cranky if I don't get my sleep."

"Well," clucked Bohadea. "All right then, Almedon. At the end of my watch, I will wake you. Come, Amburrr," she called to the girl, "we will den-down right here." Bohadea nuzzled at the soft mossy carpet spread beneath the small overhang of rock.

Amber scooped Olli up in her arms, and carried him over to their sleeping place. This would be her second night in a row away from camp. Away from her parents. It had been two days now since she'd felt a warm hug from her Dad or had a good-night kiss from her Mom. Amber felt a little hurt twitching in her chest. She missed them so much. And she knew they would be missing her, too. One silvery little tear ran from the corner of her eye. Amber took a deep shaky breath, then settled down beside Bohadea. At least tonight she would not sleep alone. Tonight she would be warm and cozy in the company of her friends.

Bohadea stretched out on her side, and Amber curled up beside her. Olli burrowed in between them. They all snuggled together for a while, then drifted off to sleep one by one.

Almedon sat by himself on the outcropping, watching the moon rise. Around him, the crickets sang, and he could hear the chirp of an occasional bat as it whooshed by, chasing after fireflies. From a nearby cliff came the howling of a small pack of wolves. They were having a half-moon ceremony, asking the Mother Moon Wolf to protect them from the Rumblers.

Hmmph, thought Almedon with disgust. Wolves are warriors. They should be preparing to do battle, not shivering like rabbits beneath the moon. Where were the warriors when you needed them? Where were the great warriors of the Sun Eagle legends? His eyes scanned the tops of the cliffs. But there was no answer from Pointy Noggins. They stood as still and as silent as they had for a million years.

The moon crept toward Hognose Cliff, its light growing brighter as it rose in the sky. Almedon noticed how oddly it lit the top of Bear Head Point. It made the two round hills that looked like bear's ears, all shiny and yellow. He could see the silhouette of a night hawk sitting on top of one of the ears. But the hawk whistled suddenly and disappeared into the dark in a whir of wings.

From the corner of his eye Almedon caught a sudden blur of golden light. It seemed to flit through the bushes. At once he was on full alert, every muscle coiled with tension and ready to spring. He scanned the scrubby cover of bush, his eyes darting into every crevice and latching onto the slightest movement: the stirring of a leaf or the flutter of a moth. There was nothing there. But Almedon did not relax. He could sense another presence. *It was there!* Someone was there.

Then it came again. Another flash of gold, closer and very low to the ground. It moved like a predator. Almedon was about to sound the alarm when a fat furry moth with orange spots darted out onto the rocks. From the edge of the bush came a sudden swish and then an explosion of gold: leaping, pouncing, dancing across the rocks in pursuit of the moth. A cat!

A very fine cat indeed, thought Almedon. He had long reddish gold fur, a seashell pink nose, and a tuft of pure white at the tip of his tail. Almedon considered the prancing cat for a moment. He was annoyed at it for having startled him, but relieved too. This cat offered no threat to his companions who snuggled together beneath the overhang.

Almedon cleared his throat loudly.

It was the cat's turn to be startled. He stopped dead in his tracks and stared up at the eagle while his moth flitted off into the dark. "You dumb bird," he snarled, "you made me lose my moth."

"You would've lost it anyway," Almedon snapped back. "You hunt like a fledgling."

"A fledgling!" huffed the cat. "I'll have you know I am a very good hunter. An excellent hunter. The best hunter on all the Cliffs of Pointy Noggins."

"And what is it you hunt?" sniggered Almedon. "Small winged bugs that can't fly too fast?"

"Birds," said the cat pointedly, looking straight at the eagle. "I hunt birds."

At this, Almedon threw back his head and roared with laughter.

"What's so funny?" demanded the cat. "I don't see anything funny about that."

"Well," wheezed Almedon, barely able to contain his laughter, "that sounded like a threat to me, but as you can see, I'm quite big enough to eat a cat if I had a mind to."

The cat laid back his ears and swished his tail from side to side. His pink nose twitched as he regarded the eagle. Abruptly his tail stopped swishing and his ears stood back up. The cat had decided that this was not a topic worth pursuing. "So what's with the big pile of sleeping animals?" he asked Almedon, gesturing toward Bohadea, Amber, and Olli.

"My friends," said Almedon.

"One of them's a squirrel," announced the cat suspiciously, as if this was news to Almedon.

"My friends," said Almedon, more firmly this time, and with a hint of menace in his voice.

"Hmm," said the cat. "Weird."

"We're looking for Half Moon Peak. For the cave of Istarna," said Almedon. "Do you know where it is?"

The cat perked his ears right up high, padded across the rocks closer to Almedon, and rubbed up against a smooth boulder, his back arched and his tail held high. But he didn't answer the question.

Almedon blinked and frowned, silvery eyelids flickering in the moonlight. He watched the cat for a moment, then said: "You wouldn't happen to be called Pudd-Wudd-something-or-other, would you?"

"Princeling," said the cat, turning around and rubbing his other side up against the boulder. "Pudd Wudd Princeling."

"You're him?" said Almedon, his eyes wide with surprise.

"He is me," said Pudd Wudd with a courtly bow.

"Then you must know of a place called Half Moon Peak. We seek Istarna there. Can you tell me where to find her?"

"For what purpose?" asked Pudd Wudd.

"For strong magic," said Almedon. "To stop the Rumblers."

"Ah, yes," said Pudd Wudd. He had begun to prowl about the rocks in a distracted way. "Yes, there are many who would wish to see Istarna."

"But we're … we're…." Almedon couldn't quite bring

himself to say it, but then he just blurted it out: "We are the Tribe of Star Bear. We *must* see Istarna."

Pudd Wudd turned back to Almedon, his pretty little tiger face and yellow jeweled eyes caught in a moonbeam. "Don't ignore Half Moon door," he said.

"What? What door? What are you talking about?"

Pudd Wudd tiptoed across the rocks toward the bush. "Meow," he said to the moon. To Almedon he said: "Rum-tum-tiddle, no time to diddle." And then he vanished in a streak of gold through the lattice of twigs and leaves.

"Rum-tum-tiddle indeed," grumbled Almedon. "Silly cat." He turned back to Hognose Cliff and saw that the moon was almost right above it now. He spread his wings and coasted down to where Amber and the others slept. He pecked gently at her shoulder. "Human," he whispered. "It's time to get up, Human."

Amber rolled over and yawned. She sat up and stretched. "I wish you would call me Amber," said the girl. "My name is Amber."

"Amber," repeated Almedon grumpily, but he couldn't tear his eyes away from the squirrel. The squirrel was sleeping upside down, on his back, with all fours stuck up in the air. And he was snoring loudly. "I didn't know squirrels snored," said Almedon absently. "Come. You must climb to the outcropping for your watch."

Amber yawned again and combed her fingers through her long unruly curls. "Wish I had my hairbrush," she mumbled to herself, and then set off to climb up and around to the top of the outcropping. It was quite steep and she had to dig her toes into the dirt and pull herself up by grabbing at bushes and rocks. She hauled herself up from one tree to the next.

How remarkable, thought Almedon, that a creature as clumsy as that could manage to survive at all. But he didn't say anything rude. He just watched until she crawled over onto the top and then he spread his wings and flapped up to meet her.

"I will sleep in this pine tree right here beside you," said Almedon. "If there is any trouble, wake me at once."

"Okay," agreed Amber. She settled onto a large rock that made a rather bumpy seat, but it was better that standing up the whole time, or sitting on the bumpier rock-strewn ground.

After a while she heard Almedon begin to snore and it made her smile. She leaned back, gazed at the moon, and hummed a tune she had learned from her music teacher. She hummed it over, five and a half times, and then abruptly stopped.

It was something she had seen.

Amber leapt from the rock and shouted at the top of her lungs: "Almedon. Bohadea. Olli. Look! Look!"

Almedon tumbled out of the tree and almost landed right on top of Amber's head. Bohadea leapt from her mossy bed, and very nearly squashed Olli flat. Olli squealed in terror and flung himself after Bohadea who had already begun to run up the hill.

"Look!" shouted Amber. "Look!"

"What? What is it?" yelled Bohadea in a panic.

"What? What? What?" screamed Olli, charging up the hill.

"Where? Where?" screeched Almedon, his head swiveling like a pinwheel in the wind.

"Half Moon Peak," shouted Amber, pointing up. "There it is."

Olli practically flew right up onto Amber's shoulder and he looked out over the top of her hand to the place where her finger pointed.

Almedon turned to look too, and blinked in disbelief at what he saw.

"Where? Where is it?" puffed Bohadea, out of breath.

"There," said Amber, more quietly this time. "See how the moon lights it up?"

It was an amazing sight. For the moon had shot out a thin beam of clear blue light that traveled across the Cliffs of Pointy Noggins. It passed directly between the bear ears, at the top of Bear Head Point, and then traveled across to the peak of a rather ordinary medium-sized cliff. The tip of that cliff shone like a frosty blue iceberg, for there, reflected from the rocky face, was a half moon, as perfect and as bright as the moon itself.

"Half Moon Peak," breathed Bohadea. "I knew it. I knew it was there."

"I wonder ...," mused Almedon, "do you suppose that could have something to do with the door?"

"What door?" asked Amber.

Almedon glanced at the place in the bushes where he had last seen a glimmer of gold. Everything had happened so quickly that he had forgotten to mention Pudd Wudd's visit. "That Pudd Wudd fellow was here," he said.

"What?" bellowed Bohadea.

"Pudd Wudd Princeling!" cried Amber. "That's the one Corny-Q told us about!"

"Pudd Wudd the cat?" yapped Olli. "How big is he? How big is he? Big enough to eat a squirrel?"

"Why didn't you tell us sooner?" growled Bohadea.

"I didn't have a chance," Almedon explained. "You were all asleep. I didn't want to wake you up."

"Well? What did he say?" demanded Bohadea.

"Now, let me see." The silvery eyelids flickered. "He said he eats birds," chuckled Almedon.

"Yuck," hooted Olli.

"About the door," Bohadea prodded him. "What did Pudd Wudd say about the door?"

"Oh, yes." Almedon gazed up at the moon, as if Pudd Wudd's words might be written there. He frowned, and then said: "'Don't ignore Half Moon door.' Yes. That's it. That's what he said: 'Don't ignore Half Moon door.'"

"What door?" Olli wanted to know.

"What else?" Bohadea quizzed. "Did he say anything else?"

Almedon thought a minute and said: "It was silly. The rest was silly."

"It doesn't matter. Say it anyway."

"Well, what was it now? Ahh ... oh yes. 'Rum-tum-tiddle, no time to diddle.' That was it. But I think he just meant that he had to get going."

"We leave now," said Bohadea firmly. "We must get to Half Moon Peak right away." She began walking.

"But it's dark out," said Olli anxiously. "It's time to sleep."

"I don't like to fly in the dark," said Almedon.

"My father told me never to go hiking after dark," said Amber. "We could get...." She was going to say lost, but then realized that she already was lost. So instead, she said: "hurt! We could fall into a hole or something and get hurt."

But Bohadea was paying no attention to any of them. She was jogging in the direction of Half Moon Peak.

Amber looked at Almedon, then shrugged her shoulders and followed Bohadea. She would walk directly behind Bohadea, she decided, and only put her feet in the places that Bohadea had already stepped. That way, she wouldn't fall into any holes.

Almedon looked uncertain for a moment, then sulkily flapped his wings and lifted off. But he snagged the tip of one wing on something that made him swerve and crash-land in the pine boughs. He thrashed and knocked about and grumbled angrily at the tree.

Bohadea swung back around to see what all the commotion was about. "Almedon?" she called. "Are you all right?"

"I think he got stuck in a tree," said Olli, rather too gleefully.

"I am not stuck," snapped Almedon. "I just didn't get clear of the treetops is all. I told you, Bohadea, I don't like to fly in the dark," he yelled.

"You could ride on my back," offered Bohadea.

"Pfufff," snorted Almedon. "Don't be ridiculous." Filled with determination, the eagle launched himself into the air and this time he did clear the treetops, sailing out into the dark night sky.

As he rose up, the trees seemed to sink away into the darkness, and then disappear. Almedon realized it would be too dangerous for him to attempt a treetop landing in the dark, so he decided to follow the moonbeam straight to Half Moon Peak, where he could land on the brightly lit cliff top.

From the ground, Amber watched the eagle, who seemed to float on that ray of moonlight like a dandelion puff caught in a sunbeam. She watched as he winged his way toward Half Moon Peak. Later on, she looked up again just in time to see him land in the half moon that shone from the cliff top.

"I wish I could fly," she said wistfully.

"What did you say Amburrr?" asked Bohadea. She had been very quiet on this night walk, concentrating on her footing, looking up only occasionally to track the moonbeam and to calculate the shortest route to Half Moon Peak.

"Almedon is at Half Moon Peak already," said Amber. "I just saw him land."

"Good," grunted Bohadea, and she was quiet again.

Olli stirred in Amber's pocket where he had curled up into a soft round ball, and promptly fallen asleep. His weight made the whole top of Amber's jumper billow and sag and the straps bite into her shoulders, but she didn't care. She loved the way the squirrel made a warm spot over her heart. And his snoring reminded her of the purr of a cat. She reached up a hand and gently stroked the lump in her pocket, tracing her fingers along the curve of Olli's back.

The sudden hoot of an owl startled Amber. She caught her toe on the edge of a rock and stumbled, tipping forward and then jerking back to keep herself from falling. Everything seemed so different in the dark, Amber thought. It was damp and misty. The woods were filled with musty earth smells, with tall looming shapes and dark hidden places, and low whispery sounds, things that squished and crackled underfoot, things that slithered through the night. Amber definitely preferred the daytime.

She gazed up at Half Moon Peak and frowned. In the indigo sky, the light of the half moon seemed thinner somehow, and more crescent shaped. "I think we'd better hurry," she said to Bohadea. "I think the light is going out."

Bohadea stopped to look up at the peak, and Amber bumped up against her back end. "Dear me," fretted the bear. "Oh dear me. The moon has risen so fast and the moonbeam must follow it or it will be lost. We must hurry. We must go as fast as we can. Before the light of Half Moon Peak is gone altogether."

She swung her head around to Amber, her brown eyes shining in the moonlight. "Climb onto my back," she told the girl. "We must go very fast now."

"I rode a pony once," said Amber doubtfully, "but I've never ridden a bear before."

"Quickly," said Bohadea.

Amber edged up beside Bohadea, who was not as tall as a pony, but seemed very tall for a bear. She took a deep breath, then swung one leg up. She leaned forward, grabbed onto a handful of fur, and wiggled all the way up onto Bohadea's back, being very careful not to squish Olli, who still slept soundly in her pocket.

"Hang on," said Bohadea.

Amber leaned forward, burrowing her fingers deep into the thick fur at Bohadea's shoulders.

Bohadea whispered softly, her eyes cast up to a spray of stars that swept the roof of the forest: "May Star Bear guide us," she said. And then they were off, loping through the shadows, the wind rushing by, ruffling Bohadea's fur and dancing through Amber's hair.

It took a few moments for Amber to stop bouncing and catch the rhythm of Bohadea's stride. But once she did, it was as smooth and fast as a galloping horse. Amber had never imagined that a bear, a big lumbering old fuzzy-bear like Bohadea, could run so fast. She leapt over logs and potholes as sure-footed as a mountain goat. Bohadea ran through the dark, over the hills and through the gullies, racing against the moon.

The half circle of moonlight that lit up the cliffside grew thinner and thinner, and Bohadea ran faster and faster, her heart pounding in her chest. Her breath grew harsh and ragged. Her powerful muscles tensed and quivered beneath the weight of the girl. But Bohadea would not stop to rest. She would not stop until they had reached Half Moon Peak. Or until it went dark.

Pudd Wudd's words raced through her head: "Don't ignore Half Moon door." Half Moon door. *Moon door. Moon door. Door.* Was it a door? Was the moon lighting up a doorway that went into Istarna's cave? Bohadea didn't know. Maybe. Maybe not. But it was the other thing that Pudd Wudd had told Almedon that made her run.

"Rum-tum-tiddle, no time to diddle." *No time to diddle.* No matter what Almedon thought, that part was clear to Bohadea. Pudd Wudd had meant for them to hurry.

Bohadea spared another quick look up. She could see that they were drawing closer. Half Moon Peak was no longer so distant. It was becoming clear and distinct. With a fresh burst of speed she lunged forward, then suddenly was stopped short.

"Oh, no," she cried.

"What's wrong?" Amber swung one leg over Bohadea's back and hopped down onto the ground.

"Listen," said Bohadea. "Down there."

They were standing at the top of a steep drop-off that ran a long way down into a deep, dark ravine. And from somewhere far beneath them came the unmistakable sound of rushing water.

"A river?" asked Amber.

"A very deep, very fast river," said Bohadea glumly.

"Can't we swim across it?"

"No. It would be much too dangerous. We must find another way."

"In the dark?" asked Amber doubtfully.

"Oh dear," sighed Bohadea, "we'll never make it now." She began to pace frantically back and forth along the edge of the drop-off.

"Olli," Amber nudged the squirrel.

He grunted.

She nudged him again. "Olli. Wake up."

He stumbled halfway out of the pocket and then let himself sink back in again. "I wanna sleep," he said crankily.

"Olli," insisted Amber. "Get up. You need to go up a tree and see if you can find some other way to get across the river from here."

Grumbling crossly, Olli dragged himself out of Amber's pocket and looked around. "It's pitch dark out," he complained.

"I know," said Amber. "But we need to get over there." She pointed out into the dark toward a barely visible tree-line on the other side of the ravine.

"Way over there?"

"Just go!" she ordered the squirrel. "We don't have much time."

Olli allowed himself one very big, very huffy sigh, and then he leapt from Amber's shoulder to the low-hanging limb of a hemlock tree and disappeared into the dark.

Bohadea was still pacing at the edge of the drop-off, and Amber went to join her. "We must get across, we must, we must," muttered Bohadea.

"Olli will find a place for us to cross," said Amber with certainty, although she wasn't entirely sure that he would.

They both stood still, looking out at the thinning light of Half Moon Peak. Nothing moved for a long while, but then, from the deeper shadows, a figure emerged. It was Almedon. He walked awkward and birdlike into the now slender shaft of light, and looked back over the forest. He seemed to look directly at them, although it was much too far away and much too dark even for an eagle to see.

The shadows around Almedon seemed to shift, as if shapes were moving and changing, like curls of smoke. Amber thought she saw a girl hidden in a cloak of shadow. Bohadea thought it was a bear. Then the silhouette of a cat. It drifted toward the edge of the light, crept closer to Almedon, then sank back into the shadows.

Almedon opened his wings as if preparing to take off, but he stood right where he was and beat his wings faster and faster. He stopped, rested for a moment, and then did it again. He lowered his wings, and then raised them for a third time, flapping again, harder and faster.

"He's sending us a message," said Bohadea. "He's telling us to hurry."The sudden scurry of squirrel feet drew their attention away from Almedon, who was fast disappearing back into the shadows of Half Moon Peak. "Olli?" called Amber.

"Ollidollinderi the Great," the squirrel shouted as he leapt from a dark cluster of hemlock branches onto Amber's shoulder. She was getting used to these surprise attacks and hardly even flinched as he thumped down.

"Did you find anything?"

"Yup," said Olli proudly. "A place where it's only a tree's length apart from our side to over there," he nudged his nose at the tree line.

"But how do we cross?" asked Amber. "We need a bridge of some sort."

"No bridge," said Olli matter-of-factly. "But there is a broken tree. Half fallen over with its roots stuck up in the air. All we have to do is push it over and we've got us a bridge-thing." Then, very self-importantly, Olli raised his little paw and pointed in the direction he had come from.

Bohadea galloped off at once. Amber ran after her, and Olli bounced along on her shoulder. "Hey, this is bumpy," he protested. "Too bumpy." He jumped off and scurried up a tree trunk.

Amber was the last one there. Bohadea already had her shoulder pushed up against the upturned roots and she was shoving with all her might. Amber went around to the other side and added her small weight. Olli stood up on his haunches and yelled directions.

The tree swayed back and forth, and just when Amber thought it was an impossible task, that the tree would never fall over, Bohadea gave a great bellowing grunt, and

Amber could feel the whole tree shift. She yelped loudly and threw herself into the task. There was a great grinding, ripping sound and the huge tree fell. It seemed to go over in slow motion, and then its top end hit down on the other side of the ravine, making the ground shake.

"Tchee, tchee, tchureee," yelped Olli. He bounced onto the fallen trunk and skittered straight across to the other side of the ravine. "It works," he shouted back. "It works!"

Amber wiped her forehead with the back of her hand. Slowly, she picked her way over the underbrush toward the edge of the ravine. She was not nearly as eager to cross over on the fallen tree trunk as Olli had been. She knew it was a very long way to the bottom of the ravine.

Bohadea brushed up beside her. "Best not to rear up on your hind legs when you cross," she said. "Go over on all four paws and keep your eyes on the tree bark."

There was no point in stalling. Amber leaned over and pushed one hand up against the fallen tree trunk to try and jiggle it. It didn't move. She straightened up and shoved the heel of her boot at the trunk as hard as she could. It didn't budge.

"Hey! What's taking everybody so long?" shouted Olli.

"Okay, I'm going now," Amber said, more to herself than to anybody else. She got down on her hands and knees and began crawling.

The bark grazed the skin of her hands and scratched against the knees of her jumper. The wind whistled softly around her, speaking of danger, as it so often does in very high places. Amber was glad it was dark. Glad that she could not see the river or the rocks below. She kept her eyes on the outline of the tree trunk and moved slowly out across the ravine.

Behind her, Bohadea held her breath and watched. She didn't think that humans were very good at doing things that involved balance, and she knew she would never forgive herself if anything happened to Amber. But Amber moved steadily across and Bohadea breathed her relief when she saw the girl scramble back up onto her hind limbs, safely on the other side.

The trunk was very large and solid, and Bohadea had no trouble crossing. She just dug her claws in with each step and made-believe she was walking over the old log that lay across the stream at Hog's Hollow.

Amber squealed her delight. She wrapped her arms around Bohadea's broad neck, and planted a kiss right at the top of the bear's nose. Bohadea nuzzled the girl and smiled. She wasn't used to human ways, but she knew that this was a display of affection, and it made her heart grow big and warm.

"We must hurry now," said Bohadea.

Amber flung one leg over her back and wiggled up. Olli scrambled up and settled down between her hands, looking out between Bohadea's ears.

As the trio moved swiftly through the woods, the thick pine forest grew more and more sparse, the spaces wider and wider, until finally, Half Moon Peak loomed up in front of them across a barren meadow.

The thin splash of light on the cliffside was fading more quickly now. Its faint glow outlined the dark shape of Almedon, his wings flapping wildly, urging them on. Bohadea charged across the meadow at a speed that even she did not know was possible. She clambered up the rocks, and fell in an exhausted heap in the last dim flicker of moonlight. Amber and Olli spilled onto the ground beside her.

"Yikes," squealed Olli. He froze at the sight of two huge eagle feet, their great black talons digging into the earth right in front of his nose—a thing most squirrels would not live to tell about.

"The light falls from a door," said Almedon. "It opens only when struck by the blue light of a certain half moon. It's almost closed. We must go! Right now! Or we forfeit our only chance."

Exhausted, Bohadea leapt to her feet. Amber, seeing that Olli was still very frightened, scooped him up and tucked him into her pocket.

Almedon led the way, rushing toward the place where a thin beam of light spilled out of the cliffside. His wings clapped at his sides, his feet barely scratched the ground. Bohadea loped along behind him. Amber ran as fast as she could. Olli gripped at the fabric of her pocket to keep from bouncing out.

The doorway did not look wide enough for someone as big as a bear. And even as they watched, the rock face shifted, closing the gap even smaller. Amber looked at Bohadea. Bohadea looked at Almedon. No one wanted to go first.

"How will we get back out?" asked Amber. It was a thought they all shared.

"On faith," said Bohadea. She stepped forward, reared up onto her hind legs, and squeezed through, grunting with effort.

Almedon quickly followed.

"Onto my shoulder," Amber commanded Olli. She was afraid she might squash him if he stayed in her front pocket. He slipped out and climbed up, his tail pushing against Amber's cheek as he snuggled in close to her neck. She slipped though and one second later the rocks slid together and the doorway shut fast behind them.

4

Drawing Down the Stars

Ghostly music played in the shadows of the vast cavern. Bohadea's ears pricked up at the sound of a spirit drum: *The beat of Istarna's drum!*

The walls were fashioned of a blue crystal, so deep and rich that it appeared black in some places, and glimmered bright blue in others. From the tall creviced ceiling dripped long crystal spikes, many of them tipped with fiery blue lights that twinkled and danced among the shadows. The floor was smooth and bright, and as clear as the surface of a water pool. Up ahead, the cavern narrowed into a long dark tunnel that ended in a burst of brilliant white light. This was the direction from which the strange music came.

"Who goes there?" sang a shrill little voice from above.

All four looked up at the ceiling, unsure of what they had heard. Bohadea's nose twitched as she squinted into the forest of blue crystal. Almedon scanned the dips and spikes as he would have surveyed a rocky cliffside for prey. But he could find nothing that moved.

"There's someone up there," whispered Olli, his teeny hands clutching at a lock of Amber's hair. "Someone sneaky."

"Intruders!" shrilled the voice from above, more loudly this time.

"Intruders. Intruders. Intruders." The sharp, thin sounds seemed to echo from every nook and cranny of the ceiling. And this time Almedon did see something.

Something that made his downy feathers stand up on end: the twinkling blue lights were in pairs that flared and dimmed in rhythm with the voices. "Eyes," said Almedon in a deep low murmur.

Olli slunk down low on Amber's shoulder and silently slid into the safety of her front pocket. Amber stepped closer to Bohadea and leaned into the bear's warm furry bulk. Even Almedon took a step or two nearer his companions.

A ripple of sound, like the crinkling of cellophane, swept across the ceiling. The blue lights blinked brighter and brighter. More and more of them twinkled among the crystals, until the whole cavern began to glow. As the four travelers watched, one of the crystals stirred, a set of wings unfolded, and what had only a moment before looked like a crystal icicle, suddenly peeled free of the ceiling and swept down in a whoosh of blue.

Bohadea hopped backward in fright, and Amber raised her hands like a shield. They could both feel the rush of cold air as a flurry of blue wings flashed past.

"Bat," said Almedon, bravely standing his ground. "Some kind of bat."

"Who goes there?" shrilled the crystal-blue bat as she swept around Bohadea's little tribe. "Who goes there?"

"We're the Tribe of Star Bear," croaked Bohadea, but her voice was so creaky and frightened that all but her first two words were lost in the whirl of fiery-blue bat wings.

"Who goes there?" shrieked the bat.

"Who goes there?" Her call was echoed from the ceiling by hundreds of bat voices raised into one single ear-piercing shriek.

"Tchip," squeaked Olli, shuffling deeper into his hiding place.

The clink and rustle of glassy wings filled the cavern as the ceiling came alive. The long crystal spikes unfolded, one after another, and bats came wheeling down from their roost in tens and dozens. Down they came, filling the cave with sparks of blue light that glittered in the clear crystal of their webbed wings and slender bodies, like countless blue sparklers drawing pathways of light in the air.

The bats swirled, fluttered, and whirled. "Who goes there? Who goes there?" They drew in closer and closer, flying in formation now, circling round and round, like a carousel of giant blue butterflies, their voices growing louder and louder: "WHO GOES THERE?" they demanded.

Bohadea opened her mouth to speak but nothing would come out. Amber had her eyes squeezed shut and her hands pinned over her ears. And Olli had squirreled himself as deep as he could get into the bottom of Amber's pocket, jamming his head beneath the orange fungus treasure. This left Almedon to give an answer. But he was so flustered by the angry mob of bats that he had forgotten the name of the tribe and all he could think to say was *feather fleas*. He hollered out, loud and clear, and at the very top of his lungs for everyone to hear: "FEATHER FLEAS."

Almost at once the bats scattered, breaking the circle and gathering again at the place where the cavern narrowed to a tunnel. They shimmered and shook and formed themselves into a crystal wall so deep and so solid that no one, not even a feather flea, would have been able to pass through. Even the beat of Istarna's drum could not penetrate the wall of bats.

Two little paws appeared at the edge of Amber's pocket. A wiggly nose followed. "Hey," whispered Olli, "what's going on? How come it got so quiet?"

Amber pointed at the blue crystal wall just in time for Olli to see the gigantic face of a single bat rise out of the crystal blockade. Two enormous eyes, as big as dinner plates, burned like blue fire. Crystal blue lips parted to show a set of teeth as large and as sharp as spires of sapphire.

"WE ARE THE GUARDIANS OF ISTARNA'S CAVE," boomed the voice of the bat. "WHAT IS YOUR BUSINESS HERE, FEATHER FLEAS?"

Bohadea's teeth were chattering, but this time she found her voice: "We're not really feather fleas," she said apologetically. "I don't know why my friend said we were. I think he was just nervous." She looked over at Almedon who was looking at his feet and pretending not to hear.

"WHAT ARE YOU THEN?" demanded the bat.

"Well," said Bohadea, clearing her throat and speaking with more confidence now, "my friend here is an eagle. He's the only one with feathers. But I'm quite sure he hasn't any fleas," she added hastily. Then nudging Almedon she said: "You don't do you? Have any fleas I mean?"

"No, of course not," snapped Almedon crossly.

Bohadea nodded her relief and turned to Amber. "This one with the heather-colored pelt and the yellow mane is a human," she said. "And that little red person in the human's front pouch is a red squirrel." Bohadea turned back to face the huge bat. "And I," she said proudly, "am a bear."

"WHAT IS YOUR BUSINESS HERE, BEAR?"

Bohadea stood up taller, her face set alight with the strength of a warrior bear. "We are the Tribe of Star Bear," she announced in a deep steady voice, "and we have come to see Istarna, Wise Old Bear of the Forest, Last Descendant of Star Bear. We seek strong magic to defeat the Rumblers, who have risen from the Pit of Darkness." And then Bohadea took a gamble and hoped she was right. "Istarna is expecting us," she said boldly. "You must let us pass."

The bat closed her great dinner-plate eyes as if in meditation. Her crystal blue face deepened to an inky black color. From behind each of her closed eyelids came a low pulse of blue light. The cavern fell silent. Then, quite suddenly, the pulsing light exploded into twin sunbursts and her eyes snapped open. "YOU MAY PASS," she boomed. And with that, the bat's face dissolved back into the wall of crystal, which shimmered and shook and finally splintered into a thousand little bat shapes. The glassy wings took flight once more, swooping and glimmering in the air. Like a brilliant blue cloud they rose higher and higher up to the cavern ceiling, where their wings and bodies melted back into spikes of pure blue crystal. The tribe stood stock-still, all eyes darting across the ceiling from one crystal spike to the next. But everything was just as it had been when they first stepped into the cavern. Only the slow steady beat of Istarna's drum echoed from the still blue walls.

Almedon broke the spell: "Come on," he said, "let's go." His talons clicked across the smooth crystal floor as he led the way toward the dark tunnel and the splash of white light at its end.

Amber could feel the thumping of her heart as she stepped into the tunnel and the darkness closed in. She kept one hand twined in the fur of Bohadea's shoulder and used the other hand to reassure Olli, who had begun to shiver.

They moved slowly with Almedon in the lead. He was not used to traveling on foot and couldn't get much of a grip on the slippery crystal floor. Bohadea wanted to suggest that he ride on her back, but she knew he was too proud to accept. So she trudged quietly along behind him, marking her steps to the beat of the drum.

As they drew nearer the white glow, their pace quickened. Little pools of silvery light started to glimmer on the floor and wink from the dark walls. Ahead of them, the white crystal of another cavern began to take shape. Almedon suddenly clapped his wings and skittered along the ground, half walking and half flying, until he could contain himself no longer and took off into full flight. A few powerful wing beats set him on a course straight through the middle of the tunnel and a moment later he coasted into the bright, white cavern and disappeared from sight.

Thud! Squawk! Kerplunk!

Bohadea broke into a run. "Almedon," she called anxiously. "Almedon, are you all right?" Amber took off after Bohadea, slipping and sliding along the glassy floor, jostling Olli back and forth. They burst into the cavern just in time to see Almedon dusting off his feathers.

"This is a very bad place for birds," he said crossly, giving himself a shake. "There are no perches, the ground is like winter ice, and the walls are nearly invisible."

The clear crystal cavern was no color and all colors at once. Tiny bright stars floated beneath the ceiling, each one bursting with great splashes of light that danced through the walls like rainbows in soap bubbles. The strange music was louder here and seemed to vibrate from somewhere deep inside the walls themselves. Amber thought she could actually *see* the music, and squinted her eyes at the bright flecks of color that grew brighter with each beat of the drum.

The ghostly music stopped abruptly, and, as silence descended, the brilliant light of the cavern seemed to waver and then drain away.

Olli blinked. "Tchip! Tchip! Now what's gone wrong?" he murmured, wiggling his nose anxiously.

"I don't like this," grumbled Almedon. He shifted awkwardly, his wings hitched up and down with agitation, his bright eyes searched for some way out. "There are no openings in here except the one we came through, and we know the cavern is sealed at that end. And there is no sign of a bear in here. I don't like it at all." His downy undercoat bristled beneath his golden feathers for it was quite against an eagle's nature to hike into the depths of crystal caverns and Almedon longed for a warm gust of wind that would take him up into a wide blue sky.

"We could be trapped," whispered Amber in a tiny voice. The search helicopters would never find her in here!

"No," Bohadea shook her head. "Istarna is …," but her voice trailed off as the last of the light flickered away, leaving them in the dark.

Goosebumps rose on Amber's arms. She reached into the blackness, her hands patting empty air as she searched for the place where Bohadea had stood. "Bohadea?" she whispered fearfully.

Olli crept up onto Amber's shoulder and knotted himself in the fall of her hair.

"I'm right here," came Bohadea's voice, somewhere to Amber's right.

"Something's happening," Almedon warned.

And as he spoke, an angry red light began to pulse from beneath their feet. It grew brighter and more insistent with each beat, casting an eerie red glow across the four figures.

"It feels wrong," said Almedon. He clacked his beak twice, making a hard, jittery sound. "I think we should leave here at once!" he said as he hurried back toward the tunnel.

Bohadea stood her ground, squinting down at the bright ruby floor.

"Where will we go?" asked Amber, her eyes flicking from the bear to the eagle, who was now nearing the tunnel entrance.

"Where will we go?" echoed Olli. "Where? Where? Where?"

"Wait!" called Bohadea. "Look!" Her nose pointed down at the floor. "I think I can see something down there."

Almedon hobbled back to Bohadea and leaned over to see what she had found. Amber squatted down, and Olli scrambled out onto the platform made by her knees to get a better look.

Beneath them was an entire city. A city made of blood-red crystals. The buildings were squares and rectangles. Some of them were short and squat. Some were spectacular towers that jutted so high into the air they almost scraped the ruby red floor through which the four gazed. And right in the middle of this incredible place, was a deep, dark, square pit that seemed to burrow into the very core of the earth.

Around the pit were enormous, lumpish creatures with red eyes as big as cabbages, and pointed teeth like giant silver icicles. Their long powerful arms, which seemed to have far too many joints, ended in giant snapping claws. They moved on huge rear legs that hugged close to the ground. Clumsy and lumbering, they scaled the walls of the pit and marched out of the red city in all directions.

Some of the humungous creatures were driving tiny apish animals who were furred in a very unusual shade of flamingo pink. The little ones walked on their hind legs like humans, but threw their weight from right to left in a slow, shambling gait.

"What are they?" asked Amber, her eyebrows knitted together in puzzlement.

"The big ones," said Bohadea without hesitation, "are Rumblers."

"Ohhh," murmured Amber and Olli in unison, their faces glowing red in the reflected light, their eyes wide with horror.

"I recognize them," said Almedon uneasily. "They killed the Forest Council. But what are those puny pink things that skitter like rabbits?"

"Those," said Bohadea, "are Saroos."

"Saroos?"

"Remember the Star Bear story of how the Rumblers got out? It was the Saroos who did it: the ones who left the forest to find a square place to build all their square things. What you see down there are the things they built from their precious red crystals. The hole in the middle is where they dug out all the red stones. And at the bottom of that hole is the Pit of Darkness, where Dreeg, King of the Rumblers, lives."

This was the City of the Saroos. This was the pit from which the Rumblers had crawled up into the sunlight. A terrible silence settled over the tribe.

Almedon suddenly screeched and snapped his beak at the ruby city beneath his talons. "They are killing our people and eating up the forest, and here we are, trapped in this stupid cave doing nothing to stop them. We've got to get out of here!" He flapped his wings furiously, rose several feet up into the air, and then came crashing down on the crystal floor. As he landed, the City of the Saroos began to fade. The ruby light dimmed.

"Oh, oh," said Olli. "Tchip, tchip."

"It's going dark again," said Amber, edging closer to Bohadea's side. She did not want to lose her in the dark. But the light only softened, fading from red to pink and back to white again.

The air was suddenly electric, filled with tiny silvery specks that danced to the rising strains of spirit music. The specks began to form into a wide spiral around the cavern. Trails of light twisted and spun upward into an open night sky. It was as if the ceiling of the cavern had evaporated. They could see tiny globes of purple, red, and green, spinning circles high above them. Clusters of stars twinkled, and silver crescent moons winked in and out from behind the globes. The spiral twisted faster and faster like a beacon of light piercing the indigo sky above.

"Wow," breathed Amber, "you can see the whole universe from here."

Olli purred with amazement.

Almedon swayed back and forth, his sharp brown eyes scanning the strange night sky. He started in a little lunge upward, as if to take off, but then drew back in hesitation. The sky did not look the same as the one that glowed above the Cliffs of Pointy Noggins. He cautiously rose into the air and banked sharply to the left, purposely brushing the tip of one wing at the place where the cavern's ceiling had been. A crackle of electricity licked back at Almedon and sent him lurching down to the cavern floor. The others watched anxiously as he shook out the wing, then noisily ruffled his feathers and folded his wings back into place.

A silvery tinkle of laughter drew their attention back up into the strange, beautiful night sky. There, looking down at the them from the rim of the cavern, was Pudd Wudd Princeling, his seashell pink nose twitching with mirth and two reddish-gold paws dangling casually over the edge. Spirals of light twisted up and swept past the cat.

"The great eagle explores the unknown like a kitten," sniffed Pudd Wudd. "But at least a kitten will grow into a cat: the mightiest hunter of them all. A cat is clever. A cat can make himself invisible. He will fit through small places that an eagle cannot go. He is a trickster. Sure-footed. Quick-witted. A shape-shifter."

Almedon ground his beak, his eyes glinting dangerously at Pudd Wudd's perch on the rim. "If you are such a great trickster," he said, "than trick your way down here into this cavern. Let's see how *you* pass the invisible barrier that spits flames."

Pudd Wudd rose idly, arched his back into the shape of a C, then slowly stretched forward into a long graceful pose. He unsheathed his curved white claws, and yawned a huge lazy cat yawn showing a neat row of sharp pearly teeth. Gingerly he stepped forward tracing his way along the edge of the rim.

"Mr. Princeling," called Bohadea urgently, frightened that he might leave. "We were told that you know the way to Istarna's den. Please," she pleaded, "we must find Istarna. Right away! Can you tell us how to find her?"

"Ride the light," said Pudd Wudd. "Ride the light, away from the night."

"Ride the light, indeed," sneered Almedon. "Why must you jabber in riddles? Personally, I can do without this foolish cat-advice. I just want to see Mr. Pudd-Head here ride the light down into this cave."

"Almedon! Shush!" commanded Bohadea. "Mr. Princeling," she said, her nose pointed back up at the rim where Pudd Wudd paced. "I apologize for my friend's rudeness. We appreciate your advice, it's just that we don't quite understand it. Perhaps you could show us the way to Istarna's den."

Pudd Wudd abruptly sat down still as a statue, staring up into the stars. As the spirals of light rushed past him, his silhouette faded then brightened again like a pulsing neon sign. *Ride the light, away from the night.* His words echoed through the cavern, yet Pudd Wudd did not move his lips, for not even a whisker twitched.

Bohadea knitted her brows together in concentration.

"What's going on?" whispered Amber in confusion.

"Tchip," whispered Olli. "Light. Night. Light. Night."

Suddenly Pudd Wudd sprang from his place on the rim and dove down into one of the spiral pathways. In a flash of golden light, he was gone. Golden sparkles swirled down into the cavern following the silvery trails of light and disappeared.

"Where'd he go?" Amber searched the rim for signs of Pudd Wudd.

"Into the light," said Olli. "He went into the light."

"Ride the light, away from the night," said Bohadea, marking each word carefully as she began to circle around the cavern, nosing at the trails of swirling light.

"How'd he do that?" demanded Almedon crossly.

Bohadea stopped short. "The floor," she said absently. "Are those whirls of light coming up through the floor?"

Almedon turned an eagle eye downward. "From deep down," he said. "It goes down as far as it goes up." He looked up at Bohadea. "You're not thinking ... that we should jump into the light like Pudd Wudd Princeling did?" finished Amber. "It looks dangerous," she frowned.

"Jump into the light," squealed Olli. "It'll be fun!"

"You first, squirrel," said Almedon sarcastically.

Olli marched back down into Amber's pocket. "I'll go with her," he said, jerking a thumb up at Amber. He squeezed his eyes shut. "I'm ready," he announced.

Bohadea and Almedon looked pointedly at Amber.

"I thought you were kidding," she said to Almedon. "You're not serious?" she asked Bohadea hopefully.

"Just make sure you jump downward," instructed Bohadea. "Away from the night. That's down."

"You mean head first? Dive down head first?"

"Yes, I suppose," said Bohadea. "Head first."

"But I'll crack my skull open on the floor!" exclaimed Amber. She jabbed her heel twice into the solid crystal floor to prove her point.

"I don't think so," Bohadea wagged her head. "But I'll go first. Just in case." And with that, the huge bear dove head first into a thin whispy little trail of light. At the very moment that her great furry bulk hit the light, Bohadea disappeared, and in her place was an explosion of black-gold, a flurry of tiny specks that spiraled down, down through the floor, deeper and deeper until they could no longer be seen.

Amber looked at Almedon with frightened eyes.

"Let's go! Let's go!" yelled Olli, jumping up and down with excitement.

Amber cupped both hands over Olli, took a deep breath, closed her eyes, and dove into the spiral. Bright pink, red, and gold sparkles shimmered in the air, swirling quickly downward like specks of dust caught in a whirlwind.

Almedon was left on his own. He jerked his head around nervously. He looked up at the dark sky, then down into the floor, shook his head once more, sighed deeply, and dove.

It was like floating. Like riding a moonbeam. Like soaring through the sky on dream wings. There was light everywhere. Bright silvery light that flowed through the veins of every feather. And in his mind's eye Almedon could see the Great Sun Eagle, a bird of pure golden light, flying beside him. Together they coasted downward on dream wings and Almedon felt like the mightiest warrior eagle that had ever lived. Soon he had the sense of it being time to land, although he could see nothing specific to land on. He simply extended his feet, dream-like, and the next thing he knew, he had grasped a smooth hard branch of unfamiliar bark. He shook out his feathers and looked quizzically at the wondrous landscape that surrounded him.

Almedon found himself perched in a tree of clear white crystal. The sparkling branches reached into an immense diamond-shaped cavern and the glassy roots stretched toward a flowing stream of light so bright that the eagle had to avert his eyes. It was the river of light that made the strange music they had heard in the cavern above. But perching this close to its source made Almedon's body vibrate with a gentle hum, and the river's song was so beautiful that Almedon imagined it was the voice of an eagle angel, and for a moment he wondered if he was dead.

After all, he had seen the Great Sun Eagle! Almedon could not recall any other living eagle having flown with the Great Sun Eagle. Where had the Great Sun Eagle gone? He turned to look at a spot on the ground not far from his tree, but there stood a bear! A bear of Bohadea's kind, but so ancient that she had turned completely white and her fur shone like sunlight rippling across the water. She looked up at the eagle with gentle blue eyes that filled Almedon with such awe, he did what no eagle would ever do before any other than the Great Sun Eagle. He spread both his wings and lowered his head in a deep respectful bow.

"Welcome," said Istarna, her voice like angel song.

Bohadea stood facing Istarna, her face alight with wonder as she gazed at the last living descendant of Star Bear. Amber stood by Bohadea's side, a smile of amazement lighting up her face.

Almedon gave a little twitch of surprise when he spotted Olli sitting upright in a branch of the crystal tree, not far from where he had perched. The red squirrel chirped happily as he fidgeted with a diamond-shaped fruit. He did not seem the least bit bothered by the sudden appearance of the huge golden eagle. Almedon frowned at the squirrel, but discovered that he really wasn't all that annoyed, in fact, he was actually rather pleased to see that the squirrel had arrived safely. Almedon cast an eye across the cavern. There was no sign of the cat. A look of puzzlement crossed his face and then Pudd Wudd was forgotten, for Istarna had begun to speak.

"Tell me why you have come?" Her voice was an echo that seemed to vibrate from all directions at once.

"We have come for strong magic to fight the Rumblers," said Bohadea.

Istarna nodded. Her gaze passed over each of the travelers." Draw closer," she said, gesturing with her nose for Olli and Almedon to join the others on the floor.

Olli slid down the crystal trunk, nose first, hollering with glee at the smooth ride he got on the glassy bark. Almedon puffed up his wings and glided down without effort. The four stood staring at the ancient white bear, filled with anticipation.

"What do you fear?" said Istarna.

"RUMBLERS!" said Olli and Bohadea in unison.

"Being lost forever," said Amber.

Almedon remained silent.

Istarna shook her magnificent head and it seemed as if little sparks flew from her fur. "No," she said. "One at a time. Close your eyes, take a deep breath, and then tell me what it is you fear most."

Olli squeezed his eyes shut, took a deep noisy gasp of air, and then hollered out at the top of his lungs: "NUT WORMS! Everybody says you can tell if a nut's got worms in it from the outside," he told Istarna. "But I can't tell. And I always seem to get the wormy nuts. I hate wormy nuts. They're squiggly and horrible and teeny tiny so sometimes you can hardly see them till it's too late. I'm scared to get nut worms in my mouth. I have bad dreams about nut worms coming out of bad nuts and chasing me up a tree. YUCK!" Olli huffed with disgust and plunked his little paws down on his hips.

The wise old bear smiled kindly and the light in the cavern grew brighter with her smile. "And tell me what you like best, Olli. What makes your heart sing?"

Olli cocked his head to one side and grinned. He cast his eyes down shyly and said: "I like your fur. It's pretty. It's like sunshine in a puddle. I like to watch the sun playing in puddles under my tree. I have a very fine tree you know. It's pine and it has nuts and a puddle underneath when it rains. And when the sun comes back out: I like that best. I like how it plays in my puddle."

Istarna laughed; it was the sound of a thousand tiny bells, of wind chimes, of baby squirrels at play in a pine tree. She reached one great paw up into the air and flicked her wrist sending a hundred fiery sparks peeling into the cavern. She turned her paw up and reached to show Olli what lay in her palm. "This is your lucky charm," she said. "It will help keep the nut worms away. And it will keep your world bright with sun-filled puddles."

Olli leaned solemnly forward and carefully lifted a tiny silver acorn from Istarna's paw. "Oooh," said the squirrel. "It's very very beautiful." He stared down at the amulet, carefully cradling it in his two little paws. "But how will I carry it with me," he looked up at the ancient white bear, with wide innocent eyes.

Istarna drew a single strand of fur from her own coat and threaded the silky string through the tiny top stem of the silver acorn. Then she lifted the charm from Olli's paws and placed it around his neck. "Oooh," said Olli. "Tcheee, tchureee."

The old white bear smiled then turned to face Amber. "What do you fear?" she asked.

"Well," Amber hesitated. "I guess it's kind of silly. But when Olli told us about nut worms, all I could think of was spiders. I'm really scared of spiders. I don't know why. I just am and my Dad says it's silly, he says the spider is more scared of me than I am of the spider, but I can't help it, I'm still scared of spiders."

"Close your eyes and tell me of your favorite thing," said Istarna.

Amber pressed her eyes closed and a slow smile spread across her face. "Purple," she said. "I love purple. I like the purple coneflowers by our well in the front garden. And I love violets, they're my favorite flower. And the quilt on my bed is purple. And my mom let me paint my whole room purple. It's really beautiful. And my favorite dress is purple. I'd have all purple clothes except my mom says I have to have some stuff in other colors, too. But when I grow up I'm gonna have everything in purple. Mom says I should have been called Amethyst instead of Amber 'cause amethyst is purple and amber is yellow. But amber fits too 'cause that's the color of my hair. Dad says I'm his precious gem." Amber blinked up at Istarna.

With a flourish of her forepaw, there appeared an amethyst crystal gem in the shape of a small exquisitely carved spider squatting in the palm of Istarna's huge white paw. Amber leaned forward. She looked at Istarna and then back at the amethyst spider that the great bear held out in her paw. "Why, it's beautiful," said Amber, her voice filled with awe. "Who would've thought a spider could be so beautiful!" She picked it up and held it in her hand. "And I'm not scared of it, either. It's too beautiful to be scared of."

This time the bear took several strands of fur from her coat and wove them into a stream of silver onto which she strung the amethyst spider. "Banish the fear," said Istarna as she placed the amulet around Amber's neck, "and you will see how the light makes everything beautiful."

She turned to face Almedon. The eagle shifted uneasily from one foot to the other, avoiding the shining blue light in Istarna's eyes.

"What does the eagle fear?" asked Istarna.

"An eagle fears nothing," mumbled Almedon, looking at his feet.

"Even eagles are mortal," said Istarna kindly. "In mortality there is separation. In separation there is fear."

"But I am a fearless hunter. I fear no living thing."

"You are indeed a fearless hunter," said Istarna. But I can see a deep hurt in your heart. You guard it closely, but still it throbs like a wound in your chest."

The eagle gasped at Istarna's words. He ruffled his feathers and one small downy plume floated to the ground to lay at his feet. Almedon stared at it a moment then began to speak: "I had a mate once," he said. "She and I were joined through the rites of the Great Sun Eagle for life. We passed through many summers and winters together, and together we raised five young eaglets. Her name was Ledonnia, and she was a daughter of the Herondic Tribe, the greatest eagle hunters that ever lived."

The cavern fell silent as even the river of light had ceased to sing its song.

"One day, Ledonnia and I were hunting the Valley of Rich Rabbit, and we decided to fly out along the edge of Loon Lake. Suddenly, there came a great clap of thunder from the ground. I saw a flash of light and a puff of smoke from where the thunder came, and then Ledonnia fell from the sky. She went limp. I could see much blood on her feathers. There was a hole in her chest. She fell like a rock to the waters beneath. I went down with her, calling to her, and imploring the Great Sun Eagle for help. But she was already dead. I tried to drag her body from the waters." He sighed. "It was no use. She sank beneath the waves. And it was the last time I ever saw her.

"I will never forget how she looked just before she died," said Almedon sadly. "She was the most beautiful eagle that ever was, and I will always remember how the beams of sunlight glinted from her feathers." A single tear slid from his eye and fell to the ground. The instant it touched the crystal floor it was transformed into a sparkling diamond. It lay there on the floor next to the single downy feather at Almedon's feet.

Istarna reached forward and lifted the tiny teardrop and the downy feather into her paw. The feather she ran across her tongue and it became a thin, fine strand of gold that she threaded through the teardrop. She nudged gently at Almedon's left foot and he lifted it from the ground. Istarna placed the little teardrop ring she had fashioned around the middle talon, and the river resumed its song.

"Bohadea Bear," Istarna turned to face the young bear. "Tell me what you fear."

Bohadea hung her head as she spoke: "Too many things," she shook her head sadly. "But the worst is when someone is hurt and I can do nothing to help. Many moons past, at raspberry season, there came a terrible epidemic when many bears fell sick. They became restless and tired and weak. Their breath came like a slow ragged wind and their fur became coarse and dry. Soon they could no longer go out to gather food. My mother was one of these sick bears.

"My sister, Potelia, and I, we gathered extra food to bring to mother; but she became weaker and weaker and after a time she could not eat at all. I collected the roots of itchweed and the leaves of rattlebush and plucked sticky-head flowers and gathered the seeds of hen-bell, and all of these I made into medicines. But nothing worked. Mother only got sicker, until one night, Dark Bear came out from behind the moon and took her spirit away to the stars."

Again the river had ceased its song.

Bohadea sighed deeply. She looked sadly up at Istarna, then her head drooped again as she remembered yet another time of unhappiness. "And then there was Honeydrop," she said. "My sister had two beautiful little cubs. Snowberry was the boy, and the little girl was called Honeydrop. One day Snowberry and Honeydrop were playing chase games on the rocks at Cedar Bend, right on that little outcropping that overhangs the rapids of the White Water Run. I suppose Honeydrop was too busy playing to pay much attention to where she was going. She stepped too close to the edge, and as Snowberry chased her, she lost her balance, and fell onto the rocks in the river below.

"One of her forelegs was broken badly and I had to help Potelia bring her back to their den. It was terrible," Bohadea shook her head and choked back the tears. "From the full moon to the new moon that poor little cub lay in the den growling and crying from the hurt. The bone had pierced her flesh and the flesh could not be healed. We made many medicines of our own, but none was strong enough, and so I ran all the way to Whisker Ridge to find old Ramanod the Medicine Bear. But by the time we returned to Potelia's den, Dark Bear had already taken Honeydrop to the stars.

"Oh, how I wish I could have found the right medicine for little Honeydrop." Bohadea looked into the eyes of Istarna. "I am so afraid," she said, "that Dark Bear will come again to take away someone I love because I cannot find the right medicine to make them well again."

The wise old bear nodded with sympathy. "Poor Bohadea," she said. "I see a lovely pink light that shines from your sweetest of hearts. You are a good bear, Bohadea." Istarna paused, she reached out a paw and the others saw a stream of light run from the ancient bear toward Bohadea. It made Bohadea smile, and as she did, the river of light took up its song once more.

"Know that Dark Bear does not bring sorrow to those she takes away," said Istarna. "What do you see when you look at the stars?"

Bohadea smiled shyly. "I love the stars," she said. "They're beautiful. And I have one picked out that I think is my mother. And a little one that I call the Honeydrop Star."

"Look up to the stars," instructed Istarna.

Bohadea looked up and the others followed her gaze. The great cavern had been transformed into a huge circle of enormous carved rocks that reached up into a sky of the blackest velvet, bejeweled with a million twinkling stars.

"Draw down the stars, Bohadea," Istarna whispered, her voice seemed to come from far away.

Bohadea reared up onto her hind legs. She stretched her nose skyward and reached both forepaws up to the sky, and as she did the stars began to streak earthward. Small and large, bright and dim, all the stars in the sky raced down toward Bohadea. The bear cupped her great paws together and the others watched in wonder as she caught one star after the other. Bohadea stood almost motionless, staring into the brilliant heap of tiny twinkling stars that collected in her paws and spilled over onto the crystal floor like diamonds.

"And now the sky," said Istarna. The travellers watched with amazement as the black night sky appeared to collapse into itself and fall to earth. Amber and Olli both drew back. But Almedon and Bohadea did not even blink as Istarna drew the black velvet sky down into her paws and formed it into a small velvety pouch.

"You hold the strongest magic of all in your hands," Istarna told Bohadea. "There is no medicine more powerful than star dust."

Bohadea blinked at Istarna with wonder.

"Pour it in here, back into the sky," said Istarna, holding open the black velvet pouch. Bohadea carefully slid the precious heap of star dust into the pouch, careful not to spill one single glittering sparkle. A thin film of star dust clung to her paws and made them glow like fireflies.

Istarna drew the pouch closed and strung it carefully around Bohadea's left ear, tucking it into the fuzzy hollow of her ear. The ancient white bear stepped back and her eyes swept across all four of the travelers.

The entire cavern began to reverberate with the sound of a drum slowly beating out the mystical rhythm of the very Star Bear song that Bohadea had sung to the them in the clearing at Lookout Rock. Yet no one was there to play the drum. The river of light began to sing the song of Star Bear that told of the tribe of warriors who would defeat the Rumblers. And even though the words were not in a language that any of the forest people spoke, they all understood it perfectly.

Istarna's form began to waver like a mirage, as if she was made of a fine thin crystal that might shatter at any moment.

"Oh, no!" cried Bohadea. "Please don't go," she pleaded.

"Go without fear," whispered Istarna.

"But where should we go?" asked Bohadea.

Istarna only smiled. The light of her body became so bright that all four of the tribe had to shield their eyes.

"How do we fight the Rumblers?" Bohadea called out to her, fighting down the panic.

The drum beat harder, the river sang louder, the light of Istarna no longer held the shape of a bear. Suddenly there was a tremendous flash as the wavering light reached out toward the river and with it became one.

"Oh, my," breathed Bohadea. "How do we find our way out of here?" she asked, looking around the doorless crystal cavern.

"On the wings of your dreams," said the crystal clear voice of the river. And then all was silent.

"Now what?" said Amber. Her voice sounded hollow in the sudden quiet of Istarna's cave.

Almedon stood very still, gazing at the river. "It was like a dream coming down here in that spiral of light," he said. As he spoke the river began to hum very softly. Its light began to fade.

"We must do it quickly," said Bohadea. It was as if she could read Almedon's thoughts, for she knew in an instant that he was thinking of flying into the river of light. "The light is fading and there is no other way out."

The eagle glanced at Bohadea then looked back at the stream of fading light. "On the wings of your dreams," he repeated.

"Just close your eyes," chirped Olli. "Close your eyes and you can dream."

"Sometimes you don't even have to close your eyes," added Amber. "I have daydreams all the time in French class. I dream of riding my bike to the park after school."

Almedon turned to look at the others. "Before you jump, close your eyes and call up a dream from the spirit world. A good dream."

"Go," urged Bohadea.

Almedon's eyelids flickered, he spread his great wings, lifted off the ground, and dove into the stream of light, leaving only a trail of golden sparkles that rippled across the river.

"I'm a flying squirrel," bubbled Olli happily, his front paws splayed out and flapping like two stubby little wings.

He took a running leap at the river of light and flung himself in head-first, disappearing in a burst of shimmering red light.

"Go now," Bohadea nudged Amber toward the river. The girl dove in, dreaming of being a cliff-diver in Mexico. Bohadea quickly followed.

5

On the War Path

Bohadea swam beneath the crystal waves as if in a dream, as if she could breathe underwater. She could see Almedon and the others ahead of her and she paddled effortlessly behind. A small bright form appeared to her right and Bohadea turned to find herself face to face with Honeydrop, her sister's cub. Honeydrop smiled and Bohadea was amazed to see that her coat had turned from blackish- brown to a soft golden white. She was the most beautiful cub Bohadea had ever laid eyes on. Bohadea nuzzled her little niece and Honeydrop nipped playfully at Bohadea's ear. It made the bear so happy she thought her heart might burst with joy. The pressure in her chest grew stronger, and she realized she could not breathe underwater after all. She surged upward, breaking the surface, and gasped for air.

Amber was flapping her arms in the water nearby, heading for the rocky shoreline while Olli clung to her shoulder like a drenched mouse. Almedon had already balanced himself on a rock and was shaking the water from his wings.

Bohadea spun around, slapping the water with her paws, desperately searching for Honeydrop. But the little cub had vanished. She shook her head in puzzlement, checked the water once more, and then paddled toward the grey rocks that shone in the first faint light of dawn. Her fur laden with water, she dragged herself dripping onto the shore.

Olli shook out his tail, sending a wet spray into the air. "Quit it," grumbled Amber. Olli shrugged his shoulders and huffed off to climb a gnarly old cedar that leaned low over the water.

Amber wrung out her hair with both hands, then wrapped her arms around herself, shivering in the cool morning air. "Where do you suppose we are?" she asked. "It looks a bit like the river by Lake Wakimika, but I have a feeling it's not."

"Stay here," commanded Almedon, "and I will find out." Again he shook the water from his wings, then took off over the river, catching an updraft that carried him high into the whispy clouds above.

Amber ran her foot across a stretch of beach pebbles, clearing aside some of the bigger stones. She sat down, wrapped her arms around her legs, and let her forehead drop onto her knees. She was cold and wet and hungry and lost. And now weird things were happening. She was losing track of time. She could barely remember what her campsite looked like, much less where it was. Even her mother's face was a fuzzy picture.

"What's wrong, Amburrr?" Bohadea nudged her softly.

"I wanna go home," sniffed the girl.

Bohadea nodded but didn't speak.

"I'm scared, Bohadea."

"I'm scared, too."

"You are?"

"Of course I am."

"I ain't scared," shouted Olli from the cedar tree.

"Eavesdropper," Amber glanced crossly at Olli.

"Leaves dropper," Olli mimicked her, pinching off a bunch of prickly cedar leaves and tossing them Amber's way.

"Are you really scared Bohadea?" Amber blinked at the bear.

"Yes. But do you remember what Istarna told us? It was the second to last thing she said."

Amber shook her head. "I don't remember. Too much was happening all at once."

"Go without fear. That's what she said." Bohadea nosed at the amethyst spider that hung from Amber's neck.

Amber clutched the charm in her hand. It made her fingers tingle. "If it wasn't for this, I would have thought it was all just a dream. It seemed like a dream, didn't it?" Amber took a deep breath. "Well," she sighed, "I guess there's nothing to do but keep going."

Bohadea turned her nose to the sky, searching for Almedon. But it was a long while before the eagle returned.

Bohadea found some berry bushes. Olli collected some nuts. And Amber plucked the leaves of some wild mint that grew along the shoreline. She was proud of her contribution to the meal, and smiled broadly when Bohadea crammed a whole pawful of the leaves into her mouth. It was only after they had eaten their fill that the eagle's shadow finally fell across the rocky beach.

At first sight of the swooping shadow, Olli dashed down the cedar's trunk, intent on Amber's pocket. Then, just as abruptly, he changed his mind and whirled back around, back up the trunk, and out to the tip of a bobbing limb, where he stopped to watch as the eagle landed on the edge of a jagged rock. Olli wiggled his back end in anticipation, then hunkered down in the fragrant clump of cedar.

The eagle's silvery eyelids flickered once at Olli and then he turned to face Bohadea and Amber, who hurried toward his perch. "I'm so glad you're back," called Bohadea. "I was beginning to worry."

Almedon's feathers seemed to have lost some of their sheen and he hung his head like a very old eagle. When he spoke, his voice was heavy with sadness: "We are near the killing grounds," he said.

"Killing grounds?" Amber repeated the words in a quavering voice, her eyes were wide blue circles.

Olli pressed himself deeper among the spiny cedar leaves.

"It is worse than anything we could have imagined," Almedon shook his head grimly. "The Rumblers are moving out of the Pit in all directions. They have worn deep ruts into the earth, like dry river beds, and these are the paths they travel. Those terrible pink things...."

"The Saroos," offered Bohadea.

"Yes," Almedon snapped his beak. "The Saroos are working for them now. They go a long way ahead of the Rumblers as scouts, and set up traps for the forest people who are trying to escape. All the captured folk are herded together, wolf and deer, coyote and crow, duck and tortoise, and they are imprisoned inside a cage made of fire. The Saroos have fashioned the fire into fine glowing threads that form exact angles; each side makes a perfect square. It is like the webbing of some strange, giant spider. But one touch is death. I saw a robin fly into one side trying to free her mate. The webbing burst into flames where she struck it, and nothing but ashes spilled to the ground. Inside the fire-web there are ashes wherever forest folk have tried to escape. The survivors are huddled in the middle. Wolves with rabbits. Doves with hawks. It's unnatural!"

"This is unbelievable," Amber squeezed her eyes shut and raked her fingers through her hair. "Why are they keeping them prisoner?"

"I spoke with a red-tailed hawk who said that the Rumblers come to the webs to collect the prisoners. I don't know for what purpose. But I do know that those caught inside the fire-webs do not come out alive."

Bohadea blinked at Almedon, stunned. "But how will we ever defeat them? There are only four of us. And we have nothing to fight them with." She paused. "Except the talismans that Istarna gave us," she said uncertainly. Bohadea touched the little black velvet pouch tucked in her ear and wondered how a pawful of star dust could stop the Rumblers.

"I don't know how we will fight the Rumblers," said Almedon. "I only know that we must." He shifted his weight and as he did a ray of sunlight caught the diamond teardrop on the talon of his left foot, shooting a rainbow arc of light across the pebbled beach.

"One of the fire-webs is only a short distance from here," Almedon continued. "By paw, you can travel there along the river path. If we leave now, we will arrive before the sun begins its journey to the Land of Shadow Eagles."

"What are we supposed to do when we get there?" asked Amber anxiously. She curled her fingers around the amethyst spider and felt the prickle of its warmth.

"When we get there," said Almedon, "we will free the forest folk. According to the eagle's eye, Rumbler troops will arrive at the fire-web soon after the sun returns from its night's journey. On this night, we free the forest folk. Or tomorrow they die."

"But how do we get them out?" Amber wondered aloud.

Cowering in the clump of cedar leaves, Olli whispered the words to himself: *"Fire-web."* He shivered and clutched the silver acorn at his neck. Nut worms seemed like an awfully piddly thing, now that he had Rumblers and Saroos and fire-webs to worry about.

Suddenly, Bohadea reared up on her hind legs and roared at the sky. It was the mighty cry of an ancient warrior bear. Fierce and blood-curdling, it fractured the air. Olli squeezed his face into a fierce little grimace, and rattled a warning. Almedon raised his beak to the sky and his high-pitched war cry spiraled into the air. The ground quaked and pebbles on the beach began to churn. Amber could feel the earth's vibrations run up her legs and into her body. She stomped her feet, shook her head, and her little-girl voice completed the powerful spiral of sound.

Deep in the forest a band of marauding Saroos heard the distant war cries; they broke rank and scurried deeper into the woods. The clouds darkened and gathered speed over the Tribe of Star Bear. A bolt of lightning tore through the grey sky, a mighty clap of thunder jolted the earth. Rain poured onto the beach and the forest.

Bohadea dropped back onto all fours. "Star Bear heard us," she said, raindrops glistening on her eyelashes.

"Sun Eagle has left the sky to come and fight with us," said Almedon with amazement.

"My guardian angel is purple," said Amber quietly. "I saw her standing in the clouds."

"Yup," agreed Olli. "That was an angel all right. She has a very beautiful tail." He shook the rain from his coat, scrambled down the tree trunk, across the pebbles, up Amber's leg, and hopped into her pocket. Amber hugged herself, shivering from the chill of the rain.

"Your pelt does not keep the rain out very well, does it?" said Bohadea with concern. She lumbered over to the forest edge and plucked some large fern leaves, dropping them at Amber's feet. "Perhaps you can make a cover from these. The rain will not come through the leaves."

"We must go now," said Almedon. Beads of water ran over his feathers and slid from his wings.

Amber scooped up the fern leaves although she didn't know how a raincoat could be made from them.

Almedon raised his voice above the pelting rain. "It is very dangerous to travel the forest now. The Saroos and their traps are everywhere. You must not wander from each other. Stay close. I will scout ahead and if you hear an eagle cry you must hide at once for it means the Saroos are near."

"Almedon," said Bohadea. "You said they had captured birds, too. Can they take a bird from the air?"

"I don't know," said Almedon, feathers furrowed at his brow.

"Then you, too, must be very careful. Don't take any chances."

Almedon nodded. "Follow the river upstream. I will return often to guide you." He flapped his great wings and rose into the air setting flight at a lower height than usual. Bohadea, Amber, and Olli watched until he disappeared over the top of the forest canopy.

The rain was already settling down to a fine drizzle. Bohadea turned to face her companions. "You heard what Almedon told us. It's dangerous in the woods. We must stay close together. I will go first. Amburrr, you must not be any more than three or four tail-lengths behind me. And Ollidollinderi …" Olli snapped to attention at the mention of his long formal name "… you must remain in Amburrr's pelt pocket, where you'll be safe."

"It's kinda damp in here," Olli complained. "Can I go up on her shoulder if I want?"

"I suppose," replied Bohadea. "As long as you stay with her. And Amburrr," the bear looked deeply into the girl's blue eyes, "you and I, we must move like the spirits. Pay attention to where each paw falls on the forest floor so that we make no noise."

Amber nodded her solemn agreement. "Indian guides can walk like that," she said. "I'll walk like an Indian spirit guide."

"Eyes open and ears pricked," Bohadea said, then she turned and led the way to the riverside trail.

The beach pebbles had become slick with rain and they scrunched underfoot despite Amber's best effort to move in silence. In the short space between her and Bohadea a round glittering stone caught her eye. Amber tucked the bunch of leaves Bohadea had given her under her arm and swooped to pick it up, careful of Olli who was still in her pocket.

"Tcheeez!" he complained anyway, his fuzzy head popped up like a groundhog checking for winter's end.

Amber examined the stone between her fingers: it was pretty with curls of pink and grey, but would have been rather ordinary if it weren't for the tiny white crystals embedded inside. Amber wondered if the crystals might be real diamonds. She decided to keep it and dropped it into her pocket beside Olli.

"Hey," yelped Olli, "whaddya think you're doing?"

"It's my pocket," said Amber, "I can put things in it, too, you know."

"Hush," Bohadea turned to warn them. "We must keep quiet or the Saroos might hear us."

Olli and Amber fell silent again as they stepped from the beach onto the riverside trail. It was easier to walk quietly on the forest floor. Amber watched for dried leaves and twigs and avoided them. She became quite good at finding the bare spots of dirt and began moving swiftly, making very little sound.

The rain had slowed to almost nothing beneath the forest canopy and Amber had nearly decided to discard her bunch of fern leaves when the skies opened up and it began to pour again. As she walked, she braided and twined the stems and was about to ask Olli for something from his treasury to tie the stems together with, when the piercing shriek of an eagle shattered the damp forest air. Amber searched the patch of sky above them for a sign of Almedon. Olli dove deep into her pocket.

Bohadea froze. She put her nose to the air and found there the strangest scent. *Pink!* "Saroos!" she whispered. Desperately she searched both sides of the trail, sniffing rapidly, ears twitching back and forth. She shot an urgent look at Amber and gestured for her to follow. Moving quickly and with hardly a sound, she led the way into the bush toward the river. The bank was steep but without pausing, the bear slid down, dislodging small stones, which rolled and plunked into the river. Amber flung aside her braided fern leaves and slid down the damp bank on her rear end.

A dead tree with a cave-like bundle of dried old roots hung over the river. Bohadea led them straight into the water, where she crouched beneath the protective roots. Amber squatted down beside her. Olli hunkered low in her pocket.

Amber shook with fright at the sound of the creatures approaching along the riverside trail. Bohadea gently placed her paw over Amber's mouth. Amber squeezed her eyes shut and nodded to Bohadea that she understood. Then she reached gently into her pocket, stroked Olli's fur, and gently tapped her finger twice against his nose. Olli, too, understood and clamped both paws over his mouth.

The crunching of paws and a low jabbering sound grew louder as the creatures drew nearer, and soon Amber could tell that they were right on the path, directly in front of them, in the exact place that Almedon had shouted his warning to the tribe. The Saroos had stopped there!

Why! Amber's heart pounded in her chest. She looked up at Bohadea and saw how frightened the bear was too.

Then, the thing she feared most happened: she heard the sound of branches snapping and twigs crackling under-foot as the creatures turned from the trail and came toward the river, straight for their hiding place. Amber's breath caught in her chest as she heard them pause on the bank directly above the fallen tree.

There was a small sliver of space in the twine of roots above her, and Amber craned her neck to catch a glimpse of the dreaded Saroos. There was a flurry of flamingo-pink fur. They were taller than Amber had expected. At least five feet tall. Their bodies were very wide and burly, their limbs long and spindly. They had wide thin mouths, big ears, and long knobby fingers. The three that Amber could see through the chink in the roots carried red crystal wands that they clutched between their bony fingers. The sight sent a shiver up her spine.

The Saroos were jabbering to each other in a language that Amber could not understand, and she almost gasped when she realized what had caught their interest. It was the fern leaves she had been braiding. The leaves she had tossed aside just before sliding down the riverbank.

A fourth Saroo came into sight. This one seemed to be in charge, for he began gesturing and snapping orders that made the others scurry about. *They're looking for us now,* Amber thought with horror. If only she hadn't left those leaves behind.

Bohadea and Amber pressed in closer to the tangled muddy roots. A tiny grey spider scuttled across Amber's arm. She gritted her teeth to stifle a scream. She squeezed her eyes shut and clutched at the talisman at her neck. At once she felt the warm vibration of the amethyst spider soothing and calming her. She opened her eyes in time to see the real spider slip away along the root bundle. And in time to see a flash of flamingo-pink to the left. The Saroos were searching the bank. It was a matter of seconds before the tribe would be discovered.

Suddenly, downstream, from the far bank of the river, came the splash of a large stone hitting the water. The Saroos stopped in their tracks and turned toward the sound. Another stone hit the water. Amber saw the flash of an eagle's wing. Almedon broke from the woods and shot straight up into the sky, moving with amazing speed away from the Saroos and into the cloud cover. The Saroos began to shout and run in their clumsy shambling gait toward the spot where they had seen Almedon break cover. Amber gasped as a beam of red light shot up in the air after Almedon. Several beams followed with sharp zapping sounds, but none hit Almedon for the eagle had already disappeared into the stormy grey clouds.

The Saroos ranged along the riverbank in a frenzy, moving away from the tribe's root cover. Bohadea shoved Amber toward the bank. The girl scrambled up on all fours with Bohadea beside her and they both dove for cover in the bush.

"Onto my back," hissed Bohadea.

Amber flung herself up and they were off, Bohadea weaving through the bush with hardly a sound. When she hit the trail, she turned and galloped upstream fast as an antelope, running a long time, until her breath came in short ragged gasps.

"Do you think we're safe now?" whispered Amber anxiously.

Bohadea slowed to a trot, sniffing at the air. "I don't think so," she shook her head. "Their scent is still strong." She stopped and turned her nose to scan the inland terrain. "There are more coming. We cannot stay on the trail. It's too dangerous."

Olli poked his head up. "We'd better go up in the trees," he suggested. "It's too dangerous down here."

"You didn't see their red zapper sticks," said Amber. "They're like ray guns. No way are the trees safe. They'll just point their red sticks at you, and *zap*, you're fried."

"Fried?" Olli quivered.

"Fried," nodded Amber.

"We travel by river until Almedon finds us," said Bohadea. "Then we go deep into the bush."

Amber dismounted, Olli cautiously climbed up onto her shoulder, and Bohadea led the way back to the riverbank. The bear poked her nose out of the bush at the river's edge and sniffed carefully in both directions. "It's harder to catch a clear scent in the rain," she said, "but I think we'll be safe for now."

Bohadea led the way down the bank's gentle slope and splashed into the stony shallows setting a course that ran against the current. Amber moved in close to Bohadea and sloshed through the ankle-deep water, thinking how lucky she was to have a pair of water-logged sneakers between her feet and the slippery stones of the riverbed.

What would her mom say if she could see her now? Soaked from head to toe with rain and mossy green river water. Her skin and clothes smeared with dirt. A red squirrel living in her jumper pocket with a heap of fungus and nutshells and other forest junk. Her hair wild and tangled. It had been ... how long? Over two days since she had run a comb through her hair.

It made her think of her holiday in Jamaica. A Rastafarian man called Jerome had brought them green coconuts every morning for breakfast. She had wanted to have her hair done up in dreadlocks just like Jerome's. But her parents wouldn't allow it.

She cast her eyes along the shore, spotting a muddy place ahead where the bank rose up in a tangle of tree roots. Jerome had told her that he'd made his dreadlocks by twisting his hair together with mud. So as they passed by the muddy spot, Amber veered in closer to shore, scooped up a big glob of mud, and began twisting and pasting.

"Whatchya doing?" Olli asked after a while.

Bohadea turned to glance at the girl. "Why Amburrr, your head fur is almost as dark as mine. It looks as though you have many tails growing from your head," she laughed.

"I think she's trying to get the stink off," said Olli. "She keeps getting more mud and putting it in her fur."

"That's not how you take a mud bath," Bohadea snorted with good humor. "You must roll your entire body in the mud to get a good bath."

"It's not a bath," frowned Amber. "I'm putting my hair in dreadlocks."

Bohadea looked confused. Olli shrugged. "Oh well," he said, "the main thing is that you smell better now. The mud helped."

"It has nothing to do with how I smell," said Amber crossly. "It's a new hairstyle."

A sudden flurry of wings startled all three as Almedon coasted in, landing on a nearby larch tree at the water's edge. "You are making too much noise," he scolded them. "What if the Saroos had been nearby?" He turned to look at Amber. "What have you done to your mane?"

"She was getting some of the smell off," offered Olli.

"Was not!" protested Amber. "I put my hair in dread-locks. Dreadlocks are … they're ah … it's the way that human warriors wear their hair. I decided that if I'm to be a warrior, then I should look like one. And later, when night comes, I'll put mud all over my face and my hands and arms. For camouflage. So I blend in with the night."

Almedon looked impressed. "It is good to look like a warrior," he said by way of praise, "but you must act like one, too. Twittering like a flock of starlings is not the warrior way. You must learn silence."

Bohadea was back on guard, her nose scanning the shoreline for a whiff of the Saroo scent. Satisfied that they were not near, she turned to Almedon. "You risked your life to save us, Almedon," the bear said solemnly. "Thank you."

"I saw the Saroos try to shoot you down with their red zapper sticks," said Amber. "I'm glad they missed."

"Fried!" hissed Olli. "Or you wouldda been fried!"

Almedon ruffled his feathers, hitched up his shoulders in a distracted way, then smoothed his feathers down again. "We are a tribe now," he said. "As strange a mix as we are," he looked pointedly at Olli, "our lives have been bound together. Our war cries brought Sun Eagle down from the sky to fight by our side. Now we are destined to fight together—to death if need be."

"Tchip," whispered Olli. "To death?"

"It is the most noble of deaths to die in battle," said Almedon. "Or to die in the defense of one's tribe."

"I don't know about that!" Amber frowned, her head cocked to one side. "In history class we learned about all the wars. People killing each other because they don't like the other guy's ideas, or because they want what the other guy has. I don't think it's noble. I think it's stupid."

"Humans spill blood for sport," said Almedon, his eyes as bright as two matched garnets. "Your kind play games that require bloodshed. Do not confuse the pawns of your games with warriors, young Human. A true warrior dances with Sun Eagle, he brushes his wings against the stars. A warrior has no past and no future. A warrior never sets wing tip or talon outside the circle of life, he follows the Path of the Rainbow."

"I'd like to walk on a rainbow," said Amber. She touched the amethyst spider and absently stroked the glit-

tering purple gem. Then her brow furrowed, she locked
eyes with Almedon: "But I still don't see why dying is so
noble."

"The warrior's lifeblood is a gift from Grandmother
Earth. When the time comes, the warrior gladly returns his
blood to the earth and flies home on his spirit wings."

"Hush!" Bohadea urgently sniffed at the air, her ears
twitched. "Hush up or we'll all be flying home on spirit
wings."

Almedon stiffened, his head swiveled toward the forest. Olli stood rigidly on Amber's shoulder.

"Wolf," whispered Bohadea. "Quickly Amburrr, stand
by my tail."

Amber leapt to the bear's side. "Tchuk," squealed Olli,
he dove into the pocket.

"She's broken cover," said Almedon. "I see her."

"Fear! The wolf is scared," said Bohadea, her nose
probing the air.

"I can't smell anything," said Amber, nervously twisting one of her new mud-caked dreadlocks.

"She runs swiftly," said Almedon. "But not hunting.
She's heading right for us."

"Where? Where is she?" Amber was searching the
treeline for some sign of the wolf, when a silver streak
burst onto the riverbank.

The tribe stood motionless, staring, as the she-wolf
skidded to a halt. Her brown eyes flashed wide with shock
as she took in the black bear, the muddy, heather-pink
human, with a head full of tails and a small red squirrel
stuck in her front pocket, and the golden eagle perched
overhead on the gnarly limb of a larch. The wolf's lips
twitched up and down, there was a flash of sharp white
teeth, a low rattle in her throat. Then she yipped one high-
pitched yelp, turned tail, ran two steps, stopped, flipped

right round facing them again, and stood her ground. She blinked at them, still panting hard, but not speaking.

"From whom do you run?" asked Almedon.

The sleek silvery wolf swung her head toward the eagle but she didn't answer him.

"Speak!" commanded Almedon. "If the Saroos are headed this way we must seek cover quickly."

The wolf perked up her ears. "The Saroos. They took us by ambush. Captured the whole pack. They killed Ruffis, my mate." Her shoulders slumped, her head hung low. "They took Shaleena and Eldiveera, my daughters. They're only pups."

"*Pink!*" cried Bohadea, her nose scenting at the forest.

The wolf jerked her head up in alarm and sniffed the air. "They're still on my trail," her voice was a snarl.

"Oh, no," wailed Amber, her eyes wide with fear. "Where will we hide this time?"

"Oh no, oh no, oh no," squeaked Olli.

The wolf cocked her head at Amber and Olli, her ears twitched. She quickly sniffed the air again, then turned to the tribe: "I was heading for an old wolf den by Weeping Rock. It's not far from here and well hidden, but it was abandoned because it was too dark and wet for the pups. It will be a good hiding place. You can come with me, if you want."

"Weeping Rock," murmured Bohadea. It was just as Star Bear had predicted: With *fear they'll walk, by Weeping Rock.*

"That is in the direction of the fire-web. We leave at once," said Almedon. "With all speed."

Bohadea nodded at Amber and the girl leapt onto her back. Olli scrambled out of Amber's pocket and latched onto a clump of fur between Bohadea's ears. The wolf watched in amazement, then turned and ran. She splashed across the river, and turned upstream on the far bank. Bohadea ran very fast, but she couldn't keep up. The wolf was glad to slow her pace: she had run long and hard, she was tired and grief-stricken, but strangely, pleased to have the bear's tribe for company.

Almedon cruised low over the river using the forest canopy for cover. On every twelfth wingbeat, he would rise above the trees to catch a glimpse of the flamingo-pink spots that marked the locations of the Saroos. In addition to the Saroos tracking the wolf, there were at least three large bands operating in the area. One band was moving slowly, herding a group of captives in the direction of the fire-web. There were wolves among the prisoners and Almedon wondered if the wolf's pups were among them. The second band was moving away from the river, and a third smaller band was ranging upstream close to the river. The river rangers were the ones that worried Almedon. Soon, Bohadea and the wolf would have to pass by the rapids where the Saroos seemed to be concentrating.

A flock of starlings rushed across the canopy screaming with panic. They dove low over the river then swung up over the trees and scattered in all directions. Almedon banked to the right turning back downstream. He had to warn the tribe of the danger ahead. He saw dapples of silver and black ahead: the wolf and the bear. But the pink seemed wrong, much too—

A zap of red light, sharp as a talon, tore at the crest of Almedon's wing. The eagle screamed, sparks flew from his feathers, and the stench of fire filled the air. Too late, he realized that the splotch of pink was not Amber. His tribe had been captured by Saroos.

He veered sharply to the left and dove deep into the sheltering limbs of an ancient hemlock. A sharp glassy pain

stabbed at Almedon's injured wing. It hung limp and useless at his side. The bone was shattered, the muscle torn
away, the feathers burnt to cinders. It was an injury
Almedon knew he could not survive. A careless moment
and now it was over. Now he would perch in this hemlock
tree until death overtook him. His tribe would be herded
into the fire-web and killed. The Rumblers would march on
and destroy the whole of the forest. He hung his head in
misery and let his eyes drift shut.

The face of beautiful Ledonnia, his dead mate, drifted
before him. Her eyes were as bright as the sun, her beak as
sharp and black as an obsidian arrowhead, her golden face
like a shield against the pain that racked his body. His
heart leapt with joy, for in a short while he and Ledonnia
would fly together again, in the spirit world.

"Not yet," Ledonnia said. "You are the chosen one of
the Great Sun Eagle, Almedon. You have a mission and
you must first complete it."

"But I am dying," protested Almedon. "My wing has
been torn apart. I cannot fly. There can be no mission for
an eagle with only one wing."

"You are an eagle of great power. Your spirit shines
with the force of the Great Sun Eagle," said Ledonnia.
"Draw the strength that is within, My Love, for your fight
has hardly begun."

"I am tired. I have only one wing. I do not understand
what Sun Eagle wants me to do."

"Tchip," said Ledonnia. Almedon's eyes snapped open
to see Olli shivering on a clump of hemlock directly in
front of him.

"You're fried," said Olli sadly. "Fried bad." His teeth
chattered so loudly that Almedon could barely make out
the words.

"How did you find me?" Almedon asked the squirrel.

Olli fidgeted nervously with his fingers: "When those awful Saroos caught us, the human grabbed me up in her paw and threw me down in her pelt pocket. On my head," frowned Olli, ruffling the fur between his ears. "But the Saroos didn't find me and the next thing I knew, she scooped me up again and threw me in a bush and the Saroos still didn't see me. I didn't move for a long time. Then I went high up in the trees and I followed them. I saw when they stopped and one pointed his red stick that shot fire in the sky. The fire hit you and you screamed and I saw you go in this tree. So I came here as fast as I could through the treetops." Olli shrugged his shoulders and began to shiver again.

Almedon blinked at Olli. What an upside-down world it had become. Two moons ago it would have been unimaginable that a red squirrel would seek out a golden eagle on his perch. "Did the Saroos see where I landed?" he asked the squirrel.

"I don't think so," Olli shook his head. "They were too too low to the ground. I was up high."

"Good!" Almedon ground his beak against the stabbing pain in his wing.

"But they're coming this way. Straight here. Soon!" said Olli, his tail swished from side to side. "Tchip! The trail goes right under this tree."

"Good!" said Almedon.

"Good?" Olli cocked his head curiously at the eagle. "Don't we want to get away? We'd better get away. Far, far, far away."

"How many Saroos are there?"

Olli crinkled his nose to one side, concentrating: "One nut. Two nut. Three in all," he said.

"Who walks in front?"

"One Saroo walks in front," said Olli. "Then the wolf, Bohadea, and Amber. Then two Saroos with red sticks pointed at their backs; they come last. I hate red sticks. Tchurrr!"

Almedon gritted his beak. "Ledonnia said I still have a mission to accomplish. This must be it."

"I think we'd better go now," said Olli uncertainly.

"Yes," said Almedon. "You'd better hurry. Go and hide yourself in the top branches of the pine tree behind this one and stay there until the Saroos have passed."

"But ... tchip, tchip ... aren't you coming, too?"

"I will stay," said Almedon, he winced with pain. "GO!" he snapped his beak at the squirrel.

Olli flinched, blinked at the eagle, then raced headfirst down the trunk of the hemlock. But he didn't go into the pine tree. Instead, he turned around and peered up at where Almedon was perched. The eagle was well hidden. It was hard to see him even from directly underneath. Olli fearfully glanced over his shoulder to see if the Saroos were coming. They weren't, so he slunk around to the opposite side of the trunk and very quietly crept back upward, settling into a spot not far from Almedon's perch.

It wasn't long before the first Saroo came into sight. Olli stiffened and froze. He did not look at Almedon but he could sense that the eagle had seen the Saroo too.

The lead Saroo looked straight ahead with hard black eyes that never seemed to blink. He carried a red stick at his side. Next came the wolf, her silver head hung low, her tail dragging behind her. Bohadea walked tall and straight, her nostrils flaring, her eyes flashing: She smells us, thought Olli. Amber looked scared and kept one hand trailing on Bohadea's rump. The last two Saroos were jabbering at each other in some language that Olli did not understand.

The first Saroo passed beneath the hemlock and Olli slowly cowered down, pressing himself hard against the trunk. The wolf passed. Bohadea was directly beneath them. Suddenly there was a flash of gold from the branch where Almedon perched. Olli watched with terrified eyes as Almedon flung his battered body downward ... falling ... hard as a rock, talons reaching forward like a guinea cock about to fight. In an instant, Olli understood what Almedon intended to do. He also understood what he, Ollidollinderi, must do, and it filled him with the biggest terror he had ever felt in his life. A hot silver spark flew from the squirrel's acorn talisman and hit him square between the eyes. He clenched his tiny fists, gritted his teeth, and with a high shrieking battle call he flew from the tree.

Almedon hit his target first. The Saroo at the rear, closest to the riverside, was struck full in the face by the eagle's talons. A split second later the Saroo was blind. The second Saroo had begun to turn toward his companion, to raise his red crystal wand, when he too was struck in the face. Olli dug his teeth, and the tiny claws of all four feet, into the part of the Saroo that stuck out the furthest, his snout. The Saroo screeched in pain, but Olli hung on, clinging with all his might to the Saroo's snout.

The lead Saroo turned, red wand raised to strike, and the wolf leapt, tearing out the Saroo's throat with the practiced skill of a predator. Bohadea roared and charged the Saroo with Olli on his snout. He went down hard, Olli jumped clear, and Bohadea slammed all her weight down on the arm with the wand. The Saroo screamed as the bones cracked.

The blinded Saroo beat at the eagle with his paws, and with the hard crystal wand. Amber delivered a powerful kick to the Saroo's knee. His leg buckled. "Leave him alone," she cried. She sank her teeth into the hand that held the wand. The Saroo dropped his red wand and stumbled to the side. Almedon fell to the forest floor in a bloody heap of tangled feathers. He didn't move. Amber rushed to the eagle's side. The wolf moved in on the injured Saroo and without hesitation, she killed him. Then she turned to face the last Saroo. Her lips curled upward and a raging snarl rose from the depths of her belly. This Saroo she knew. It was he who had killed her mate Ruffis. Bohadea moved aside and the Saroo scrambled backward, cradling his broken arm. The wolf roared in fury and made her final deadly strike.

"Bohadea!" Amber was crying, tears streaked down her cheeks. "He's dead! I think Almedon's dead!"

"NO!" howled Bohadea. She rushed to Amber's side. Gently she prodded at Almedon, her nose on his face, on his neck, his chest. "No, he's not dead. Not yet. There's time!" With trembling paws and faulty breath she unfastened the pouch from her ear and dipped the tip of her nose into the star dust.

The tiny brilliant sparkles glowed on her nose with an unearthly light. Bohadea began to hum. She touched her nose to the crown of Almedon's head, to his forehead, his throat, his heart, his belly, his tail, and the tips of each wing. At each place the bear touched, a magical white starlight began to dance, spiraling round and round, and the light sang in the same clear voice as the river in Istarna's cave. The eagle stirred. His silver eyelids flickered.

Bohadea turned her attention to Almedon's ruined wing. She carefully nuzzled the eagle's wound until the starlight became so bright that she had to back away. As the bear, the girl, the squirrel, and the wolf watched, the light flitted and weaved across the eagle's body, singing its healing song. Tiny bursts of starlight twinkled and then disappeared, one after the other, until all was silent.

Almedon rose from the ground, ruffled his feathers, flapped his two perfect wings as hard as he could, and folded them back across his body. "Ledonnia says I must stay and fight," he announced. "She was a warrior of the Herondic Tribe, you know," he added with pride.

"You have very powerful magic," the wolf said to the bear.

"From Istarna, descendant of Star Bear," said Bohadea.

"It worked!" said Amber.

"Of course it worked," said Bohadea, fitting the pouch back into her ear.

"Look!" said Olli. He scrambled up onto Amber's shoulder, and safely tucked himself between her dreadlocks before pointing at the fallen Saroos: "The light of their fire-sticks is not as bright anymore."

Amber stepped over to one of the crystal wands and bent to pick it up. Olli clung to a dreadlock.

"No!" barked Bohadea.

Amber stopped and she gave Bohadea a puzzled look. "But...."

"No," said the bear. "The sticks hold bad magic. We must not touch them."

"But maybe we could get them to work. Then we'd have weapons, too. We'd stand a better chance."

"No, Amburrr," Bohadea said firmly. "Then we would become like the Saroos. We fight only with our teeth and claws and with the magic of Star Bear."

"Okay, I guess," Amber shrugged her shoulders and turned away from the crystal wand. "What do we do now?"

"We go to the den at Weeping Rock," said Almedon.

"What for?" asked the wolf. "The Saroos are no longer tracking us. Besides, I must go to find my daughters now. I will not leave the forest without my pups."

"Your pups have probably been taken to the fire-web," said Almedon. "But there are bands of Saroos everywhere. It is not safe to travel by sunlight anymore. We must get to the den and stay until Sun Eagle leaves the sky. Then we go to the fire-web. We will free your daughters together."

6

Spirits of the Rainbow

They crept with their bellies low to the ground past the rapids that ran beneath Weeping Rock. The Saroos were everywhere, beating the bushes, flushing the forest people into the open, herding the prisoners away with the crystal wands. The air crackled with sharp thin zaps of crystal fire. The smell of terror and death hung like a black cloud over the woods. The wolf, who knew the terrain well, was in the lead, pulling herself along the ground. She threaded her way through a dense thicket of brambleberry, the thorns raking her fur like bear claws.

It was too dangerous for Almedon to fly. Too dangerous for Olli to run through the canopy. Almedon had no choice but to accept Bohadea's help. He flattened himself against the bear's back and rode through the tangle of thorns. Olli clung to Amber's dreadlocks, using the furry new tails as a shield against the sharp brambles.

The wolf crawled to the edge of the thicket and stopped. "We go up through the rocks now," she whispered. "The den is not far."

On the riverside was a sheer cliff where the water fell over the rocks, pounding into the rapids below. The wolf turned in the opposite direction, keeping to a sparse cover of bushes. Bohadea slunk low to the ground and Amber followed in a deep crouch. Suddenly Bohadea stopped short. "They're coming this way!" she hissed.

The wolf broke into a run and dove behind a large boulder. Almedon swiftly took flight. Amber sprinted after the wolf, legs churning, arms pumping, keeping her head low; Olli clung to a dreadlock swinging precariously over one shoulder. Amber dove in beside the wolf, Bohadea flung herself on top. They stayed that way, motionless, as a small band of marauding Saroos passed by.

As soon as they were out of earshot, the wolf jumped to her feet and began to run uphill, winding her way between bushes and boulders. Amber scrambled after her, nimble as a mountain goat; if she had paused to think about the loose gravel footing she would have faltered.

The wolf disappeared into a dense clump of bushes. Amber hesitated, then cautiously parted the twisted branches. There in front of her was the jagged entrance to a den. The tip of the wolf's tail vanished into the dark and Amber hurriedly followed, dropping onto all fours to clear the low overhang of rock. Olli hung like an acrobat, swinging from the fall of her hair.

It was dank and eerie inside. The walls pressed inward, the ceiling hung low and threatening, as if the weight of the world above was about to break through. A trickle of water crept darkly through the cave. Only the faintest dusty grey light allowed Amber to see the shadowy form of the wolf moving ahead. Olli's anxious breath brushed at her neck as she stepped deeper into the den. She could hear Bohadea and Almedon push in behind her, while the wolf tiptoed forward leading them around an old rock slide that had partially sealed the tunnel.

"*Pink!*" Bohadea snuffled at the thick damp air. "I can smell Saroos. It's awful strong, they must be—"

Amber cleared the rubble. The wolf stopped short and Amber bumped into her. The fur on the wolf's back bristled as a low menacing growl began to rumble deep in her throat.

"IN HERE!" cried Bohadea. But it was too late because they were standing face to face with two pink Saroos who looked just as shocked and frightened as the tribe did.

The Saroos threw their spindly arms up into the air to show that they had no fire-sticks. The wolf coiled into her haunches, about to spring. "No!" shouted one of the Saroos, in a tongue that was understood by everyone. The wolf shifted her weight, adjusting her striking stance. Bohadea and Almedon cleared the barrier of tumbled rocks, both charging to the attack. Amber balled up her fists.

"No!" the Saroo shouted again, his bony pink hands pushing back at the air as if to repel the attack. "We're hiding, too. We mean you no harm. We're runaways. Please don't hurt us!"

The wolf shifted her stance again, and was about to leap when Bohadea called out: "No! Wait! Let's hear their story first, then we'll decide what to do."

"Kill them," growled Almedon.

"Kill," snarled the wolf.

"No!" insisted Amber. There was something very different about these two, and somehow, she knew that they wouldn't hurt her tribe.

"We listen, then decide," said Bohadea.

The Saroo who had first spoken took the cue and began to speak at once. "I am Trub, and this is Kog," he gestured to the female that stood beside him. "The Rumblers have made our people slaves. We are forced to do what they demand."

"How so?" asked Almedon, his voice flat and cold as a slab of marble.

Trub blinked nervously, Kog visibly shuddered. "It's the red crystals," he said. "They are used for everything in our world. We get food with crystal-finders, we build our homes from crystal with crystal tools, we travel and communicate with the crystals, our medicine depends on the red crystals. Many believe that without the red crystals we could no longer survive."

"Then your people are stupid," said Almedon. "The forest provides everything that any creature needs."

"I understand," said Trub, "but our people have been away from the forest for so long that they have lost all their forest skills. We have built a world far from the forest. A world that depends on stones from the crystal pit. Most Saroos would perish if left to fend for themselves in the forest. The forest is a dead zone to the Saroos."

"A dead zone?" Bohadea asked incredulously.

"These creatures deserve no mercy," said Almedon. "They are as thick and dangerous as quicksand, and they treat our home as if it had no spirit. They cannot hear the forest spirits speak. They are blind to tree spirits and deaf to wind spirits. I'll wager they cannot even see the Sun Eagle in the sky. They are of no earthly use. Their only purpose is to destroy us."

"Kill them," said the wolf.

"Yeah, kill 'em," snarled Olli.

"No!" Amber started forward, placing herself between her tribe and the Saroos. "Let Trub finish telling his story."

"Finish fast," growled Almedon.

Trub nodded gratefully at Amber. He began to speak more quickly, his voice taking on the jabber that they had heard earlier from the marauding Saroos. "Our people thought they could dig crystals from the pit forever, but a few days ago, the crystal miners cracked the floor of the pit, and the Rumblers broke through. There were legends that warned of such an event, but our people paid no heed, no one believed such a thing could really happen. But it did, and it was only a matter of minutes before Red City was swarming with Rumblers. Many of our kind were killed before Dreeg, King of the Rumblers, summoned Yenm, our leader, to strike a deal."

"Dreeg agreed to negotiate?" Almedon narrowed his eyes at the Saroo.

"Not exactly," Trub shook his large ungainly head. "He told Yenm that we had two choices. The first was to die. The second was that if the Saroos did his bidding until the forest was conquered, then he would show us the place that holds the richest deposit of red crystal in all the universe and it would be ours forever."

"This story wins you nothing, Saroo," growled Almedon. "Your kind are greedier than a pack of bone-thin wolverines. You give us yet another reason to kill you."

The wolf curled her lip and snarled at Trub. "Your kind killed my Ruffis to get yourself more red stones? You stole my daughters to trade for another pit full of rocks?" The fur on her shoulders began to ripple, she growled deep from the belly.

"You're nut worms," yelled Olli. "A slithery, slimy, stinky, wiggly bunch of nut worms."

Trub lowered his eyes, then exchanged a quick worried glance with Kog.

Kog took one jittery step forward and spoke for the first time. "We are not making excuses for what our kind have done," she said quietly. "Many wicked things have happened, especially these past few days since the Rumblers have been in control. But you must understand that Trub and I have taken no part in destroying the forest or your people. We are opposed to everything that has happened. We tried to turn the minds of our people to fight the Rumblers, not to serve them. And before that, we tried to turn the spirits of our people back to the forest. This has made us outcasts. If the Saroos find us now they will kill us just as surely as they will feed you to the Rumblers. The only difference is that we will be killed slowly. If you kill us right now ...," she paused, "it may be the best thing."

There was silence for a moment and then the wolf spoke, her voice laced with anger: "They try to trick us with their fancy words. We have all seen what the Saroos can do. These two have lost their weapons, so they resort to trickery. But they are as wicked as all the rest. The instant we turn our backs they will summon the others and capture us. I say we kill them now—before they kill us."

"Yes," agreed Almedon, "kill them."

"Kill 'em," said Olli.

"But I believe her," protested Amber. "I think she's telling the truth."

"Yup, telling the truth," said Olli.

"I think so, too," said Bohadea. "The movements of her body were truthful. Let them live."

"Let 'em live," said Olli.

"Two in favor, two against, and one in the middle," said Amber. "We have a draw."

"This is no time to hold a council meeting," snapped Almedon. "We are a warrior tribe. Tonight, we go to the fire-web to free our people. These two can be nothing but a liability. Whether they speak true or not is of no consequence. They must die!"

"Wait!" Trub held one long bony finger up in the air. Excitedly he spoke: "If you want to go to the laser-prison, we can help! We can help you set the prisoners free. Together we could do it! And we have a comrade there who also wants to escape. We can get her out too, and then we can all go our separate ways."

Almedon cocked his head suspiciously.

Trub and Kog began to chatter in an agitated manner, waving their bony fingers in the air, sketching a plan to breach the fire-web and set the prisoners free. Soon, even the wolf's ears began to twitch with interest, for she had Shaleena and Eldiveera, her daughters, to think of.

Almedon paced restlessly. Their chances of success would be greatly increased with the help of the Saroos—*if* they were trustworthy! If they were not, the tribe would almost certainly be led to their deaths. Any error in judgment spelled doom.

"Almedon," Bohadea spoke quietly to the eagle as the Saroos chatted on. "We must trust them. It's no coincidence that we've all been brought together. Star Bear has sent them to help us. I feel it in my bones."

An uneasy truce settled over the band of fugitives and there was no more talk of killing Trub and Kog. The Saroos had laid out a risky plan, but it was better than no plan at all.

With lingering distrust, the forest people distanced themselves from the Saroos to await the rising of the moon. Almedon and the wolf, by silent agreement, kept guard over the only exit from the cave. Bohadea settled herself beneath a dry niche in the rocks for a little nap and Olli tucked himself into the deep fur beneath her shoulder, he was snoozing in no time, but the little twitches and tiny growls betrayed the monsters who haunted his dreams.

Only Amber sat near the Saroos, who perched nervously beneath a long slitted crack in the rock that let in thin needles of light and a fine mist of water. Amber couldn't help being fascinated with these two strange creatures and tried from time to time to engage them in conversation, despite the pointed looks of disapproval from Almedon. But the Saroos were skittish and no longer inclined to chatter, so they waited in near silence until the last faint needle of light had evaporated and left the cave in utter blackness.

"Is it time to go yet?" Amber's small voice echoed in the darkness.

"Soon." The eagle's voice came from his post by the rockfall.

Amber could feel butterflies begin to flutter in her empty stomach. She nervously twirled a dreadlock around one finger: a warrior hairstyle, she reminded herself. I must be brave! What would a real warrior be doing right now, she wondered, just before the battle? She patted the rocks around her until she found what she was looking for: a slick river of muck that snaked along the damp floor. She drew a finger through the mud and streaked it across her cheek. War paint! She scooped up a second clump and smeared it on her other cheek.

She held one hand up in the dark, stretching it toward the narrow slitted window in the rock. Yes, there it was, a barely visible flash of white. She must darken her skin to blend in with the night. Amber scooped out a whole fistful of muck this time. She smeared both hands and then carefully drew a striped pattern on her face. The mud felt cool and refreshing, reassuring somehow, as if it offered protection against the enemy lurking out there in the dark. She was just wiping the mud off of her hands and onto the legs of her jumpsuit when Almedon gave the command to move out.

There was a shuffling of feet in the direction of the eagle's voice. Amber had both hands stabbing at the dark empty spaces in front of her and was just about to complain about the darkness when a tiny lightning bug zipped in through the narrow slitted window. The tiny bright green body pulsed in the darkness. Almost immediately, another bug joined it, then another, and another, and soon there was a living lantern casting an eerie green light through the den.

"They have come to light our way," said Bohadea, uncurling herself from under her rocky niche.

"I'm tired," grumped Olli.

Amber stepped over to Bohadea and scooped Olli up onto her shoulder. Olli yawned widely, stretched, and shook out his tail.

Bohadea was staring at the greenish mud-streaked glow of Amber's face. The bear smiled to herself, shook off her fur, and padded toward the rockfall. The Saroos carefully fell in behind. The wolf led the way toward the den's entrance, escorted by the lightning bugs.

The wolf turned to face the group. She leveled her gaze at the Saroos. "The female comes with me," she gestured at Kog. Kog jumped in fright, then gingerly picked her way toward the wolf. "One false move," said the wolf, directing her words at Trub, "and I rip her throat out." Trub nodded fearfully.

"They'll be all right," Bohadea reassured the wolf.

"They'd better be," the wolf looked threateningly at Bohadea. "Now let's go." She turned deftly toward the den's entrance.

"Wait!" called Bohadea to the wolf. "We don't even know your name."

The wolf spun back around looking quizzically at the bear.

"We're all going to fight together, as a tribe," said Bohadea. "We should at least know each other's names."

"I am Diansha," said the wolf, "daughter of Rutalina, and like my mother before me, I am known as Chief Hunter of the Quelicot Tribe. I am a Quelicot wolf," she said proudly. "And I will have vengeance for what these invaders have done to my people." Diansha swiftly swung her head at Kog, battering her forward through the narrow

opening of the cave. Kog stumbled out into the night, her
spindly limbs quaking as though whipped by the wind.

The others followed in the haze of green light that disappeared like a mist into the night air. They stood there,
seven dark shadows in the faint light of a gibbous moon.
The only sound was the steady pounding of water that
drummed at the face of Weeping Rock.

"If we are divided," said Bohadea in a slow, dark
voice, "we will lose. We cannot go into battle as enemies.
The squirrel, the human, the eagle, the bear, the wolf, and
the Saroo, must become one with Star Bear. Or we will all
be dead before Sun Eagle flies again."

No one spoke.

"After the forest people have been freed tonight,
Diansha will rejoin the Quelicot Tribe and the Saroos will
run with their own kind. But for this one night, we are all
Tribe of Star Bear. We fight together, with one mind. We are
the Warriors of the Rainbow, each of us a different color,
each of us of a different nature, but all of us of the light.

"We must bind ourselves together in the sacred circle
of the warrior. If we are divided, our power will leak out
and we will be easy to kill. Anyone who will not stand in
the warrior's circle must leave us now. Those who want to
fight with the Tribe of Star Bear, come into the circle."
Bohadea stood very still as everyone, including the wolf
and the Saroos, shuffled into the circle.

"Now, each warrior must call the spirits down from the
stars," said the bear.

"It will be too noisy," protested Almedon. "We will be
calling for the Saroos to come with their killing sticks."

"Make the call inside your head," said Bohadea. "Then
only the spirits will hear." She closed her eyes and began
to hum a single note as she had done when she worked her
healing magic on Almedon. Amber followed, choosing the

note B, and praying for her guardian angel to bring a warrior spirit down from heaven for her.

The wolf chose a low rumbly sound and kept her eyes
fixed on the cluster of stars the Quelicots called the
Hunting Pack, while the Saroos made a high-pitched
mewling sound and stared with unblinking eyes at each
other. The eagle and the squirrel both had their eyes fixed
on the same bright, triangular star, but Almedon called it
the Eagle Talon, and Olli called it Bright Squirrel Point.

A shooting star rushed across the night sky. Then
another and another. Seven in all. And when Bohadea
opened her eyes she saw that above the head of each warrior hovered a pulsing sphere of light, each one a different
color. "The warrior spirits have come," said the bear, and
as she spoke, the spheres of light began to dance in a wide
circle above their heads, each one leaving a bright trail of
color. Faster and faster they spun, spiraling downward,
merging into one another, until all seven warriors were
caught in the swirl of rainbow light. Amber felt light-headed, as if in a dream, or on a merry-go-round.

The circle grew even brighter as dozens of tiny spheres
of a twinkling golden light gathered there. They flitted and
danced, moving into the center of the circle, and gradually
they merged into a bright golden shape. Suddenly the light
winked out and there sat Pudd Wudd Princeling, the cat.

"What's he doing here?" clacked Almedon. "He's ruin-
ing our warrior circle."

"Three by the sumac, the hunter will attack," said Pudd
Wudd, his face turned to Diansha. He tiptoed over to Trub
and rubbed up against his spindly shins. Trub leaned over
and stroked Pudd Wudd's soft golden fur. *Meow!* Pudd
Wudd arched his back with pleasure then looked up at
Kog. "At a howl in the night, strike with red light," he told
the Saroo.

To the Tribe of Star Bear, Pudd Wudd Princeling said: "Touch what you sought. Think without thought."

"Not again!" groaned Almedon.

"Rum tum tiddle, no time to diddle," he said directly to the eagle. Just then a fruit bat swept through the circle low enough to make Pudd Wudd's ears twitch. Pudd Wudd took one furious swipe at the bat and missed. "Yeeeow," he complained, and bounded off into the night.

"What did he mean?" asked Amber. "Touch what you sought. Think without thought?" She clasped the amethyst amulet, it pulsed strongly in her hand, the vibrations running up her arm and making her feel a little dizzy. "How can you think without thought. That doesn't make any sense."

"Look Amburrr!" exclaimed Bohadea. "Look at what you are touching."

"My spider?" she said.

"Touch what you sought."

"I get it, I get it, I get it," shouted Olli. "We gotta touch our magic charms."

"When?" wondered Amber.

"We'll know when," said Bohadea. "We'll know exactly what to do when the time comes to do it."

"We must hurry," said Almedon. "I will fly to the fire-web and scout it out, then I will wait for you. Those two know the way," he gestured at Kog and Trub. "Follow them, and go with eagle speed." Almedon lifted off into the night sky, his dark form an eerie silhouette against the yellow moon.

The Saroos shambled downhill through dark shadows and scrubby bush. The others followed. They fell into single file with Trub in the lead and Bohadea guarding the rear. The Saroos stopped from time to time, to get their bearings from the stars, then set a new course, leading them closer and closer to the prison camp. No one spoke a single word on their dangerous journey through the darkened forest.

They cleared the top of a heavily treed hill, moving slowly around the trunks of giant red pines. A ghostly moan pricked at the needles of the trees. A shiver ran through the little band of warriors.

The unearthly moans grew louder and more persistent. A thousand phantom voices rode on long slow waves through the forest, playing a song of death. The fur stood straight up on Bohadea's back. A growl rumbled deep in the throat of the wolf. The forest floor pulsed like the heartbeat of a frightened rabbit. A strange red glow like a ghostly fire flickered through the trees. Dark strong wings beat at the boughs of a pine overhead and Amber could not restrain a yelp of terror.

"Hush," warned Almedon, his voice urgent and fearful.

The warriors stopped, their eyes scanning the treetops for the eagle. Almedon hopped from one bough to the next, a shadowy form darting among the dark pines. Finally he perched just above their heads. "I've been waiting for you," he said. "That cat was right, we must hurry. The Rumblers are closer than I thought. They move even in the dark. They will be here long before first light."

"I must get my children," cried Diansha. "I must save my tribe."

"They will be saved," Almedon assured her. "But we have to move with great speed. The Saroos spoke true. The fire-web is just as they said it would be. At each corner is a giant red crystal that makes the fire for the webbing. There are two smaller crystals at the front of the web. These two open and close the gate, and they are guarded by two Saroos. There are ten more guards who patrol outside the perimeter."

"Where is the sumac?" asked Diansha.

"At the back," said Almedon.

"The spirit cat spoke first to me," said Diansha. "So I must strike first. I will take the three Saroos nearest the sumac."

"Then Kog and I must go with you," said Trub to the wolf. If he was afraid, he showed no sign. "We must have the laser wands if our plan is to succeed."

"You all know what to do then," said Almedon. "Follow the Saroo Trail. At the rock that bears the shape of the grouse, the trail divides into two. The path leading from the grouse's beak goes to the front of the fire-web. The path from the tail goes to the back of the fire-web. Near the middle of the Beak Path is an old rockfall that will easily hide you three for a while," he gestured at Bohadea, Amber, and Olli.

"After the wolf has taken out the three guards nearest the sumac, everyone moves into position," said Trub. He looked straight at Olli and Amber. "You will be our bait!"

Amber swallowed hard and nodded.

"Remember, when the eagle hoots once, Kog and I will lead you to the gate."

"When the eagle hoots twice, we make our final strike," said Diansha.

Bohadea nodded. She touched one paw to her ear, to the little bag of black velvet. She hoped that she could do what she knew she must, without dealing death.

Amber clutched at her amethyst spider and let the gentle vibration rise through her arm. She shut her eyes and said a prayer asking for protection and sending a message to her mom and dad: *I love you*, she told them. *I love you very much and if I get killed tonight I'm very sorry to make you sad. But I'm a warrior now, and a warrior has got to fight for what's right. So please don't be sad. I love you both*. She opened her eyes, stroked her dreadlocks, then looked at Olli who sat perched on her shoulder.

"Bait," whispered Olli, his whiskers twitching anxiously.

"Touch what you sought," she whispered back.

Olli curled his tiny fingers around the magical silver acorn. "Think without thought," he said to himself. "I can do that. I don't think much anyhow. It's like when you're eating a really good nut. You just eat it. You don't need to think about eating it, unless you don't have a nut. In that case, you probably would think a lot about nuts, but when you—"

"Shut up," commanded Almedon. "Silence! Absolute silence."

Olli clamped his mouth shut. The warriors became very still.

"Let's go!" ordered the eagle.

The warriors began their march into the red glow, toward the ghostly cries of the trapped forest people. At Grouse Rock, they paused. They looked into each other's eyes for one brief moment, then the wolf and the Saroos took the fork to the left. Bohadea, Amber, and Olli went right.

Diansha took the lead, creeping with her belly low to the ground, her ears pricked and her nostrils twitching. Kog and Trub followed behind, slouched forward so their long arms almost trailed on the ground. Their eyes were wide and unblinking, their heads inclined in the direction of the red glow, now so bright that it had turned the night sky a deep blood red.

A twig snapped. Diansha spun around and soundlessly barred her teeth, a silent warning for the Saroos to pick their footing more carefully. Kog caught her breath, her fists clenched at her sides. Trub touched her shoulder protectively.

They crept closer to the edge of the clearing where Diansha's first target stood guard. The cries of the captives sent shivers up their spines. The smell of fear was almost enough to make Diansha bolt. They were close enough to see the dark figures of the prisoners pacing and circling inside the fire-web; in some places they stood in knots, frozen in terror. Diansha searched for some sign of her daughters, her tribe, but then tore her eyes away: it would only distract her from her mission. She shut her nose to all smells except the scent of the Saroo guards.

At the corner of the fire-web was a giant red crystal, a stone of extraordinary beauty made sinister by its evil purpose. It was angled upward, and shot a razor-thin beam of red light to the topmost corner of the fire-web. A Saroo guard stood no more than four leaps away. Diansha and her companions crouched down in silence.

The wolf scanned the perimeter. A second Saroo stood a fair distance off with his back turned, and a third Saroo was stationed by another generator crystal at the far end. Diansha shifted her weight. A dried leaf crunched underfoot. The Saroo guard turned and looked directly into the eyes of the wolf. She sprang from the sumac and was on the Saroo before he could open his mouth or lift his fire-stick in defense. An instant later she was dragging his body back into the sumac.

The dead Saroo still gripped the fire-stick in his paw. Trub pried his fingers off the wand. Kog looked down at the dead Saroo, her face so drained of color that she appeared white even in the red glare of the fire-web. Trub grabbed Kog by the hand and dragged her quickly back into the bush.

Diansha was already slinking toward the second guard who paced idly back and forth, lost in a daydream. She slipped into position behind a sumac with low-hanging limbs and focused so intently on the Saroo that she could feel the rhythm of his heartbeat and see in her mind's eye the flow of his sharp barbed thoughts. She knew that he was angry with another Saroo and was hashing out what he would say the next time he saw her. The guard walked to within a leap of Diansha but was too caught up in his own thoughts to see the wolf or the two Saroos crouched behind her. Diansha allowed him to pass by.

He stubbed his toe on a rock, faltered for an instant and cursed. Diansha waited no longer, she sprang at him from the rear. He fell forward and the fire-stick flew from his hand, landing near the fire-web. He struggled to turn and face his attacker, but Diansha was swift, and a moment later she was dragging her second kill back into the bush.

"The stick is lost," whispered Diansha.

"We'll get the next one," said Trub.

There was a disturbance inside the fire-web. Some of the captives had seen the wolf attacking. They began to mill around excitedly near the back of the web. Diansha was agitated. This would draw the attention of the other guards if they didn't stop. Suddenly a wolf pushed his way through the crowd, searching the sumac for some sign of movement. Diansha's heart leapt: it was Prakna, Chief Healer of the Quelicots, and brother to her dead mate Ruffis. *He's alive!* She acted on impulse and risked breaking cover to show herself to Prakna. She gestured with her nose for him to back away from the fire-web, then she quickly withdrew into the sumac.

Prakna understood at once. He began to bark quick, sharp orders and within seconds all the captives had dispersed. They began to act normally again, but the atmosphere had shifted dramatically. News was buzzing around the compound in secretive little circles, the cries were changing from desperation to hope. The scents were changing, too: from hopeless fear to fighting fear.

Diansha and the two Saroos made their way to the final target. Although the captives were not gathered at the back of the fire-web, or staring into the sumac, Diansha knew that they were still tracking her every movement through the bush. When she reached her position at the far corner, there was a scuffle inside the web. It drew the Saroo guard into perfect striking position. Inside the blink of an eye, the wolf's third strike was pulled back into the bush.

But the fire-stick had fallen from his paw a few paces from the sumac. Trub darted out, scooped up the wand, and darted back in again. The sight of the sprinting Saroo caused another commotion among the captives, but one warning bark from Prakna, and all was calm again. Or as calm as could be expected.

The wolf and the two Saroos quickly back tracked along the trail. Diansha snorted a parting salute to her companions. She broke off the path into the bush, and took up a new position by the left side of the fire-web where she would await the final signal to strike.

Kog and Trub, each carrying a red crystal laser wand, hurried back to Grouse Rock and turned onto the Beak Trail. They scrambled over the rockfall and slipped down into the hollow where Bohadea, Amber, and Olli were hiding. No one spoke. They only nodded at each other. Bohadea nuzzled Amber under the chin then slipped into the darkness, heading for her position on the right side of the fire-web.

Amber, Olli, and the two Saroos waited silently. Olli fiddled nervously with the fuzzy end of a dreadlock. Amber could hear a rush of blood in her ears that thrummed with each beat of her heart. An eagle hooted once.

Amber's hand flew to her amethyst spider. Kog and Trub stood up and pointed their crystal wands at Amber and Olli. Amber sucked in her breath and stood up. Olli sat

up on his haunches and clutched at the dreadlock. They
moved out onto the trail, heading for the front gate, taking
no trouble to conceal the noise of their passage.

The voice of a single Saroo rose in a loud question-
ing jabber, cutting through the heavy red air. Trub called
back in the same jabber. Again the Saroo guard called
out. Again Trub answered. Amber turned to look at him
anxiously. Trub shook his head and gestured for her to
look forward: a warning that she should not show any
familiarity with him or Kog again. Amber marched. Olli
hung on.

Moments later, a Saroo guard scuttled down the path to
meet them. It was a tall female with very large eyes and a
thinly drawn mouth. She gasped her surprise at the sight of
Olli and Amber and began to jabber excitedly to Kog and
Trub. She ushered them quickly along the path, her quick
sharp eyes darting between Olli and Amber, Kog and Trub.
She suddenly jabbered something at Kog, her eyes narrowed into slits. Amber could tell that the question had
made Kog nervous, but the Saroo guard seemed satisfied
with Kog's answer because she turned and led them on
without looking back again.

The Saroo made an abrupt turn and the woods parted
to reveal an enormous blazing red cube—the fire-web. It
burned like a terrible jewel, the black ash at its base a tes-
tament to other brave warriors who had come here to save
their loved ones, and failed. Amber was stunned at the
enormity of the red generator crystals at the corners, for
each one was as large as a full-grown man.

Two Saroos stood at attention directly in front of the
fire-web's gate. One of them flushed a deep cherry red
color at the sight of Kog and Trub. It was Radg: the rebel
Saroo whom they had come to collect. Radg nodded once,
then stared straight ahead and waited.

Inside the fire-web, the captives surged forward. The air was electric. The scent of the prisoners had become strong with something that was making the Saroo guards jumpy. There was a sharp bark from a wolf inside the web. The captives broke off to the sides again, but currents of danger still ran among them.

A wolf howl pierced the blood red night.

Amber and Olli twitched with fright. So did the Saroo guards.

At a howl in the night, strike with red light.

At once, both Trub and Kog remembered the words of Pudd Wudd Princeling. They attacked. There were two sharp zaps of red light. Two guards fell. Radg took the cue. She swung around and sent out a third beam of light. A guard by one of the generator crystals fell. Trub shot again, and a fourth was down.

The eagle hooted twice.

Bohadea bounded from the bush. At the same moment, on the opposite side of the fire-web, Diansha sprang to the attack, taking down her target without a struggle. But Bohadea hesitated. She had no heart for killing and tackled the guard like a wrestling cub. The Saroo let out a high-pitched whistle of alarm.

Another guard swung around, weapon at the ready. He shot at the bear. A razor-thin beam zinged past her, close enough to singe the fur on her shoulder. *Jump!* Istarna's voice rang in her ear. Bohadea leapt to the right just as a second beam whizzed by. A third beam cut a fiery trail across her side, this one shot from the weapon of the fallen Saroo. The downed guard whistled a second alarm. Two more Saroos rounded the corner at a full gallop. *I'm sunk,* thought Bohadea. But the new Saroos pointed their weapons at Bohadea's attackers. Bohadea hit the ground.

Zaps of fire shot overhead, acrid smoke filled her nose and stung her eyes.

The spindly pink legs of two Saroos moved toward her. She blinked up at them and coughed. "Are you okay?" Kog asked the bear.

"Fine," said Bohadea scrambling to her feet, her eyes locked on the second Saroo, the stranger who stood by Kog's side.

"This is Radg," explained Kog. "The one we told you about."

Flashes of fire and whistles of alarm rang out from the other side of the fire-web. A wolf barked in a sharp signal of victory.

Tremors of excitement surged through the fire-web. Kog and Radg broke into a run back to the front gate. Bohadea loped behind. Trub and Diansha rushed in from the other side.

Amber and Olli watched wide-eyed as Kog and Trub began to turn one of the gate-crystals around so that it pointed toward the huge corner generator. Bohadea helped Radg turn the other one. And as the crystals arced around, an opening began to form in front of the fire-web. At first it was so narrow that only the littlest people—finches and mice and butterflies—could escape. But as it became wider there was a surge of larger and larger animals rushing through the opening to freedom.

Suddenly a terrifying rumble shook the ground—*The Rumblers were coming!* The scent of terror reared up like the head of a cobra, and the captives began to scatter in all directions.

Diansha was swept forward by the furious rush of prisoners. "Shaleena! Eldiveera!" she called, but her voice was drowned in the thunder of hooves and paws. Bohadea was bumped and jostled and finally forced off to one side.

Amber and Olli were pushed this way and shoved that way, but managed to go neither forward nor backward.

Another rumble shook the ground.

Screams of terror burst through the forest and frenzied wings beat at the night air. There seemed no end to the flood of forest people, but at last the deluge began to subside and the beating of hooves grew fainter. But Bohadea could see that an angry mob had gathered at the place where the gate crystals stood. She reared up to see if she could find Amber there, but the girl was lost in the crowd. Diansha worked her way closer to the gate, bobbing and weaving through the tangle of forest people, calling the names of her daughters, her tribe.

Two young wolves broke from the mob and rushed to their mother's side. Diansha nuzzled her pups, her brown eyes moist with joy. "Where is Prakna?" she asked the little ones. "Where are the Quelicots?"

"They want to kill those three bad pink ones," said Shaleena, jutting her little black nose in the direction of the gate. "But there is another funny creature who also walks on her hind legs and a squirrel who say the pink ones are not bad."

"Wait right here," frowned Diansha. "Don't move," she ordered the pups. The wolf pushed her way to the center of the crowd, arriving just as Bohadea shouldered her way in.

Amber had both arms stretched out behind her, trying to shelter Kog and Trub from the raging mob. Olli was jumping up and down on Radg's shoulder, his little fists balled up and stabbing at the air.

"What's going on here?" demanded Bohadea, taking her place at Amber's side.

Diansha closed the protective circle around the Saroos. "These ones are on our side," she announced.

"They are not to be killed," screamed Almedon, he was gliding overhead in slow sweeping circles.

Prakna, the Quelicot wolf, stepped forward. "If Diansha says they are on our side, then it's true. We leave them be," he ordered. And the mob began to back away.

A tremor shook the earth. The Rumblers were closer. Much closer! The gnashing of teeth and claws slashed through the night. A wave of fear shimmered in the hazy red air. The remaining captives turned on their heels and fled. The Tribe of Star Bear stood alone with the Quelicots and the rebel Saroos.

The earth trembled again. Diansha turned to Prakna: "Take our tribe to Beehive Bluff, where they'll be safe," she said. "I'll meet you there." Prakna nodded; he galloped over to where Shaleena and Eldiveera stood whining with fear and nudged them forward. He glanced back at Diansha, then led his people into the dark cover of the forest.

"The Rumblers are over the next hill," Almedon screamed his warning. "Hurry!"

Trub ran into the fire-web. Kog and Radg shadowed him on the outside, meeting him at the first generator crystal. Each Saroo touched a different facet of the terrible red crystal with the points of their wands. Hot red sparks sizzled in the night air. There was a burst of bright red light and the generator crystal winked off. As did one quarter of the fire-web. They raced to the next generator and repeated the process. Half the web remained. They shut off the third and the fourth. And the web was gone. All that remained was a thin red glow from the two gate crystals.

"Hurry!" called Almedon. The Rumblers were dangerously near. Trees were being snapped like twigs, and whole trunks were being crunched up like beetles.

The Saroos quickly completed the ritual with the gate crystals, and the night was once again lit only by the pale yellow light of the moon.

Almedon sounded the alarm: "They know something has gone wrong here. They're on the march. Hurry! Hurry!"

The crashing grew louder and louder as trees were felled in the path of the Rumblers, but they no longer paused to eat them. They were headed straight for the clearing.

"Help me! Quickly," Trub cried.

Kog and Amber ran after him, back to one of the generator crystals. Olli hung on. Bohadea, Diansha, and Radg ran to another. Using every ounce of their strength they lowered the giant crystals onto the ground, then slid them together, nose to nose. They raced to the other two generators and slid them into position, so the four formed an X.

"No time," screamed Almedon. "No more time."

The Saroos exchanged panicked glances. "Activate," yelled Trub, his voice jabbery with fright. Kog and Radg struck up their lasers. The Saroos raced around the crystal X, striking a certain pattern at the base of each gigantic crystal. One by one the generators whined back to life, glowing ruby red. The four beams met, spitting and sizzling at the center of the cross. The crystals began to vibrate faster and faster. The others backed away as sparks flew from the growing fireball at the center of the X.

"Go!" shrieked Almedon. "There is no more time."

Trub cast a fearful glance at the forest than looked back at the gate. "Let's get those last two," he called, and broke into a run.

The others raced after him and helped Trub turn the smaller gate crystals so that they, too, were laid point to point.

"NOW!" screamed Almedon. "RUN FOR YOUR LIVES!" A tree crashed into the clearing, shaking the ground.

"Go!" shouted Trub. "GO!" He shoved Kog toward the path. Amber leapt onto Bohadea's back. She grabbed Kog's arm and yanked the Saroo up behind her. "Trub," Kog screamed after her mate. Diansha swung her head at Radg. The Saroo froze. "Get up," yelled Diansha. Radg jumped onto the wolf's back. They ran like the wind.

Trub turned his attention to the gate crystals, and just as the first one buzzed back to life, an enormous set of flashing red eyes broke through the sumacs. A roar like an exploding volcano shattered the air.

"RUN!" Almedon screamed at Trub as he wheeled one last time through the air, then raced after the tribe.

Trub stepped over to the second crystal, and with shaking hands he traced a pattern on its base. The crystals began to spit and whine, a small fireball began to glow between them.

Another Rumbler roared his fury and broke into the clearing. Trub looked to where he had last seen Kog and the others. For a moment, it seemed as though he would run, but instead he turned back to face the Rumblers. There was no way he could escape on foot. Not now.

A dozen of the huge red eyes flashed at him. Sharp steel teeth gnashed at the air, giant claws snapped at the earth. Trub calmly pointed his laser at the crystal X, sending another bolt of energy through the generators. The last thing he saw was the razor-like spines of a Rumbler claw reaching toward him as it blew up into a thousand pieces.

The explosion was so powerful that Amber and the Saroos, already a distance of ten meadows away, were thrown to the ground. A red fireball the size of a small mountain lit up the sky. A second explosion followed close behind. The Tribe of Star Bear, the Saroos, and the wolf, stared up at a blood-red moon.

"*Trub,*" called Kog, picking herself up off the ground. "*Trub!*"

The red glow faded from the sky and the night fell silent.

7

The Medicine Bear

In the pale pink light of dawn a lone crow flew over Beehive Bluff. She arced above the grassy meadow at the bottom edge of the cliff, then banked sharply to the left, rising over Beehive Bluff and out of sight. Almedon followed her flight from the limb of a white birch near the base of the cliff.

Bohadea lay curled asleep at the entrance to a small wolf den; Amber was snuggled into her fur like a young cub, and Olli was tucked in somewhere between the two. Prakna and some of the other adult Quelicots were curled up close to the bear because the wolf den was too small to fit such a large tribe. Only Diansha and her daughters slept inside along with another mother wolf and her three young pups.

Kog did not sleep. She sat in a crumpled heap of wilted arms and legs. Her bony fingers clutched at her face, her head hung low. She had spent the night weeping over the loss of her beloved Trub. Beside her, Radg was stretched out on the ground, arms flung helter-skelter, fast asleep.

"Saroo," said Almedon.

Slowly, through hooded eyes, Kog looked up into the silver-green of the tree where the eagle perched. She blinked, then turned away and stared at the ground again.

Almedon cleared his throat. "I just wanted to say that your mate was a brave warrior," he said.

Kog looked back up at the eagle. Her eyes were dull with sorrow.

"My mate was killed, too," said Almedon. He cast an eye down at the diamond teardrop that sparkled from his talon. "She was a great hunter. From the Herondic Tribe."

Kog nodded. Her furry pink chin quivered.

"Your mate spoke true. He fought bravely."

Kog's breath hitched in her chest.

"I think it would cause him much sadness to see you like this," said Almedon. "I cannot speak for his spirit, but I think he would want you to be a strong warrior. To fight even harder than before. To avenge his death."

A small spark flickered in the dullness of Kog's eyes.

"Did you live in the city of red crystals?" Almedon asked her. "Before ... all this ...," his voice trailed off.

"We lived at the edge," said Kog, her finger traced an aimless pattern on the ground. "We didn't like to live near the Pit. It was too busy. And there were no trees or any green things there." Her eyes flicked up at Almedon. "Most Saroos thought that trees were too messy and too much trouble to keep up."

"Keep up?" said the eagle with disbelief. "Were they so stupid that they didn't know trees could stand up on their own, without any help from a Saroo?"

A trace of a smile flickered on Kog's thin lips, then disappeared. "They wanted trees to grow in straight lines and geometric shapes. It involved a lot of work to grow a tree in the shape of a cube."

Almedon shook his head. "It sounds like your people were bitten by the brain-fever."

"Yes," Kog agreed. "That's what Trub and I thought. And Radg, too," she gestured at the Saroo sprawled out on the ground. "We could hear the voices of our ancestors calling out to us from a time before the Saroos had built

Red City. They were calling us back to the forest and warning us that if we did not change our ways there would be a catastrophe that would put a violent end to our tidy square world. And they were right," she said, her head bowed in sadness.

"How long a journey is Red City from here?" Almedon asked her.

"A long way," said Kog, blinking up at Almedon. "Trub and I were on the run a long time before you found us."

"In which direction is Red City from here?" he asked the Saroo.

Her head jerked up hard, her eyes were wide: "You're not thinking of going there, are you?" she asked the eagle.

"Dreeg, King of the Rumblers, directs his army from deep inside the Pit of Darkness, does he not?"

"Yes, but …"

"Then that is where my tribe must go." *Down into the Pit, to battle the Rumbler King.*

"It would be suicide!" exclaimed Kog. "You'd never even get near the Pit. How would you get by the Saroo patrols? Past the Rumbler lines? Through the Silver Desert—"

"Silver Desert?" Almedon interrupted her. "I've never heard of such a place." Kog shrugged. "It's the in-between land that separates the forest from the redlands that lead to the city. But it's a strange, scary place. The air shimmers in a silver color. It's thick. Almost solid. And very hard to breathe. You wouldn't survive for long in that silver air.

"There's no sound either. None at all. Nothing makes a noise. And really weird things happen there. We have so many stories about strange and dangerous creatures who materialize in and out of the thick silver air. Hundreds of Saroos have disappeared from the Silver Desert without a trace. You have to be very careful."

"Can you see Red City from there?"

"Once you get out of the Silver Desert you can. It's beautiful to look at from far away," Kog said dreamily. "Like a crown of red jewels." Her face abruptly changed back into a frown. "But you can't really be thinking of going there."

"In which direction do we travel?" Almedon asked again.

Kog sighed and shook her head. She knotted her long bony fingers together and stared at the eagle. "You must know of the Point Star," she said, "it's at the top of a group of stars that look like a bird."

"Yes, of course," said Almedon. "Beak of the Night Eagle."

"Yes! And at the opposite end is the Tip Star. It sets first, as if the bird is going down tail first," said Kog, looking to Almedon for confirmation.

"I know the one," he nodded.

"The place where the Tip Star touches the earth just before sunrise, that's the direction you have to go. When you pass the front lines of the Rumblers you'll find deep ruts and way-pits gouged into the earth. At first, they'll seem to criss-cross in all directions. But if you keep moving toward the setting Tip Star, you'll find that the ruts begin to join together to make a wider and deeper gouge, like a canyon. The deepest canyon will take you straight through the Silver Desert to Red City."

"And the Pit is in the middle of the city?"

"The very center. There is a great square there. A square of red crystal spires and gates that surround the pit."

"And we must pass through this structure before we can descend into the Pit of Darkness?"

"Through the gates, into the mining pit. When you have descended to the very bottom, you'll find a place where the earth has cracked open. This is the door." Kog shook her head. "I can't imagine how you plan to survive such a journey. It's a suicide mission."

"Is that the only way in?" Almedon asked, ignoring her warning.

Kog sighed. "The crack is the only opening into the Pit of Darkness. But there are several narrow channels that lead underground to the main mining site from other parts of the city. One comes from beneath the tall tower with the triangle on top. One from—" Kog stopped short. She gazed up at the honeycombed rocks of Beehive Bluff and sighed. "Maybe, with the help of other Saroos ...," her voice trailed off.

She turned sharply back to face the eagle. "'Agida,' is the rebels' call to arms. Now that my people are enslaved by the Rumblers, they may be more willing to answer such a call. Remember the word 'Agida.' It will identify you as a friend of the rebels. But it's risky. The 'Agida' call will bring a swift death if it's uttered in the wrong place, at the wrong time."

Caw. The crow made another pass over Beehive Bluff. Almedon turned one eye up to the hazy pink sky. He watched as the crow circled overhead, then lifted up over the cliffs, out of sight. A moment later she was back again, making another circuit over the meadow.

"That crow's up to something," said Almedon, more to himself than to Kog. "Will you take over my watch?" he asked the Saroo.

She nodded and pulled herself up off the ground, shaking out the gaggle of arms and legs. A pall of sadness fell over her face again.

Almedon unfurled his wings and lifted off. He caught a small updraft and rode it up after the crow.

"Cawww!" As soon as the crow spotted Almedon, she closed her wings and dove down fast, then abruptly pulled out of the dive, and swept up behind Almedon. "Caw," she nipped at his tail.

"Don't start up with me," Almedon cautioned the crow. "I'm not in the mood."

"Caw," the crow said, but she didn't nip at his tail again.

Almedon cruised over the bluff in the same circular pattern the crow had flown. He glanced toward the horizon, toward a faint puff of grey smoke that came from the place where the fire-web had stood the night before. He could see that a new wave of Rumblers had arrived there and knew it was just a matter of time before they began the march toward Beehive Bluff.

The crow paced the eagle. He ignored her for the moment; something else had caught his attention. Throughout the forest there were stragglers, tiny bands of forest people, and small flocks of birds, who seemed in no hurry to escape the Rumblers. Instead of running deeper into the forest, they were simply camped here and there, or moving slowly, toward Beehive Bluff. *But why?* Why weren't they running away?

"What are you doing here?" Almedon snapped at the crow. "Why aren't you flying away?"

She flinched and fell a little further back. "I'm looking for the Tribe of Star Bear," said the crow matter-of-factly. "I think that strange flock down in the meadow might be them. You came from there, didn't you?"

"I did."

"I want to join up," said the crow earnestly. "I want to fight with the Tribe of Star Bear."

The feathers on the nape of Almedon's neck pricked with surprise. "Come down with me then," commanded the eagle. "And get off my tail!" he snapped at the crow. Almedon sailed downward, then adjusted his tail feathers, flattened out the dive, and coasted in for a landing. The crow followed, but not too closely. She chose a juniper tree near the wolf den for her perch.

Diansha had just emerged from the den with her daughters. She stretched out her long sleek body and yawned. The pups followed suit, yawning dramatically with pink tongues curling outward, little paws stretching further and further forward until they collapsed down onto their chubby bellies.

A coyote yelped from the forest's edge.

Bohadea blinked awake and lazily rolled herself upright, spilling Olli and Amber onto the ground.

"Tchip," complained Olli. He shook himself out and fluffed up his tail.

"Ohh," groaned Amber. "I can't believe it's morning already. Feels like I just fell asleep." She stretched out her arms and yawned loudly.

Bohadea sneezed a big sloppy bear-sneeze, then sniffed the morning air.

The crow cocked her head curiously, scanning from one to the other, trying to take it all in at once. "Is that the head bear?" she asked Almedon.

Bohadea poked her nose up at the juniper tree. "Who are you?" she asked the crow.

"I'm Tae Ola," said the crow with a little bob of her head. "The forest is filled with the news that the Tribe of Star Bear saved many forest people from the Rumblers last night. It is said that you destroyed the fire-web, killed the Rumblers, and took some Saroos prisoner." Tae Ola stared curiously at Kog and Radg.

"They're not our prisoners," said Bohadea. "They're rebel Saroos. They fought with us."

"Oh?" said the crow, not quite convinced. "Well, the reason I have come is that there's another fire-web at Muskrat Marsh, and many of my people have been imprisoned there.

Including my sisters," she said sadly. "I want to go there and free them. Can you help me free my sisters?"

Bohadea looked up at Almedon.

"We must go to the Pit," said Almedon. "It is foretold that the Tribe of Star Bear will enter the Pit of Darkness to battle the Rumbler King. It's where we must go."

"What about Tae Ola's sisters?" said Bohadea. "And all the others trapped at Muskrat Marsh. I have friends there, too!"

"You will save them, won't you?" pleaded Tae Ola.

"Maybe Muskrat Marsh is on the way," suggested Amber.

"It's in the opposite direction," said Almedon.

"But we are the Tribe of Star Bear," said Bohadea, "we can't just ignore them."

"Of course we can't," agreed Amber.

"Course we can't," echoed Olli.

"The Quelicots can help," offered Diansha.

"And the rebel Saroos, too," said Kog. Radg's head bobbed up and down in agreement.

"I must tell the others," Tae Ola shouted joyfully. "I must tell them I've found the true Tribe of Star Bear. My sisters are saved! The forest is saved!" She darted up into the air, over Beehive Bluff, racing for the forest: "CAW! CAW! CAW!"

"Now look what you've done," Almedon snapped angrily at the group. "She's off to tell the whole world that we'll rescue all their friends and relatives. There are dozens, maybe hundreds of fire-webs out there. How do you suppose we're going to save every single forest person and fight the Rumbler King at the same time? It's impossible!" he spit furiously at the tribe.

"Yip!" called a coyote. There was a scuffle of activity as the coyote leapt out of the forest and pranced skittishly at the edge of the meadow. He stopped stock-still and stared at the gathering beneath Beehive Bluff. An entire pack of coyotes materialized behind him. "Tribe of Star Bear?" called the lead coyote.

"We are," Bohadea bellowed back.

The lead coyote gave a signal and the entire pack loped across the meadow toward them.

"Tchip," squealed Olli. He raced up Amber's leg and plunked himself on her shoulder. "Tcheeez," he wheezed, "that's an awful big pack of coyotes."

A trail of dust flew up in the wake of the charging pack and they skidded to a halt as they reached the group gathered in front of the small wolf den. The lead coyote made a snippy little bow. His eyes skipped from Diansha to Prakna, then settled on Bohadea. He bowed again, this time more deeply, his nose almost sweeping the ground. "We are the Tribe of Jalep," said the coyote to Bohadea. "We heard of the great battle under the last moon between the Tribe of Star Bear and the Rumblers. The Warriors of Jalep humbly offer their services to the Tribe of Star Bear." Again the coyote made a deep bow.

"Why does everyone assume the bear is in charge?" grumbled Almedon.

"'Cause we're called the Tribe of Star Bear," Amber whispered back, one hand shielding her mouth from the coyotes. "You know, 'bear.' There's a bear in the title so they figure that ..."

"I know what they figure," Almedon hissed.

"Ah-hem," Bohadea cleared her throat, looking sharply from Amber to Almedon.

Almedon crankily fluffed up his feathers and stomped one foot against his perch.

Bohadea bobbed her head in a little bow to the coyotes. "We are very pleased that you've come to fight with the Tribe of Star Bear," she said.

"Look!" Amber shouted, pointing across the meadow at the forest fringe. From all directions, warriors of every species were converging on Beehive Bluff. They were coming in singles and pairs, in little groups and whole tribes. There were groundhogs, bats, hawks, wolverines, bees, sparrows, bobcats, ducks, mice, butterflies, deer, ferrets, squirrels, raccoons, bears, dragonflies, all manner of forest folk from every neck of the woods.

Tae Ola soared across the treetops leading back a flock of crows thick and black as a storm cloud. They were ringed in a bright shimmering blue, cast by the enormous flock of blue jays that followed behind them. The birds jangled the air with their raucous cries.

"Oh my stars!" exclaimed Bohadea.

"Well," snorted Almedon, "it's about time."

"Fibbertygibbertyboo!" Olli hopped excitedly from one foot to the other, his tail slapping up and down on Amber's shoulder.

"Oh! Look! Look at that!" cried Amber. She was pointing at a black bear lumbering toward the bluff with a small red squirrel perched on his back.

"Snowberry," cried Bohadea. "It's my nephew, Snowberry."

"Tullywanooli," shouted Olli. "That's Tullywanooli on his back."

Bohadea ran to meet her nephew, bellowing with excitement.

"Go, go, go," Olli tugged on one of Amber's dreadlocks. "MOVE IT!" he shouted at her.

"Knock it off, you little pest," Amber frowned at Olli. "I'm not a golf cart, you know. If you want to run over to meet them, then run over there yourself."

"Aw, come on, tchee, tchee, pleeeze," he cajoled. "That guy's from the Kingdom of Tumbling Puffball. He's a big acorn. Plus, there's too may coyotes and ferrets and hawks out there. I could be eaten. Then you'd be sorry."

"Oh, all right. But I'm not running." Amber stomped off after Bohadea.

Olli fidgeted and fussed, fluffed up his tail and wiggled his whiskers.

Bohadea and Snowberry nuzzled each other, grunting and purring and sniffing happily. Tullywanooli held on to Snowberry's back, watching with concern as Bohadea heaved up against one side and then the other. Then he spotted Olli coming toward him, riding atop Amber's shoulder.

Tullywanooli waved his tail in greeting. Olli waved back. "Permission to come aboard your human," he saluted Olli with his bushy red tail.

"You'll have to ask her yourself," said Olli, jerking one thumb up at Amber. "She's kinda touchy today."

"Ohhh," said Tullywanooli with wide round eyes. "Tchip?" he said to Amber.

Amber stepped closer to the bears, leaned over, scooped up Tullywanooli, and plopped him down on the shoulder opposite to Olli. Tullywanooli latched onto a dreadlock, then peered across under Amber's chin at Olli. "This is my first ride on a human," he said.

Forest people thronged across the meadow toward Beehive Bluff. The trees were growing thick with birds, in some places there were so many that it appeared as if the leaves had turned deep blue or jet-black. Bohadea turned and led her nephew back toward the wolf den. Amber followed with the two red squirrels twitching excitedly on her shoulders.

"Is Potelia safe?" Bohadea asked Snowberry.

Snowberry did not answer at once. His head drooped and Bohadea knew the answer to her question before he spoke. "My mother is dead," he said. The words came slowly and sounded flat.

Bohadea's heart hitched inside her chest. It was as if a little piece of her heart had broken off and flown away. A thousand pictures of Potelia flashed through her mind. She remembered how they had wrestled together as cubs, splashed in the water of Big Trout Stream, had their noses stung by bumblebees. Together. Always together. Even after they were supposed to have gone their own ways as grown-ups, she and Potelia had never parted for long.

"She stood up to the Rumblers," said Snowberry proudly. "She stood her ground. And when they kept on coming she charged them. It was over quicker than a flash of sky fire."

"At least it was fast," said Bohadea, her voice unsteady.

"I ran away," said Snowberry, his words heavy with shame. "And then I heard that the Tribe of Star Bear had struck. It gave me hope. So I came to fight."

"I'm glad you came," Bohadea nudged him under the chin. Then she stuck her nose up in the air and sniffed at Tullywanooli. "And you, too," she bobbed her head at the squirrel.

"I came to fight, too!" said Tullywanooli. "Rumblers knocked down the Kingdom of Tumbling Puffball." His little red face crumpled up with sadness. "And then they ate it," he snorted with fury. "I ain't got nothin' left to lose."

"I guess that's true of all of us in one way or another," said Bohadea sadly.

She sniffed out at the crowd that was gathering at the foot of the bluffs. It was a startling scent, a startling sight. The idea of "natural enemies" seemed to have evaporated. Eagles and squirrels, ferrets and ducks, wolves and groundhogs, all together in the same small space. No one snapped or snarled or threatened the other, no matter the tribe, no matter the species. The terror of the Rumblers overrode all other fears.

"Now what?" Almedon flapped in bewilderment. He hopped excitedly from one branch to the other. "What do we do now? What do we tell them. Impossible! It's impossible to organize this many people."

"Almedon," said Bohadea, "calm down. We just need to think for a minute. Imagine what we can do with this many warriors. Why we have as many warriors as there are berries in a berry patch. We could free the prisoners from many fire-webs—all at the same time."

"And what about Dreeg?" Almedon wanted to know. "What about the Pit of Darkness? It is foretold: The Tribe of Star Bear must go into the Pit to defeat the Rumblers. Into the Pit. To battle the Rumbler King."

"Why can't we do both?" said Amber.

"Do both," said Olli and Tullywanooli in unison. They looked at each other and giggled.

Almedon shot them a withering look.

"How can we do both?" asked Bohadea.

"We divide up into groups," said Amber. "We already know how to destroy a fire-web and free the prisoners. And we know how to wreck their big red crystals. We even saw how the crystals could be turned on the Rumblers, so we know they can be destroyed. We just tell the new warriors everything we know. Then Kog and Radg and the Quelicots can lead the new groups, and we can go take care of this Rumbler dude in his pit."

"The Jaleps could lead a group too," said Bohadea. "And Snowberry," she nodded at her nephew.

Snowberry looked over at Tullywanooli. "Are you game, little buddy?"

Tullywanooli looked around as if the bear was addressing someone else, then realized with a start that he was being asked to help a bear lead a warrior group. "Oh, tcheeez, tchip, yyyup, yup. I'll help," he said in a tiny voice. He leapt off Amber's shoulder, flew gracefully through the air, and landed on Snowberry's back with a skid that nearly sent him careening over the other side.

Almedon hitched up his shoulders, then ruffled his feathers and flattened them down again. "It's a good plan," he grumbled to Amber. To Bohadea he said: "We will make the announcement from over there." He gestured to a rising platform of rock that jutted from the bluff just beyond the entrance to the small wolf den.

Bohadea and Amber picked their way across a tumble of boulders that led up to the ledge, tailed closely by the pair of Saroos. Kog glanced uneasily over her shoulder at the growing crowd.

Snowberry, Tullywanooli, and Diansha squeezed onto the ledge behind them. The rest of the Quelicots and the Jaleps spread themselves out in a protective ring around the platform.

Almedon unfurled his golden wings, flew to a small outcrop above his tribe, and sent out a call for silence. An eerie quiet fell across Beehive Bluff just as the sun burst over the horizon in a blaze of bright yellow light.

Bohadea began to speak. She told of their journey from Lookout Rock to Pointy Noggins, from Istarna's Cave to Weeping Rock. When she spoke of the Saroo attack in the woods, the crowd hissed and snarled. When she told how Diansha had made short work of them, they yelped and cheered. This made Kog and Radg very nervous. They kept their eyes lowered and shuffled from foot to foot, knotting and unknotting their long bony fingers.

But Bohadea made a special point of telling how Trub and Kog had helped the tribe to plan their attack. And she told the story of brave Trub who had given his life in a final act of courage that had destroyed not only the crystals, but the Rumblers themselves.

There was a sudden flurry of wings as a flock of crows fluttered into the air near the edge of the meadow and began to circle. The crowd parted as a very old bear trudged slowly forward. Noses twitched and the forest people fell back as the old bear passed by. Bohadea could sense the uneasiness of the crowd, she could smell it hovering in the air. She raised her head and sniffed more forcefully. *Blood!* A strong scent of blood hung over the bear. He was badly injured.

Bohadea's eyes widened at a twinkle of light that flashed from the bear's neck, for there hung the telltale necklace of the Medicine Bear. "Ramanod!" she exclaimed. "Why it's Ramanod, the Medicine Bear."

The old bear cast her a glance and paused. He nodded, as if affirming something to himself, and then carried on, dragging himself toward the rocky ledge.

Bohadea and Snowberry pushed their way out toward Ramanod. The old bear stopped. His head bobbed slightly as if it were too heavy a weight for him to carry. Bohadea sniffed at his belly where the blood came from. It was very bad. There was a gash two bear-paws long where a loop of intestine had spilled out. Ramanod would not live long in this condition.

The two younger bears pushed up against his sides taking some of his weight. They began to move forward with Ramanod held between them. Tullywanooli's whiskers twitched, but he didn't fidget or fuss, he stood on Snowberry's back as still as a rock.

"I have been sent by Star Bear herself," said Ramanod. He grunted with the effort of his words. "I must speak with you, Bohadea, the chosen of Star Bear, before it is too late."

"Don't speak now," said Bohadea. "I have very strong medicine, given to me by Istarna. First, I will heal you, then we will speak."

Ramanod shook his great head but allowed Bohadea and her nephew to press him forward, moving toward the wolf den. As they passed the ledge, Bohadea paused and called out to Almedon: "You must organize the warriors into groups. Tell them to destroy all the fire-webs in the forest and to hold the Rumblers back for as long as they can." She turned to Snowberry and asked him to stand with Almedon in her place. Alone, she led Ramanod into the den, where he finally collapsed with a painful groan.

"What happened?" Bohadea asked him, as she prodded gently at his gaping wound.

"I had a vision," said Ramanod.

"No, I mean your wound. How did it happen?"

"Ah." Ramanod's eyes drifted shut. He opened them again with much effort. "I was ambushed by a Saroo patrol. They had already captured two bear cubs and a young female." He raised his face to look at Bohadea, then dropped his head back to the ground. "The cubs reminded me of you and your sister."

"Potelia is dead," said Bohadea flatly.

Ramanod grunted.

Bohadea began to unfasten the pouch of star dust from her ear.

"I fought the Saroos so the others could escape," he said.

"Did they?" asked Bohadea as she opened the pouch.

"They did. But when I reared up, the last Saroo cut me down with the fire-stick. I escaped with a little magic," he said quietly. "I knew I had to survive long enough to speak with you."

"You will survive longer than that," said Bohadea, reaching a paw toward the star dust. "This is the most powerful healing magic I have ever seen. It will fix any wound. Even one such as yours."

"No," said the old bear. He lay one paw over hers to stop her from touching the star dust. "You will need every speck of that star dust to heal the great damage that has been done to the earth."

"Don't be silly, Ramanod. I have enough to heal everyone who needs it. And right now you need it the most. If you don't let me sprinkle Istarna's medicine on your wound, then Dark Bear will soon seize you and drag you up to the stars."

"I do not fear Dark Bear," snorted Ramanod. "She is the twin sister of Star Bear. They are identical, only Star Bear dances in the light of the moon, and Dark Bear dances behind the moon."

"I don't care where Dark Bear dances," said Bohadea defiantly. "She has cheated me twice before. And today, I learned that she has taken Potelia as well. She will not have you, too. Not today." Again she reached for the star dust. Again Ramanod stilled her paw.

"Dark Bear is like an old friend to me now," said Ramanod in a deep slow drawl. "I am a Medicine Bear. I have spent my life in the light of Star Bear, and in the shadow of Dark Bear. There were many times when I thought I had opened myself to channel the healing light of Star Bear only to discover that Dark Bear had come instead. And now ...," he paused, "now I am old. So many of my tribe have gone to the stars with Dark Bear."

Bohadea's shoulders hitched, tears stung her eyes. She felt like a cub stuck inside a hollow tree trunk, the wood pressing in on her from all sides, the rising panic of being stuck all alone inside a dark narrow space.

Ramanod gasped for a breath. He squeezed his eyes shut and a small groan of pain escaped his lips. "When someone you love dies," he said, "they take a piece of your spirit with them. When too many of your tribe have gone to the stars, a day comes when you realize that there is more of your spirit dancing in the stars than in the forest. The spirit in the forest becomes thin and sad and longs to be whole again."

Bohadea was silent. Tears wound their way across the maple-sugar fur of her muzzle, leaving darkened rivulets.

"My spirit longs for the stars, Bohadea," said Ramanod.

Bohadea tossed her precious pouch of star dust, the sacred talisman of Istarna, to the ground. It slumped there on the rocks, a dark stain of black velvet. A few tiny specks of star dust escaped from the pouch and twinkled in the pale grey light.

Ramanod watched her with gentle weary eyes, but when he spoke, his voice was strong and clear. "I had a vision," he told Bohadea. "Star Bear came to me. She touched me at the place of my third eye and I saw the Tribe of Star Bear assembled here beneath Beehive Bluff. I saw you and me, in this den, as we are right now. And with us were the spirits of Star Bear and Dark Bear. They had come to help us perform the final ceremony of the Medicine Bear. And when it was over, I followed Dark Bear to the stars. You followed Star Bear into battle."

Bohadea snorted back her tears and blinked at Ramanod. "The final ceremony of the Medicine Bear?" she asked in awe. "Me?"

"Us! Together," said Ramanod. "Bohadea, help me sit up."

Bohadea hiccuped and swallowed the last of her tears. She leaned over and gently eased the old Medicine Bear up onto his haunches. Ramanod moaned and Bohadea winced as she saw the purplish loop of intestine bulge a little further out from the gash in his belly.

Ramanod closed his eyes and began to chant in a low bear-song voice. Bohadea closed her eyes and sang with him. It went on for several minutes and when Bohadea opened her eyes again, the den was filled with such a soft pearly light, it seemed as though the moon herself had come to rest inside Beehive Bluff. Ramanod lifted the Medicine Bear necklace from around his huge neck. It was made from strings of braided willow bark, and beaded with hard red berries, small brown mushrooms, and spikes of clear white crystal. In its center was a little woven birch-bark basket, made thin and deep for carrying medicines.

Ramanod plucked two of the withered little mushrooms from the necklace. One he handed to Bohadea, one he put in his own mouth. Bohadea took the mushroom into her mouth and chewed slowly. She felt dizzy and light-headed, as if her mind was floating around just above her head. Ramanod lifted the necklace high in the air, he no longer seemed to feel the great pain that wracked his body. Bohadea dipped forward and Ramanod placed the necklace over her head.

"This was given to me by Anthor, the Medicine Bear before me. He got it from Drathea, the Medicine Bear before him. And now I, Ramanod, give it to you, Bohadea, the Medicine Bear whom I choose to succeed me."

Bohadea clicked one of her claws against the little medicine basket that hung from the crook of the necklace. Dreamily, she searched the ground until she found the black velvet pouch filled with star dust. She retrieved it, carefully brushed it off against her fur, and tenderly placed it inside the medicine basket.

"It is a more practical way to carry your medicines than in your ear," said Ramanod. A little smile played on his thin black lips. "How could you hear with that thing stuck in your ear?"

"I can hear better now," said Bohadea. She looked deep into his wise brown eyes.

"Then listen with both ears. And listen from the place of first-sound deep inside your heart," said Ramanod. "A true healer always walks in the light of Star Bear, but never turns her face from the shadow of Dark Bear, for without Dark Bear there would be no stars."

Bohadea sighed and nodded her understanding.

"To be chosen to the Tribe of Star Bear, you must be both healer and warrior. You must move from light to dark and back again. You must be fire and water, earth and air, predator and prey. You must understand the nature of all things. You must *be* all things."

"I'm not sure I understand your words," said Bohadea.

"Ignore my words," said Ramanod. "Only listen to the sounds. And when you look at something you wish to understand, let your eyes drift shut, let the shapes become hazy, then you will see the form of the spirit world behind them. Then you will see their true shape. If you think too hard, you will never understand it. You must *feel it!* Listen to the spirit world. See it. Feel it. Then anything is possible. Bears can fly and eagles can move mountains."

"Bears can fly," repeated Bohadea.

"A single squirrel can bring the stars crashing down."

"Crashing down."

"One little human can build a whole new world."

"New world."

"There are a few specks of star dust, there on the ground beside you," said Ramanod. "Gather them up and place them upon your heart."

Bohadea's head was swimming. Ramanod's fur, which had laid flat against his skin, so lank and dull, seemed to bristle, shiny and full of life again. He looked big and strong and young. And ever so handsome. Bohadea's head lolled to one side, her eyelids fell heavily shut and she jerked them open again, her eyes latched onto the spot where three tiny specks of star dust glittered. She swiped it up and onto her chest, just as the old bear had bidden. When she looked up again she saw a dark shadow looming up behind Ramanod. The shape of a black bear. *Never turn your face from the shadow of Dark Bear.* With wide eyes she watched as Dark Bear laid a paw on Ramanod's shoulder. Ramanod slumped over. His body lay motionless, but his spirit rose up, strong and beautiful, and smiled at Bohadea.

"I will not take a piece of your heart to the stars," said Ramanod. "Instead, I will give you a piece of mine to keep in the forest." Ramanod reached into his chest and withdrew a small heart-shaped diamond that sent sparks of rainbow light arcing across the den. He reached toward Bohadea, his spirit growing stronger and brighter. His paw moved through her like a fish through water and he placed the diamond at the center her heart. A light pulsed from the diamond filling her joy.

She could feel her own spirit grow bright and strong. She reached to touch Ramanod's paw. Dark Bear smiled, then turned, leading them up through the solid rock of Beehive Bluff. They exploded into the sunlight, flying high above the meadow. Higher and higher they went. The shapes of the warriors beneath grew tinier and tinier until they faded away into the emerald forest, and then the forest itself disappeared into a bright swirling globe of blues and greens. Stars began to twinkle ahead of them, and Bohadea could feel her heart growing lighter and brighter with every passing moment. She didn't look back and would have kept on going if Star Bear had not reached out to her with one bright white paw, and led her back down to the little wolf den. *"Not yet,"* the spirit bear whispered in her ear. And then it was over. Bohadea was sitting on her haunches looking across at Ramanod's body crumpled up on the floor of the den.

She sat there a long time just looking at the old bear. And when she was ready, Bohadea rose and padded over to him. She laid a paw on his head: "Thank you," she whispered with tears in her eyes. Then she turned and walked out of the den. An ancient white bear followed her to the mouth of the den, then disappeared.

8

Shadowland

Outside, everything seemed so clear and bright. The sky was so blue, the clouds so fluffy and white. The air was filled with the sounds and smells of excitement like right before a Bearsong Fête. Warriors bustled about the meadow, busy with final preparations. Bohadea counted twelve clans in all. With the Tribe of Star Bear, that made thirteen.

She noticed that her nephew Snowberry stood at the head of one of the clans, and a swell of pride rose in her chest. Kog and Radg looked very dignified too. They had divided up and each one stood smartly at the front of her own clan. The Quelicots and the Jaleps headed two more groups, and a hodgepodge of forest people that Bohadea did not know stood ready to lead the others.

Bohadea could see that the ragtag of warriors was still a tiny force compared to the Rumblers and their army of Saroos, but the power of the rebels was growing! She could feel their strength in her bones, and in the brave, strong beat of her heart.

Almedon's shadow floated over Bohadea. She gazed up and watched as the eagle swept onto the outcropping that hung above the rocky ledge. Behind him sailed Tae Ola and a noisy battalion of crows returning from a scouting mission. The crows scattered across the face of Beehive Bluff perching on every available jutting of rock.

A second wave of bluejays, cowbirds, grackles, hawks, and eagles followed. The birds scattered across the meadow covering the trees and bushes in a glistening blanket of feathers.

"The Rumblers are closing in on Beehive Bluff," shouted Almedon. Hushed whispers, twitters, and growls rippled across the troops.

"Closing fast," crowed Tae Ola.

"We must leave at once," called the eagle. "The birds of each clan will guide you along the safest path to your fire-web."

There was a great shuffling of paws and ruffling of wings. Bohadea hurried back up to the rocky ledge to join her tribe.

Amber spotted the Medicine Bear necklace at once. "Where'd you get that from?" she asked, her finger lightly brushing the string of braided willow.

"Ramanod gave it to me."

"You are a Medicine Bear now," said Almedon respectfully. "It is a great honor."

"What happened to Ramanod?" Amber asked Bohadea, her brow knotted in a little frown, crinkling her war paint.

"He's gone off with Dark Bear," she said.

Amber dropped her eyes. *Another death!* At first it had all seemed like a game. Like a day trip to Wonderland to ride the coasters. She had figured it would be an adventure, and then it would be over and life would go on as it had before. She wasn't so sure anymore.

"Look!" whispered Bohadea. She pointed at the sky. "The spirits are gathering."

Above the warrior clans stood the oddest cloud. It was egg-shaped and separate from all the other clouds, and it shimmered in a most magnificent tone of silvery violet.

Twinkles of light like dragonflies winged toward the egg, and when they touched it they vanished in glints of purple. The egg grew larger and larger. Faces in the meadow turned upward. A hush fell over the crowd. The egg began to spin.

Faster and faster it went, then in a whirl of violet light it descended into the meadow. The warriors drew back as the egg came to rest on a clear grassy patch, not far from where the Tribe of Star Bear stood. The egg hummed a sweet silvery song, and it glowed so brightly that some of the warriors had to shade their eyes from its dazzling light. A radiant purple crack appeared on one side, and a gasp swept across the crowd. Another crack appeared on the other side, and then a third one. A web of tiny purple lines blazed across the luminous shell and it cracked open in a flash of violet light.

In place of the egg, there stood a fiery bird with legs as high as a deer is tall. She had gleaming feathers every color of the rainbow, and a crest that flared like a crown at the top of her head. The air crackled with electricity and a buzz of excitement wheeled through the crowd. The great bird unfurled her splendid wings, flapped once, and rose back into the blue sky casting no shadow beneath her.

All eyes were on the firebird as she circled over the meadow leaving a trail of twinkling violet lights in her wake. She glided over to the first clan led by the Saroo Kog and hovered there, her wings spread above them in a glowing canopy of feathers. She curved her graceful neck downward and peered at the clan with dazzling cobalt eyes. The splendid crest of feathers at her crown unfurled in a spray of colored lights that shimmered in the air, then winked out. Rosy pink rays arced from her wing tips around the clan. She plucked one pink feather from her breast and allowed it to flutter earthward.

The birds of the first clan rose up and danced beneath the firebird. They darted, dipped, and dove around the radiant pink feather as it drifted down. Kog reached her long spindly arms up, balancing on tiptoe, and plucked the feather from the air. "Agida!" she sang out, her voice strong and sure. Kog's new clan echoed the battle cry.

The firebird's wings rippled in a graceful arc of pearly light. She swept across the meadow, the birds of the first clan winging behind her. The crowd on the ground parted, opening up a path for the warriors of the first clan as they galloped after the firebird, their battle cries echoing across the bluff. At the edge of the forest, they plunged into the trees and vanished. The form of the firebird seemed to waver for a moment as she floated there, watching over the departure of the first clan, but then her wings arced upward in a spray of violet light and she glided back to the second clan.

Here, she did as she had done for the first clan, and again she plucked a single feather from her breast. This time a turquoise one. The firebird plucked twelve feathers in all: one of pink, red, orange, yellow, green, turquoise, blue, purple, magenta, silver, copper, and gold. And as each clan peeled off from the crowd, she led them to a different path, each headed in a different direction, until no one remained but the Tribe of Star Bear.

The four stood transfixed as the firebird cast her bright cobalt eyes down at them. "Go in the light of Star Bear," said the bird, her words chiming like silver bells. "And carry with you the Feather of the Phoenix, that you may rise ... on the wings of your dreams." She plucked a pearly white feather from her breast, and let it fall from her beak.

Amber stretched up to catch the drifting feather, then turned and carefully threaded it onto Bohadea's Medicine Bear necklace. The girl turned back just in time to see the firebird vanish in a pinwheel of colored light that rained down on the tribe. They held up their faces and paws to catch the magical drops as they fell.

And then, quite suddenly, it was gone. Not a single bird cheeped, not a single gnat buzzed. All was still in the growing heat of the day. All but the terrifying drone of approaching Rumblers. As a great tree was felled somewhere in the forest, its death moans drifted over the bluff on a soft summer breeze.

"We'd better get going," said Amber, restlessly eyeing the top of the bluff.

"Where?" cried Olli, flinging his arms up in the air. "Tchip. Tchip."

"Straight toward the Rumblers," said Almedon. "That is the direction we are supposed to go."

Bohadea turned to search the sheer face of Beehive Bluff. "I know a legend about this place," she said. "It tells of how a giant race of bumblebees once lived here. Long ago, in the time of the dragons, when there were flowers as big as rocks and grasses that grew as tall as trees. It is said that the bees had sentries posted in all four directions to guard their store of golden honey. At Bearsong Fêtes, they often sang of an ancestor Cave Bear called Hermatof who tricked the bee sentry at the back gate and gorged himself on honey until he was so stuffed he couldn't move. When the bees discovered him, they rolled Hermatof into the bumble nursery, sealed him into a waxed crib, and turned him into a bee."

Amber and Olli giggled at the picture of the fat bear being rolled around by giant bumblebees.

"Get to the point, Bohadea," said Almedon impatiently. "The Rumblers will be on us in a blink."

"The point," said Bohadea, "is that if the bees had to put sentries in all four directions, then there must be tunnels leading in and out of Beehive Bluff. And there must be at least one right here in the cliffside. If we could find it, it would lead us past the Rumblers—underground."

Almedon surveyed the cliff face. "When I flew over earlier, I did notice several caves near the top that looked quite deep," he said. "Like bat caves. But I don't see how you or the girl could reach them. You would need wings to get in there." He glanced at the squirrel. "Although a very small, agile climber might do it, I suppose."

"I can do it. I can do it," squeaked Olli, bobbing up and down.

"All right," Bohadea said to Almedon. "Then you and Olli check out the caves while Amburrr and I figure out how to get up there."

"Tchureee!" Olli leapt off Amber's shoulder and began to scale the cliff, leaping, crawling, balancing, tiptoeing his way up.

Almedon took flight, skimming across the face of the bluff. He landed in a niche at the farthest top corner.

"We need a rope," said Amber. "Or a long fat vine. Something strong enough to anchor onto a tree at the top. Then we could climb down on it."

"A fat vine," mused Bohadea. "I dunno." It was a frightening prospect. Her paws could not grip a vine like a human paw could. It would be risky business for a bear.

Amber was looking at her. "Wanna do it?" she asked the bear.

"I guess so," said Bohadea. The whine of an approaching Rumbler echoed across the bluff. She sniffed the air. "We'd better hurry."

By the time Amber and Bohadea had discovered a hank of vine and hiked to the top of Beehive Bluff, the thin cover of forest was trembling from the terrible crashes and drones that drew so near. A foul scent poisoned the air.

Almedon skated overhead: "Hurry," he called. "Follow me." He banked in a sharp sweeping turn, then beat his wings in three hard determined slaps and flew off to a place halfway along the top of the bluff.

Amber ran awkwardly, clutching at the heavy coil of vine that flapped and trailed at her feet. Bohadea jogged along beside her, casting fearful sideways glances at the forest. She thought she might have seen a flash of red eyes between the trees.

Almedon hopped impatiently back and forth as the two huffed to a stop. Bohadea and Amber peered over the edge. There, on a teeny tiny ledge part-way down the cliff, perched Olli. He jumped up and waved his arms fiercely. "I found it," he shouted. "I'm the one who found it. And it's an excellent tunnel. An awesome, excellent, and very very very good tunnel. Come on down."

Bohadea and Amber looked at each other, then looked back down at the sheer drop that ended in a stony stretch of meadow far, far below. Amber looked around, her head jerking right and left in a panicky search for the tree that would anchor their line. But there was no tree. Why hadn't she noticed that before? There was not one single tree out here on the ledge. Nothing but stones. Not even a rock big enough to hold their weight. "What will we tie the rope to?" she wailed. "There's nothing to tie it to."

Bohadea's head swung around, her eyes jumping desperately from one place to the next, then settling with a stony calmness on the forest's edge—at the Rumbler that stood there, huge and metallic grey, its blood-caked gob smirking with pleasure. It didn't move. It just stood there watching, humungous red eyes flashing greedily. Its claws, drenched with sap and gore, snapped open and closed in slow measured beats. A tree crashed down beside it.

Amber and Almedon turned toward the sound, then froze. A second Rumbler broke cover; its shiny silver teeth sliced at the downed pine tree, crunching it to death in a spray of needles, bark, and sap. A third Rumbler lurched into view, ripping and shredding the bushes in its path. When this one caught sight of the Tribe perched at the edge of the cliff, it threw back its head and roared. A cloud of noxious fumes rolled across the top of Beehive Bluff.

"What's going on up there?" Olli's frightened voice called shrilly from below.

Bohadea snapped to attention. She tore the vine from Amber's rigid fingers, tied one end around her middle section, and threw the other end over the cliff. "GO!" she barked at Amber, swiping at the girl, urging her toward the edge.

Amber burst into tears. "Bohadea!" she cried.

"GO!" growled the bear.

A Rumbler roared. The stench made Amber gag. *GO!* Amber grabbed the vine and plunged over the side, rappelling downward. Her feet kicked at the honeycombed face of the bluff, her hands burned against the coarse drag of the vine.

"Hurry, hurry, hurry," called Olli, leading her to the tiny ledge that was only a wolf's-paw wide.

Amber swung back off the cliff and reached with her toes to the place where Olli pointed. Her foot caught the ledge. She heard Almedon shriek from above. She looked desperately for something to grab onto. There was nothing but a smooth hump of rock near the top of the opening. She used it to propel herself outward again. "Move," she yelled at Olli. He ducked inside and Amber flung herself feet first through the opening.

She scrambled onto her hands and knees and crawled back to the ledge. The vine was swinging just out of reach. She swiped at it and missed. She swiped, and missed again. She hissed under her breath. "We've gotta get that rope. Bohadea's attached to the other end."

Olli hopped onto her shoulder. "Try again," he said.

Amber reached for the vine. Olli crawled out along the girl's arm to her outstretched fingers. "Hold onto me!" he called. She grasped him snugly around his middle. He wrapped his two back legs around her hand and swiped at the vine, just grazing it at first, then stretching out to his maximum length and capturing it. Gingerly, Amber drew back her arm. She grabbed hold of the vine with her free hand, and Olli hopped down onto the ledge.

There were at least a half dozen Rumblers glaring at Bohadea and Almedon. The first Rumbler threw back its huge head bellowing and snorting. It lowered its head at the cliff edge, snapped its razor teeth at the air, and charged. The others followed, coming at them like a tidal wave. Their stench alone was thick and foul enough to knock a person down. Their claws clattered against the ground, eager to shred the flesh and bones of their waiting victims.

Almedon flapped his wings and screamed his fury.

"Fly away! GO!" cried Bohadea.

Almedon shrieked at the sun, then flung himself over Beehive Bluff.

Bohadea turned her back on the killing machines as they closed in on her. She looked out over the bluff into a blue summer sky. There was only one way out, and that was straight down. *Too bad bears can't fly.*

Bears CAN fly! Ramanod's voice whispered inside her head. For a moment, she thought she saw him floating in front of her, holding his paw out to her. *Bears can fly and eagles can move mountains ... can fly ... on the wings of your dreams.*

Bohadea flung both paws outwards and sailed into the air. *I can fly! I can fly!* She laughed out loud.

Almedon watched in horror as Bohadea began to fall. His horror redoubled when he saw that Amber had tied the loose end of the vine around her waist. Olli clung to the tail end like a tiny useless anchor. *The little lunatics,* Almedon cursed. Bohadea had to weigh five times as much as Amber and Olli. She would plummet to her death, dragging the human and the squirrel down with her.

The Rumblers chased recklessly after the bear. In their haste to kill, they were unprepared for the sudden stop. Fuming and shrieking they plunged headlong over the cliff after Bohadea.

Bohadea was flying! She floated down placidly, her arms spread out like bear-wings. *Bears can fly!* A great hulk of silver-red plummeted past her. A second one streaked by on her other side. But she paid them no heed. The shrieking Rumblers were nothing but a blur of color and sound to her And she was only vaguely aware of a fiery explosion at the bottom of the chasm.

Bohadea felt a tug on her middle where the vine was tied. *Oops. Gone to far.* She glanced up dreamily at the tunnel's entrance. *Fly up!* she told herself. *Just a little ways back up.*

As Bohadea flew past the tunnel, Amber steeled herself against the sudden pull of the bear's weight. She gritted her teeth, dug in her heels, and braced her arms against the rocky wall. Olli squeezed his eyes shut and gritted his teeth too. There was a tug on the vine. Not much. Not any-where near what Amber had expected. She started to reel it in, fast as she could, surprised that Bohadea weighed so little. The bear was as light as a squirrel. Olli rushed over to the ledge to see what was happening.

Almedon could not believe his eyes. *Not possible!* That little girl couldn't possibly take the weight of a falling bear. But she'd just done it! And now she was reeling Bohadea

in as though she were a bug stranded at the end of a bit of
duckweed. Almedon watched as the bear clambered into
the tunnel opening. The eagle shook his head then glanced
at the foot of the bluff just as the last Rumbler hit bottom.
They had been smashed to bits. Six or seven piles of rubble
smoked and fumed and gave off a fetid stink.

Almedon circled back to the tunnel opening. Out of the
corner of his eye he could see that a fresh batch of
Rumblers had arrived at the edge of the bluff. They were
more careful, more calculating than the others had been,
but clearly in a murderous mood. Almedon dove, then
clapped his wings tightly against his body as he glided in
through the tunnel opening.

The narrow tunnel led straight into the cliff. It had a six-
sided shape like a honeycomb cell and glowed a faint
honey-yellow. Amber led the way. She fingered the
amethyst spider, soothed by its steady calm pulse. At the
first fork in the tunnel, the pulse of the amulet seemed to
nudge her to the right, so that was the way she went. At the
next fork, it nudged her left. She followed without question
or thought, just as Bohadea and Almedon followed her.

One tunnel looked much like the next as they weaved
their way through the maze of honeycomb. It was hard to
keep track of time, and impossible to sort out direction.
Finally the tunnel widened and brightened, then opened
onto an enormous golden chamber. The walls were made
of pyrite, fool's gold, and they sparkled like a treasure
trove. In the center of the arching cavern was a splendid
structure carved entirely of pyrite. It looked rather like an
old-fashioned four-poster bed.

"The queen's chamber," gasped Bohadea. "That must
be where the queen bee sat while the drones buzzed
around and fed her royal jelly."

"I sure hope they're not here anymore," said Amber. "If that was the queen bee's bed, she must've been as big as an elephant."

They stepped carefully around the royal bed, listening for the slightest hint of a buzz. But the only sound was the padding of paws and sneakers across the golden floors.

Honeycomb tunnels led out of the chamber in all directions. Amber closed her hand around the talisman, and as she passed each opening, she closed her eyes and felt for the pulse of the purple stone. It was thready and weak until she came upon the seventh doorway, where the pulse beat fast and strong. Amber opened her eyes to see the spider glowing purple, fading and brightening with each pulse. "This one," said the girl. She turned into the narrow tunnel.

They soon passed through a second chamber that Bohadea said was the bumble nursery. The very one where Hermatof had been turned into a bee. Here, the honeycombed walls were a pale waxy yellow and gave off a sweet flowery scent, but it had the eerie feeling of the distant past, like dinosaur bones.

Further along, they came upon a third chamber, this one filled with small cube-shaped crystals. The cubes were clumped here and there, on the floors, the walls, the ceiling. They were a deep golden color, like amber. So naturally Amber had to stop and check to see if it was real amber, which it was not. It was something better. The crystals were sticky, like candy. And when she touched the tip of her tongue to one, she discovered it was crystallized honey; honey so ancient and dense that it had turned to rock. "Mmm," she hummed. "Honeyrocks."

"Honey?" Bohadea's ears pricked up. She snapped off a hunk and popped it into her mouth. "Ohhh," she grunted. Her nose wriggled with pleasure.

Amber cracked off two more clumps and handed one to Olli. The squirrel scrunched up his face and sucked noisily. She offered the second piece to Almedon, but he turned his beak up at it.

"Try it," Amber urged him.

Ordinarily, eagles were not fanciers of sweets, but it had been a long time since Almedon had a proper meal and he was hungry enough to eat almost anything. So he tucked the piece of honeyrock into his beak and swished it around. His eyes popped open with surprise. "Not bad," said the eagle.

"If I ever have cubs, I shall feed them honeyrocks all day long," said Bohadea through a mouthful of the sweet crystals. She slid her claws into a cluster of honeyrock and snapped off another chunk.

Thievzzz!

Almedon flinched at the sound. The feathers at the nape of his neck stood on end and his head swiveled around. He couldn't see anything out of place. But he could feel it. It was as if the walls had eyes.

Bzzzzzzzzzz. Thievzzz!

"Who said that?" hissed Amber. She swung around, but there was no one there.

BZZZZZZZZZZ. The walls began to swim. Suddenly, they cracked. It was like shards of broken mirror sliding back and forth creating a jumble of fractured images. And then the pieces seemed to arrange themselves into neat geometric patterns, one interlocking with the next.

Goosebumps prickled on Amber's arms; she recognized the pattern as one she had studied in science class when she was learning insect anatomy: the walls had been transformed into a shield of huge shiny eyes. Compound eyes. Bees' eyes.

Amber could see her face reflected from a thousand different angles. Suddenly, there were a thousand bears, a thousand eagles, a thousand squirrels, all staring back at her. The walls buzzed like electrical wires on a hot summer afternoon, and Amber clapped her hands over her ears.

Bzzz. Dare you zzzsteal from the Royal Treazzury?

"No!" cried Bohadea through a mouthful of honeyrock. "We are not thieves. We are the Tribe of Star Bear and we're hungry. We only took a mouthful to eat. We meant no harm."

Bzzz. If you are not thievzzz, then where izzz your offering to the queen? The compound eyes glinted darkly.

"Tchip," squeaked Olli. He dove into the girl's pocket, and in his scramble to get to the very bottom, he pitched out a stone and a nutshell that clattered to the floor.

Golden sparks danced across the huge compound eyes. *Bzzz. Not good enough! Five clumpzzz were taken. Five offeringzzz are required.*

Bohadea shot Amber a wide-eyed look and gestured to the girl's pocket. Amber stuck her hand in and fished around, picking out two acorns and a seed pod, which she carefully laid beside the stone and the nutshell.

Bzzz. Very zzzsmall offeringzzz. The queen preferzzz flowerzzz. Big flowerzzz.

Flowers? Amber dug back into her pocket. Olli quickly shoveled his stuff to one side and sat on it. "Move," Amber whispered. She shoved him off his treasure pile and fumbled around. Her fingers closed around a big slippery hunk of fungus. *Yuk!* She lifted it out. Olli tugged it back in. "Olli, let go," she hissed at him. She pulled, he tugged. She snatched it out and with a flourish, laid Olli's big orange fungus treasure in a gap of broken honeyrock.

Bzzz. Lovely. That will do. Bzzzzzzzzzz.

Without any further ado, the tribe bolted for the door

and scurried through the honeycomb, eager to be out of the glare of the gigantic bees' eyes.

Finally, the tunnel ended in a pool of pale twilight. Cautiously they left the cover of the honeycombs and stepped out into the open. They were not prepared for what met their eyes.

Nothing! There was absolutely nothing out there.

The earth was scorched black and looked dead as a corpse. Here and there stood the blackened remains of tree stumps, the odd torn leaf or twig, an occasional broken animal bone or chipped stone, but not one living thing graced this wretched place. Not even a Rumbler.

"They have killed everything," said Almedon. He looked around unable to believe his eyes.

Bohadea slumped onto the lifeless ground. "How can we possibly fight this?" She shook her head in sorrow.

"What is this horrible place?" asked Olli, blinking in confusion.

"This," said Almedon, "is what the forest looks like after the Rumblers have passed through. I'm going up," he told the others. "Stay close to the tunnel. I'll find out where we are."

"Be careful," said Amber, her blue eyes bright with fear.

Almedon nodded, then launched himself up into the flat smoky sky. His heart felt like a lump of lead. Never could he have imagined such absolute destruction. There was nothing for as far as the eagle's eye could see. Nothing but criss-crossed trails and deep gouges worn into the earth by Rumblers traveling from Red City.

He passed a way-pit where Rumblers and Saroos had gathered. It was empty. Near the horizon he sighted a small advance guard of five or six Rumblers heading for the front lines. Then he spotted a distant smudge of pink—Saroos—and an even bigger smudge of silver-

grey. More Rumblers. It would be too dangerous to
investigate any closer.

Almedon swung back toward the tribe. He saw them
huddled by the entrance to the tunnel and circled once to
be certain they were all right, then he continued on in the
opposite direction, toward Beehive Bluff. Blackened hills
rolled toward the bluff. He moved on silent wings, high
above the earth, dodging from one cloud cover to the next
until he spotted the Rumblers' front lines, and beyond that,
the living forest.

He was about to turn back when his eye snagged on a
familiar plume of smoke. There had been an explosion. An
explosion caused by the huge red generator crystals that
made the fire-webs. That meant that at least one of the new
warrior clans had been successful. The forest people had
begun to fight back!

He tilted one wing up and reversed his course gliding
along a current of warm air. He was tired. He wished for
the cozy nest that overlooked his lush green valley. He
could see in his mind's eye the sparkling ribbon of blue-
green water that wound through the valley like a fat juicy
snake, the endless meadows filled with marmots and dandelions and rabbits and the grand skeleton of an old pine
that his eaglets had always loved to play in.

He was tired indeed. He took advantage of as many
thermal currents as he could find on the way back and
landed at the tunnel's entrance just before the sun abandoned the dead zone.

The tribe decided to travel under cover of darkness. It
was the only camouflage there was. And by night they
would be able to follow the exact path of the Tip Star that
would lead them into Red City. Into the Pit.

Bohadea picked her way between blackened stumps.
Almedon bobbed along on her back, content to have the

soft curve of the bear's spine as his perch, his resting place. Amber trudged wearily behind them, drawing some small comfort from the slow steady swish of Olli's tail against her back. They soon came upon the first of the Rumbler trails. It cut into the earth ramping downward, then settled into a gouge that ran steadily at a depth of about three bears high. They did not go into the Rumbler trail, but followed it until it came to a crossroad.

Almedon glanced up at the dark indigo sky, his eyes gliding across the cosmos, settling on the Night Eagle constellation, on the star that glowed at the tip of the eagle's tail. "That way." He pointed to the trail that led to the right.

"Yes, right," confirmed Amber, her fingers curled around the amethyst spider.

Olli was getting bored and just about to head down into Amber's pocket for a quick snooze, when Bohadea stopped short. "Listen!" she whispered. "Do you hear something?"

They all froze, straining to catch some hint of the sounds that rode the still night air. It was faint, but it was there. That drone. The terrible deadly drone of Rumblers somewhere in the distance, coming along the trail.

"We gotta hide," said Amber, casting about for some place to shelter them.

But there was only black pocked earth, a tapestry of dark shadows and sharp angles. The silhouettes of the little band of warriors stood out in the silver glow of the moon like prairie dogs perched on a desert hilltop.

Bohadea looked stricken as she strained toward the sound of the faraway drone. She blinked helplessly at the flat, bleak Shadowland around her. *Now what?*

You must move from light to dark. You must be fire and water, earth and air, predator and prey. You must understand the nature of all things. You must BE all things.

Bohadea stood very still, her eyes closed tight.

In Shadowland you must BE a shadow!

Bohadea snapped her eyes open. If bears could fly and
eagles could move mountains, then bears and eagles
should have no trouble at all masquerading as shadows. "I
know," she said out loud. "I know how we can hide." The
bear padded across the barren black land, moving away
from the Rumbler trail until she found a suitable collection
of dips in the land. "Here, this is perfect," she said, turning
several times in the largest central dip like a wolf flatten-
ing out a nesting place.

"Amburrr, you lie face-down in this place," she gestured at a long shallow dip between tree stumps. "Close
your eyes, hold your talisman, and imagine that you have
become a piece of the earth."

"Dust to dust," muttered Amber. She knelt down in the
dip, clasped her amethyst spider, and stretched out. As soon
as she was settled down, she realized just how tired she
really was and snuggled in. Olli curled his fingers around
his silver acorn and nestled into the crook of her shoulder.

"Almedon, you take this one." Bohadea pointed at a
rounded shallow dip that would hold puddles during rain-
storms.

Almedon looked at her uncertainly, then down at the
little hollow.

"Become one with the earth," Bohadea encouraged
him. "The spirit world will help you."

The eagle nodded. He flattened himself into the dip
and spread out his wings so that his shape blended more
smoothly into the curve of the land; then he let his mind
drift toward the spirit world, and Ledonnia.

Bohadea marveled at how perfectly he blended into the
ground. It was very hard to tell where the ruined forest
floor ended and the eagle began. She checked to make sure

that Amber and Olli had blended in as well as the eagle, and then settled herself into the largest dip with one paw curled around her Medicine Bear necklace and its precious pouch of star dust.

The drone of the Rumblers drew closer and soon the air was tainted with the stink of death and destruction. Amber and Olli, tired out from long sleepless nights and the day-long hike beneath Beehive Bluff, had fallen sound asleep. Only the gentle rise and fall of their breath gave any hint of their hiding place. But Bohadea and Almedon were wide awake. They felt the earth tremble as the Rumblers approached, they felt it quake beneath them as the killing machines moved on the trail in front of them. Both their hearts skipped a beat when they heard the Rumblers halt on the trail. *Had they sensed the presence of living beings?*

The Rumblers were breaking out of the trail, rolling up toward the Tribe of Star Bear. Their stench filled the air. Amber flinched in her sleep.

Bohadea squeezed her eyes shut and pressed her nose into the earth. *Ramanod! Star Bear! Istarna! Please protect us.* She repeated it silently, over and over like a mantra.

There were several Rumblers: grinding, rolling, clanking, closer and closer, then spreading out to cover more ground. One was almost right on top of them. Bohadea could sense a red glow, even though her eyes were closed. Was the Rumbler scanning the ground? The red glow moved back and forth across them. And then it was dark again. The Rumbler made a bellowing sound, turned away, and began moving back toward the trail. The others followed.

They dared not move until the sound of the Rumblers' passage had faded and the earth had ceased to tremble.

"Almedon?" whispered Bohadea.

"Are they gone?" he whispered back.

Cautiously Bohadea raised her head and clambered to her feet. She looked around. "I think it's safe now."

Almedon scooped in his wings, righted himself, and fluffed up his feathers.

"Amburrr?" Bohadea whispered.

Amber shifted in her sleep, she gave a contented little snore.

Bohadea padded over and peered down at her and Olli. "Can you believe it?" she said in amazement. "They're both fast asleep."

Almedon shook his head. "It's like they say: 'Sun Eagle watches over the young and the silly.'"

"Maybe we should let them sleep a while," said Bohadea.

"No time for that," said Almedon impatiently. He twaddled over to Amber and bonked her in the head with his beak.

"Ow!" Amber woke up rubbing the sore spot on her skull.

"What?" yelped Olli. "What what what?"

"Let's go!" commanded Almedon.

"Shouldn't we wait to see if the Rumblers come or not?" Amber asked.

"They've come and gone," said Almedon.

"Huh?" said Amber. She rubbed her eyes and hauled herself to her feet. Olli managed slip back into her pocket and curl up into a tight ball without ever quite waking up.

They trudged back to the trail and once again set out for Red City, picking their way across the blackened earth. Dark shadows crept across the ruined forest floor and spooked Amber until Bohadea pointed out that they were just the shadows of clouds.

"They look like ghosts," she told the bear. She checked the sky to make sure there was a cloud to match each shadow. It was funny how different things looked in the dark. Amber remembered being scared in her own backyard once when she mistook the juniper bush by the back steps for a vampire.

Bohadea stopped and sniffed at the air. "I think they're coming back," she whispered. "Can you smell them?"

Amber closed her eyes and sniffed the air. She couldn't smell anything. But she felt something. A gnawing feeling in the pit of her stomach. A Rumbler feeling. And in her mind, she could see a fuzzy picture of Rumblers on the march. "I think they're coming again," she said in a high choked voice.

Bohadea turned tail and loped away from the trail with Amber jogging behind her and Almedon inching his wings in and out to keep his balance on the bear's back. Olli popped out of Amber's pocket. "I was having a good dream," he pouted. "You wrecked it."

Bohadea quickly picked a safe spot and the four settled into the hollows as before. But Bohadea was restless. She got up again and sniffed the air. The smell was thicker and closer, the dense vibrations of the Rumblers rattled the earth. She frowned, then glanced up at the sky.

Almedon shifted in his hollow and peered up. Bohadea's shadow hovered over him. "What are you doing?" He shuffled upright and stared at the bear.

"What's going on?" Amber rolled out of her hollow and up onto her knees.

"Yeah, what? What?" Olli wanted to know.

Bohadea looked troubled. "They sensed us the last time," she said. "The Rumblers knew exactly where to find us. They might not be as easily fooled a second time."

"Do you think they're coming back here because they know we're around?" Amber asked the bear uneasily.

"I don't know," Bohadea shook her head. "I just know that we need to do something else. Something else to mask our presence."

Circle of Light! Istarna whispered in her ear.

"Like what?" Almedon demanded.

"Circle of Light?" murmured Bohadea.

"Circle of Light," chirped Olli. "My dream angel just showed me how to make a Circle of Light. Like this! It's easy." The squirrel flipped his magic acorn over his head and, holding it by its silver cord, he dragged it on the ground in a circle around his body chanting: "Sansanjulubyoowoo. Sansanjulubyoowoo. Sansanjulubyoowoo." And as he did this, a glistening bubble of silvery pink light began to shimmer in the air around him. "There! See?" said Olli, throwing his arms up in the air as if there was nothing to it. Inside the bubble of light, he grinned from ear to ear.

"Wow!" said Amber. "Cool!"

"Watch this!" squealed Olli. He jumped about, leapt and somersaulted, and wherever he went, the bubble followed. "It's just like in my dream," he chortled happily.

"I wonder if I can do that?" Amber pulled the amethyst spider over her head. *Sansanjulubyoowoo,* she chanted, as the purple spider bumped along the ground in a circle around her. A beautiful violet bubble sprang to life and glimmered around the girl. "Oh, this is amazing!" She reached out to touch the violet light. She could feel it. It made her fingers tingle.

"How lovely!" exclaimed Bohadea. She pulled Istarna's talisman from her Medicine Bear pouch and drew her own circle. A bubble of pure white light sprang up around her.

"Look! Look!" shouted Olli. He dove into Amber's violet bubble, spun in a circle, then jumped out again. His silvery pink bubble followed him in, around, and out.

Almedon stretched his talon to the ground and traced a circle with the diamond teardrop, surrounding himself in a bubble of golden light. "Are you sure we won't be drawing their attention right to us with all these colored lights?" he asked uncertainly, and as he spoke, the light in his bubble dimmed, then winked out.

"You must have faith, Almedon, or it won't work," said Bohadea with absolute certainty. "It only works if you believe in it."

Almedon closed his eyes. *Believe, Almedon,* whispered Ledonnia. *Believe, and it is so.* Almedon took a deep breath, then opened his eyes and retraced the circle around himself chanting loudly: "Sansanjulubyoowoo, sansanjulubyoowoo." The golden bubble of light winked back on around him.

"Good!" said Bohadea.

"Do we still have to hide?" asked Amber.

"I think we should," said the bear. "It will help mask our presence better."

Again, they took their places in the little dips and hollows, making a rainbow of light that looked magical and strange in the dead darkened landscape.

The band of Rumblers moved back along the trail, heading for Red City. They showed no sign of sensing any intruders hiding among the shadows and Bohadea dared to raise her head to peak up at them. She felt sure this was not the same group that had passed earlier. These Rumblers were hauling something. Something big. But they were too far away and too deep inside the trail for Bohadea to see what it was. She only caught glimpses of odd shadows in the dark. It gave her the shivers.

The bubbles of light began to fade as the Rumblers passed, and Bohadea gave thanks that they did not wink out entirely until the Rumblers were safely out of sight.

The Tribe of Star Bear followed the Tip Star all night long, taking shelter and raising their bubbles of light whenever the Rumblers passed. They noticed that larger numbers of Rumblers were moving toward the front, often accompanied by Saroo troops. But all those moving back to Red City dragged a heavy train of cargo.

As the stars spilled from the sky and a soft pink light began to grow in the east, Bohadea grew more restless. The shadows were retreating. Soon there would be no shadows at all, no place to hide.

9

The Little Glitch

Beneath the former Saroo stronghold of Red City, at the bottom of the great central mining pit, a Saroo messenger called Ert approached the great crack that had unleashed the Rumblers. Ert had once been a powerful member of the Saroo Governing Council. In his old life, he had feared no one. In fact, he was the one to be feared. But now, he trembled in the presence of his Rumbler masters and did their bidding without question.

The crack that had first appeared at the bottom of the mining site was no longer just a crack. There had been so much traffic in and out of the Pit of Darkness, so many Rumblers passing from the bowels of the earth to its surface, that the crack had been forced into a grand gateway that would allow a whole troop of Rumblers to pass through, six abreast. The entrance was ringed by Saroo guards and each one cradled a red laser wand large enough to take out two city blocks with one strike.

Ert's new role was Head of Logistics. He had many skills and talents in organizing industrial operations, and it had been a fairly straightforward matter to shift over to a Rumbler/Saroo complex.

He had set up an effective communications and command system controlled from Red City and fanning out in all directions. It gave the Saroos an iron grip on the forest. They gathered intelligence, built fire-webs, prepared the way for the Rumblers, and helped move product back into the Pit.

Those trapped in the fire-webs were the product. Food for King Dreeg and his circle of Mighty Poobahs. Their appetite was insatiable. But even the Mighty Poobahs had to admit that Ert's finely tuned system had been delivering product tickety-boo—until now.

Ert had developed a nervous tic in his face since things had started to go wrong. One of the fire-webs had been attacked by forest rebels night before last. Seven more webs had fallen the following day, and now the forest seemed to be swarming with rebels who were tearing down the fire-webs as fast as the Saroos could put them up. There was also evidence that some Saroo troops were deserting. Perhaps even worse! Ert suspected that some of them might be fighting with the rebels.

And now ... now the unthinkable had happened. The supply of product had fallen short, and King Dreeg was getting peckish. Dreeg's top advisor, the Mighty Toothed Poobah had summoned Ert, demanding that a status report be delivered IN PERSON.

Ert's knobby knees knocked together and his snazzy pink face went tic, tic, tic as he halted at the gateway to the Pit and announced himself in the high-pitched jabber of formal Saroo language. The Saroo guards lifted their weapons and moved aside.

It was Ert's first time in the Pit. Aside from Yenm, former Leader of the Governing Council, Ert didn't think that any other Saroo had been so honored—although it seemed a somewhat shaky honor, more like a dressing-down actually.

He shambled carefully down the oddly ramped steps that had been designed for the huge clanking limbs of Rumblers. He couldn't help but notice that the steps were made of red crystal. Extremely fine red crystal. In fact, the more he looked at it, the more he thought that it was probably the finest red crystal he had ever laid eyes on. Dark and rich and lit from the inside by a red heatless flame.

The stuff in the Saroo mines would look like junk next to this. Even a small piece of such fine-quality crystal would be worth a small fortune out there on the red market. Especially if it was cut and faceted into a gem or a small tool. It did cross his mind that if his service to the Rumblers was held in high regard, he might be able to collect some of the crystal as a personal reward.

Ert began to breathe through his mouth as the stench of the Pit rose to meet his nostrils. This was his main problem with the Rumblers. They stank like a graveyard. The idea of that awful stink going in his mouth made him want to hurl. But he was a mover. A mover and a shaker who wouldn't be put off by a bad smell. On he shambled, down, down, down.

A line of Rumbler guards blocked his passage at the bottom of the stairs so he could not see what lay beyond them. "I am Ert," he called out, his voice a little too eager and high-pitched. "The Mighty Toothed Poobah has summoned me."

They stared at him with flashing eyes, red and venomous. They neither moved nor spoke. Ert felt like a luckless ant who had just blundered into a nest of ant eaters. But he stood his ground.

Ert wished he could see past the reeking wall of grey-fleshed Rumblers. There was something going on back there. He could hear the steely scuttle of other Rumblers moving toward them. Then the line of guards in front of him parted to reveal the gigantic form of the Mighty Toothed Poobah, flanked by a personal Rumbler guard. Ert had pretty much gotten used to the peculiar tastes of the

Rumblers, but he was not prepared for this: The Mighty Toothed Poobah wore a necklace of dead animals. Large animals such as deer, cats, bears, and wolves strung together with cable wire. The corpses hung there limp and greenish. Ert felt his gorge rise. He hung on to his composure by a thread, barely managing not to toss his breakfast all over the Mighty Poobah.

He felt dizzy and his head throbbed, but he gave a little bow nevertheless and plastered a big toadie grin on his face. "This is a great honor, oh Mighty Toothed Poobah," he said. "I Ert, Head of Logistics, am at your service." He gave a little flourish with his long pink bony fingers, then straightened up.

"Spare me the crap," roared the Mighty Toothed Poobah.

Ert flinched. *Tic.*

"King Dreeg wants to know why our product deliveries have been so slow. What in hades is going on?" bellowed the Rumbler.

"It seems we have a little glitch in the production line," Ert's words crept out. With lowered eyes and twiddling thumbs, he explained about the rebels and the lost fire-webs. He left out the part about the possibility of Saroos helping the forest people.

The Poobah threw back his head and spit in rage. There was steam coming out of that part of his anatomy that one would generally consider ears, although they looked more like hubcaps. "Who is responsible for this?" the Mighty Toothed Poobah demanded.

"Well," said Ert, shifting from one foot to the other, "according to our sources, there's a radical gang of troublemakers out there stirring up the forest people. This gang apparently attacked the first fire-web and then held some kind of terrorist planning meeting where they organized rebel groups to sabotage our webs and steal our product."

"And just who is this gang?" snarled the Poobah.

"Well," said Ert, clearing his throat. *Tic. Tic.* "According to our sources, there's a bear who's the leader. An eagle, a human ... um. Oh, yes, there are apparently some wolves involved ... and" he mumbled, "a squirrel."

"A WHAT?" bawled the Poobah.

"A bear," said Ert. "Their leader is a bear."

"NO, NO, NO. That last one. What was the last one you said?"

"A squirrel," muttered Ert. *Tic. Tic. Tic.*

"A squirrel? A SQUIRREL? Are you telling me that our operation is being sabotaged by a squirrel?" Foul greenish spittle flew from the spiked fangs of the Mighty Toothed Poobah.

"Well, no. No. It's not just a squirrel. This is a gang of crack terrorists. The squirrel is probably just the ... ah ... the ... ah ..."

"SHUT UP!" clanged the Rumbler. "You sniveling little twerp. This is unacceptable. Completely unacceptable. You have twenty-four hours. Do you hear me? Twenty-four hours!"

"Oh, yes. Yes, Sir. I hear you," Ert peered up at the Poobah. "To do what, Sir? What shall we have done in twenty-four hours?"

"CAPTURE THEM, YOU FOOL!" shouted the Poobah. "Deliver them to ME. Alive!"

"Yes, Sir!" Ert bowed and bobbed, bobbed and bowed.

"If you fail," said the Poobah in a steady, calm voice, "you will be hanging here next to this bear." He tapped one huge jagged claw against his putrefying necklace and sneered at the Saroo.

Ert sucked in his breath. A big brass drum throbbed inside his head. His thoughts were sharp and jumbled like shards of broken glass.

The Mighty Toothed Poobah slammed around and stomped away. The line of guards closed behind him and faced Ert. Their jaws began to snap.

Ert wheeled around and flew up those fiery crystal steps three at a time. A considerable feat for a well-padded Saroo who had spent most of his adult life pushing crystal chips around.

10

Red City

The tribe had noticed that the Rumbler trains returning to Red City did not usually have a Saroo escort with them. No Saroos, no fire-sticks. So Almedon had decided to take a double risk. He would fly a scouting mission and test out the effect of the protective light bubble at the same time. As the others watched, Almedon traced a circle in the scorched earth with his diamond teardrop. At once a golden bubble blossomed around him. He nodded at the tribe, spread his wings, and lifted off into a powdery morning sky.

"He looks beautiful," said Amber. From the earth, Almedon appeared as a golden sphere of light. He could easily be mistaken for a UFO, she thought. Maybe the Rumblers will think he *is* a UFO. Maybe they'll even be frightened of him. She hoped so.

Almedon soared across the deadlands that lay so dark and lifeless beneath the sky. It made the eagle wonder how the sky could stay so blue when the earth looked so dead. He swooped across the Rumbler trails, relieved to see that there was nothing coming toward them from Red City. But he did spot something.

There was a silver haze on the horizon. *The silver desert*, of which Kog had spoken? Almedon did not have to go far to see how oddly the air shimmered there. How thick it seemed. How very weird it looked! It was not misty or foggy, nor ill defined. In fact, it seemed to hold a distinct geometric shape and all the Rumbler trails converged there.

Almedon banked sharply to the right and swung back around to check the trails for convoys carrying Rumbler cargo back to Red City. He traveled a fair distance before finally sighting one. At first, he could not tell what the cargo was. But as he drew closer, the grisly details became clear. Never before had Almedon doubted his eyes, but this time he blinked and refocused, just to be sure. Deep inside the gouged trails, the Rumblers were dragging back floats of dead trees heaped high with the bodies of forest people.

A wave of sorrow swelled in his chest. He could feel the golden bubble waver around him and knew that he must turn back at once. He flew blindly across the ruined land wanting to get as far away from the ghastly cargo train as he could. His wings beat furiously at the air, the wind rushed at his face. The golden bubble splashed apart and disappeared. Almedon didn't even try to get it back. He was too upset to care.

As he closed in on the tribe, the eagle could see three spheres of light dancing on the ground—one of white light, a smaller violet one, and a pinpoint of silvery pink. He coasted down to a short black stump. It was the only thing left to land on. He folded back his wings. "I don't know how the three of you can be playing games at a time like this," he said crossly.

"We had nothing else to do," shrugged Amber. "We've been playing with the bubbles. Watch this!" Amber closed her eyes and frowned. The violet light faded. Then her face relaxed and the bubble brightened again.

"Did you see that?" she asked the eagle. "The bubbles are powered up by our minds. If you think scared thoughts, it gets weak. If you think happy thoughts, it gets strong!"

"Watch me!" squealed Olli. He scrunched up his face and squiggled his nose until his bubble popped. "Nut worms," he said gravely. "I was thinking about nut worms." Then, like a magician presenting his next trick, Olli flung open his arms: "And now, I will think of a ripe beechnut, as big as my head!" The squirrel squeezed his eyes shut and a silvery pink bubble began to shimmer around him, growing stronger and stronger.

"You are a beechnut," scoffed Almedon. "And what I have to tell you now will ruin all your bubbles," he frowned. As he recounted his sighting of the Rumblers' grim cargo, the spheres of light winked out, one by one, just as Almedon had predicted they would.

"We had better get going," said Bohadea sadly. "We must get to the Pit as fast as we can and put a stop to this."

"If we move with our very best speed, we should arrive at the Silver Desert before the Sun Eagle begins his night journey," said Almedon. "In any case, we must move quickly. Those bubbles might keep the Rumblers at bay for a while, but eventually, they are going to come check us out."

"I agree," said Bohadea. "We must try to avoid them as much as possible, and move as fast as we can."

"But we have to keep our thoughts light and happy at the same time, or our bubbles will burst," said Amber.

"Beechnuts," mumbled Olli.

They decided to travel the rest of the way inside their bubbles, practising to hold the light around them until the spheres became second nature. It was a poignant sight to see the four beautiful globes of light gently drifting across the ruined land.

Almedon flew regular scouting missions in the daylight and they were able to avoid almost all the Rumbler movements by zigzagging their route from one trail to the other. But as they neared the Silver Desert the trails began to merge into a single Rumbler highway leading into Red City and it became more and more difficult to pass unnoticed.

The haze of the Silver Desert loomed ahead, a densely shimmering fog. The Rumbler highway disappeared abruptly into the thick silver air.

Amber squinted at the strangeness of it. "It looks solid," she said.

"I don't think we should go in there," said Olli. "It looks scary." The silvery pink light wavered around him.

"Watch your bubble," Amber warned him. "Don't think scared thoughts."

Olli closed his eyes and the pink light grew bright again.

Just then a Rumbler platoon broke out of the Silver Desert into full view. One Rumbler stopped and looked straight at the four spheres of light perched near the edge of the highway. Then another Rumbler looked. Then a third.

"I guess we're not completely invisible to them either," said Bohadea calmly, her eyes never leaving the Rumbler troops. "I was hoping we might be."

"But the most they can see are bubbles of light," said Amber. "Maybe they'll think we're ETs and keep away."

"I don't know what an ET is," said Bohadea, "but I have a feeling that Rumblers would eat them too."

The Rumblers began to move toward them. Not a charge, but a slow, cautious, curious movement, like a cat stalking a bird.

"Oh, oh," said Olli.

"Beechnuts," said Amber in a singsong voice.

"Just keep walking," said Bohadea steadily. She began to hum.

Amber hummed along in harmony, and Olli made it a three-part harmony. Bohadea, in the lead, angled their route farther from the edge of the highway so that the Rumblers could not swipe at them.

"I'm going up in the air," said Almedon. "If they start to go for you, I'll try to draw them off. Run if you have to. Go right into the Silver Desert—I have a feeling it will be safer in there."

"Keep your thoughts light, Almedon," Bohadea warned him. "Don't let them draw you down."

Almedon lifted off into the air, his golden sphere floating over the Rumbler highway. The Rumblers paused to watch him. They made curious grunts and groans that the tribe had not heard before. Almedon circled low over their heads and then landed on the opposite side of the highway, just out of their reach. Some of the Rumblers broke out of the trail and began to march off after him. Almedon took off, flew a little farther out, and landed again. The Rumblers hesitated, then scuttled after him again. He took them on a merry chase, hither and thither. Several of the Rumblers just stood by and watched.

The rest of the tribe was nearing the silvery wall that marked the beginning of the desert. And not a moment too soon. The Rumblers were losing interest in the golden sphere. Some of them had already turned their attention back to the bubbles that floated lazily along the ground. One of the Rumblers snorted angrily. Almedon swept over their heads again and another Rumbler took a swipe at him, then bellowed.

"Time to run," Almedon called to the tribe.

They began to run, the shimmering spheres skipping along, bouncing into the silver haze. Almedon dove at the Rumblers, then set down again just out of reach. But they weren't playing that old game any more. They were going after the spheres that didn't fly. The Rumblers let loose with a series of blood-thirsty roars, and charged.

Olli clung to Amber's dreadlocks, pretending that he was swinging from his home tree. Amber leapt onto Bohadea's back, making believe she was a movie stunt rider. Their bubbles stayed strong and bright.

Bohadea imagined she was running down the hill to Hog's Hollow. A steep easy hill that made you go fast. So fast that when she and Potelia were cubs, they used to run down at top speed and fall over on purpose, sliding the rest of the way down on their rear ends. She went sooo fast! And it was sooo easy to run downhill.

Almedon was amazed at Bohadea's speed. She was outrunning the Rumblers. That was impossible—especially with Amber and Olli on her back! But there she was, doing the second impossible thing he'd seen her do in as many days. Almedon took flight over Bohadea, pacing her. He couldn't believe it: she was moving as fast as an eagle can fly.

They broke through the wall of silver haze into the desert. Beneath Bohadea's paws was a fine sandy floor of pure silver dust. The air spun and twirled with tiny silver dust motes that dashed against the light of the spheres. It was like driving in a snowstorm, Amber thought.

The Rumblers plunged in after them, bellowing and snorting with fury. They began to gain ground in the sandy silver footing.

Bears can fly! chanted Bohadea, over and over. *Bears can fly!* The sphere of white light around her began to spin and, in that very instant, she lifted off the ground and took flight.

Almedon nearly fainted when he saw Bohadea flap her burly black paws and lift off into the air.

"We're flying," shrieked Olli with delight. "We're flying! We're flying!" But no sound came out. His words rang out inside the heads of the others. But there was no actual sound.

"Ha!" laughed Amber. "If a bear can fly, then so can a girl." And with that, Amber pitched over Bohadea's back, spread her arms, and flew.

Olli hung from one dreadlock for an instant, then giggling like a fool, he peeled off and fell into formation. "We're flying," he squealed with glee. "We're flying."

Almedon was stunned. He was surrounded by a flock of forest mammals flapping their paws for all they were worth and staying afloat. The eagle laughed too. A deep belly-lurching laugh such that he hadn't laughed since before Ledonnia's death. It echoed inside the heads of the others like wind rushing between canyon walls.

Olli turned around and flapped his paws, hovering on the spot like a swimmer treading water. *We lost 'em,* crowed the squirrel. He didn't bother to move his lips this time, he just thought the words, the words formed a thought-ball, and the thought-ball was transmitted to the others at the speed of light.

The rest of the tribe turned back to see a distant crowd of angry Rumblers, almost invisible in the swirl of silver dust motes. They were about to turn back onto their flight path when two great walls of purple swam past them on either side. At first, it was impossible to tell anything about them except that they were purple. But as they glided toward the Rumblers, cutting through the thick silver air, the purple walls began to take shape. To all but Amber, the giant creatures were mysterious Other World beings. But Amber had been to Jamaica on a vacation, and she recognized them as stingrays. She'd seen stingrays when she'd gone snorkeling. Of course, they had been about a thousand times smaller than these two, and they definitely weren't purple. Nonetheless these looked just like them.

The Rumblers turned and high-tailed it for the dead zone when they saw the purple stingrays sweep out of the silver haze and dive at them. They were not used to seeing creatures bigger than themselves. As they scattered, the pair of stingrays raked the floor of the Silver Desert, whipping their long sharp tails back and forth.

"I suggest we get out of here before those things come back looking for us," Almedon sent a thought-ball to the others. He hovered in the silent silver air like a hummingbird.

"They won't bother us," Amber replied. "Stingrays like humans."

"Do they like eagles?"

"Sure they like eagles."

"I think we'd better go anyhow."

The purple stingrays did not follow, much to Almedon's relief.

The tribe could not find the Rumbler highway. The air was just too thick to see very far in any direction. So they kept close together and flew by instinct, moving in a straight line away from the dead zone. They encountered strange blurs of color from time to time, and once, when Amber turned back to look at an iridescent patch of green, she thought she saw an immense winged dragon in flight. When they hit a pink patch, Bohadea thought that they were surrounded by a flock of tiny sparrow-sized pigs. But no one else saw any flying pigs. It was hard to be sure of anything in the thick silver air.

At last they broke out of the Silver Desert onto a brilliant new landscape of red crystal. In the distance, on the horizon, Red City sparkled like a fearsome jewel.

"Oh, oh," said Olli. "I don't think I can fly anymore." He began to drift earthward like a feather caught in the wind.

"Of course you can fly!" exclaimed Bohadea, hovering above Olli's drifting pink sphere. "It wasn't the Silver Desert that made you fly. It was believing in yourself that made you fly."

"Oh!" said Olli. "In that case, I guess I can fly." He flapped his little arms again, and up he went.

The Tribe of Star Bear coasted over the fiery redlands of the Saroos. They did not fly over the road, but moved in the direction of the setting sun—a red sun that stained the sky with smears of dark color like old paint.

Flying in front of the sun was a trick Almedon sometimes used when he hunted. If the prey should glance sunward, they would be blinded by the light and completely miss the eagle. Almedon figured that from a great enough distance, their four spheres of light would look like some sort of sun-spot reflection and be ignored. As they floated across the face of the sun, the tribe was bathed in a ruby glow that tinted their bubbles shades of orange, red, and magenta.

Red City loomed larger and larger. Spires of red crystal jutted into the air and the light of the setting sun glittered on their peaks. Steely dark splotches marked where the Rumblers moved through the city. Most of the activity was around the central square at the main entrance to the Pit. Rumbler troops were moving out, headed for the forest, and a train of cargo had just arrived. Almedon thought it might be the same one he had spotted earlier in the dead zone. Saroos patrolled in and around the city, and even from some distance Bohadea could see that practically all of them carried fire-sticks.

"We'll be shot out of the air if we try to fly in over the city," she said.

"The city is heavily guarded in all directions," said Almedon. "Our best chance is still to approach by sky."

"Why don't we just circle around for a while," said Amber. "That's what airplanes do when they're waiting for clearance to land. Maybe we'll see a way in."

"Why don't we just wait till it gets dark and then fly in," said Olli.

"There is some wisdom in that," said Almedon, annoyed that he hadn't thought of it first. The eagle scanned the terrain below, spotting a spine of crystal that rose up just high enough to create a shallow valley on its far side. "There!" he gestured. "We can set down behind that ridge. We should be safe there for a while."

He led the tribe over the rise and into the hidden crystal valley. They sprawled out on the hard glassy ground, grateful for a moment's rest, and even Almedon tucked his head beneath his wings. The red sun dipped below the horizon and the shadows grew longer, darkening into a blackish red, the color of garnets.

They fell fast asleep, all four of them, and would have slept straight through the night if Bohadea had not woken with a start at midnight. The first thing she noticed was that the spheres of light had not faded in their sleep. They had grown more powerful. Now, even the sleeping forms inside the bubbles appeared to be nothing more than pulsing balls of light. But the spheres played tricks on the eyes. One moment they were bubbles of light, then they were merely shadows as they had been in Shadowland, and a moment later they appeared to take on the shape of a ridge of crystal, or a clump of rock, blending seamlessly into the landscape.

Bohadea extended a paw into the violet bubble and shook Amber. "Wake up!" Then she nudged Almedon who jerked wide awake with a snort. "What?" He shook out his feathers.

"Ohhh," groaned Amber. "I wish I could sleep for a week. Can't we sleep a little longer?"

"No, Amburrr. We have already slept too long. Look at the moon. She is already high in the sky." Bohadea pointed up at a large orange moon that hung heavily in the black sky.

Amber gazed up, then back at the towers of Red City that glowed darkly on the horizon. It didn't really look all that different from any other city. "Are we gonna fly right into the middle and land at that pit?" she asked.

"No," said Almedon. "I don't think that's wise. Too many guards and Rumblers there. It would be safer to land at the high peak with the triangle at its tip. Kog told me that there is a secondary tunnel that leads into the Pit from there."

"Then that's where we should go," said Bohadea.

"As long as we can fly," bubbled Olli excitedly, "I don't care where we go."

"Stay very close together," warned Bohadea.

"And very quiet," added Almedon. "Follow me." He spread his wings and lifted off the ground.

Olli launched himself into the air, darting along behind the eagle.

Amber and Bohadea were not quite as confident. Amber had to take a run at it before clapping her arms down hard and sailing up. Bohadea had to close her eyes and repeat "Bears can fly!" several times before rearing up onto her hind legs, bending deeply at the knees, and propelling herself upward with all her might. Olli and Almedon doubled back to circle the two stragglers until they were certain that everyone was fully aloft and on track. Then Almedon took the lead, winging toward the triangular beacon atop a distant tower.

From Red City, a few Saroo guards spotted the odd shadowy clouds that seemed to be in flight above the redlands, but they gave the sight no more attention then a curious sideways glance. One small Saroo patrol did notice when the strange clouds passed across the peak of the Triangular Council Building. They even stood and watched as the clouds appeared to spiral down to the ground. But in the end they decided that it was nothing.

The Tribe of Star Bear stood in a tight knot at the base of the triangle-topped tower. Directly ahead of them was a squat little structure that led into the side of the building. They had spotted it from the air, and decided that this was the most likely place for an entrance to an underground mining tunnel. But now, close up, it looked completely solid.

"There's no hole to get in," whispered Olli. "How do we get in?"

"There's a door," said Amber pointing to a faint rectangular outline in the red crystal facade.

"That's not an opening," said Almedon. "It's solid."

"It's a door," Amber assured him. "It looks solid, but it moves. We just have to figure out how to move it."

"Maybe a magic word," said Bohadea thoughtfully.

"More like a computer code," frowned Amber. "Or maybe just a plain old key."

"Meow," said someone else. Amber's brows arched up in surprise to find Pudd Wudd Princeling rubbing up against her leg.

Almedon was so startled at the sudden appearance of the cat that he almost squawked out loud.

"Hello, Mr. Princeling," Bohadea bobbed her head.

"How did you get here?" blurted out Almedon.

"The usual route," said Pudd Wudd.

"What are you doing here?" Almedon wanted to know.

"He's here to help us, of course," said Bohadea, her eyes never leaving Pudd Wudd.

"Fiddledeedee. Who's got the key?" said Pudd Wudd, now twining himself around Bohadea's front legs.

"Do you mean that we already have a key?" Amber asked the cat.

"Can't you just talk like normal people?" complained Almedon.

Pudd Wudd's yellow jeweled eyes sparkled as he spoke directly to the eagle. "Eenie, meenie, minie, moe." With each word Pudd Wudd strutted one step closer to Almedon. "Flick the rainbow on your toe."

"The rainbow on my toe?" Almedon looked down at his foot. He lifted it slightly and wiggled the talon that held the diamond teardrop ring.

"A twinkle of light will pierce the night," sang Pudd Wudd. Then he gave a dainty little hop, galloped off around a corner, and slipped away into the shadows.

Amber craned her neck after him, but Pudd Wudd Pinceling had vanished, as if into thin air.

"Did you hear that?" Bohadea asked excitedly. "'A twinkle of light will pierce the night.' Those are the words of Star Bear. It all has something to do with your talisman, Almedon. You have to make it sparkle." She flicked her paw back and forth in the air. "Catch the light and spin it into a rainbow."

"Flick the rainbow on your toe," Olli parroted Pudd Wudd.

"Go on," said Amber. "Flick it. Let's see what happens."

Everyone watched expectantly as Almedon lifted the talon, then leaned forward and flicked it with his beak.

But nothing happened. Not a single thing. There was no twinkle of light. No flashing rainbows. Nothing.

"Just as I thought," grumbled Almedon, plunking his foot back to the ground.

"Wait a minute," said Amber. "You have to catch the light properly. Otherwise how can you make it reflect a rainbow?" She looked up at the huge orange moon.

"But what's all this got to do with getting into the Pit?" Almedon demanded.

"Who knows," shrugged Amber. "Just try it. We've got nothing to lose."

Bohadea was examining the faint rectangular outline in the squat building. She stepped closer and poked her nose at a small square patch etched near the edge. She squinted hard, screwed up her nose, and sniffed at it. "I can't make this out," she muttered. "It's too dark. Almedon, you have sharp eyes, come and look at this thing. Tell me what you see?"

Almedon bird-stepped over and hopped up onto Bohadea's back. He poked his head forward, then cocked it to one side. "Hmm," he said.

"Well?" asked Bohadea.

"It's a rainbow," said Almedon. He spread his wings and coasted back down to the ground. "A rainbow made into a square."

Amber stepped in and leaned over to get a look. "It's a color-coded access bar," she said excitedly. "You can barely see it in the dark, but that's what it is."

"But we still don't know how to get that thing to open," said Almedon.

"I think we do," declared Amber. "Pudd Wudd said: 'Flick the rainbow on your toe.' But you have to be in exactly the right spot, and catch the light just so, for it to work." Amber pointed to a spot directly in front of the rainbow-colored square and one bear's length back. "Bohadea, you stand right here."

Bohadea shuffled into the exact spot.

"Almedon, you get up on Bohadea's back," Amber directed the eagle.

Almedon flapped his wings once and hopped back up onto the bear's back.

"I'm not sure if this will work on the first try. Or if it will work at all," Amber said uncertainly. She looked up at the big orange moon, then back at the door. "Almedon, you have to catch the moonlight with your diamond and then flick it at the bar code." She demonstrated with one hand then stepped back and watched.

Almedon shifted to one foot on the bear's back. Carefully he lifted the talon with the diamond teardrop and held it up as high as he dared. He slanted it back and forth in the orange glow of the moonlight. But as big and bright as the moon was, it still did not offer enough light to spark the diamond.

Bohadea closed her eyes and imagined the face of Star Bear. *I call upon the power of Star Bear to help us reach the Pit of Darkness,* she prayed. And in that instant, the star known as the Eye of the Bear twinkled in the black sky and shot a brilliant beam of white light earthward. Almedon reached his talon up to intercept it. The diamond teardrop splintered into a thousand glittering sparks of color. Almedon sharply flicked his foot, directing the light at the little etched square. It burst into a sequence of colored flashes, and with a grinding rumble, the door slid open. Then the light winked out and the door began to slip shut again.

"Let's go!" shouted Amber. She lurched forward through the door and Bohadea leapt in behind her. Almedon pitched and yawed dangerously on Bohadea's back, digging in his talons for balance.

"Ow!" cried the bear.

"Shush," hissed Almedon.

They were standing in a dark cubicle lit only by strips of red light that glowed from the ceiling. Ahead of them was a square shaft that plunged downward at a dangerous angle. A pulsing mechanical hum came from deep inside. Above the shaft were glowing red symbols. A small train of sleek red cars was anchored to a single bar track that sat at the mouth of the shaft. They had an unused look to them.

"Cool!" Amber whispered into the dark red glow. "It looks like some kinda carnival ride."

"I believe we will have to ride those things down into the Pit," said Bohadea with a wobbly voice. "There must be some other way down."

"I don't see any other way," said Almedon.

"But I can't fit into one of those wee red things," argued Bohadea. "They were made to fit a Saroo."

"Maybe you could fit on top of it," Amber offered.

"On top!" Bohadea padded over to the rim of the shaft and peered down. "Oh my," she groaned. "It practically goes straight down."

"Wow!" Amber was standing beside her gazing down into the shaft lit by a single continuous bar of red light. It seemed to go on forever. At least Amber could not see where it ended. "I have a feeling this is gonna be one incredible rush," she said.

"I'll be dashed to death," said Bohadea with horror.

"No you won't," said Amber. "You can fly! Remember!"

Bears can fly!

"Come on! Let's go!" Amber scrambled into the little front car, and Olli secured himself to her dreadlocks with all four paws. Almost immediately the little car revved up. One of the red symbols above the shaft began to pulse. "Hurry!" she called to the others. "It goes automatically, as soon as you sit in it." The pulsing symbol began to make a dinging sound.

Bohadea threw herself across the second small car, sprawled atop, head first, all four paws clinging on for dear life. A second red symbol sprang to life.

Amber's car began to inch forward. Almedon was seized by a moment's panic as his eyes darted from Amber to Bohadea. Then he flung himself into the third car and a third symbol began to pulse.

Gears clicked into place, Amber's car locked onto the track and slid forward. It plunged headlong down the shaft traveling at breakneck speed. She gripped the car with white knuckles and almost screamed out loud. Her dreadlocks flew straight out behind her, and she could feel the heavy lump that was Olli thumping back and forth against her back. Olli gasped in terror, then he wheezed and chuckled, then snorted and giggled wildly. Amber sucked in her breath, once, twice, then she couldn't hold it in anymore, and started laughing and whooping as the car sped down in a streak of red light.

Bohadea was not as amused. She kept her eyes glued shut, arms and legs rigidly stuck to the car. She could hear Amber and Olli whooping it up ahead of her and noted this with some amazement.

Almedon crouched deep down in his car, only his head poking up above the top, his golden feathers flapping in the wind, his eyes wide and unblinking.

The cars zipped out of the shaft one after the other and jerked to a halt inside a wide cavern that glowed a deep murky red. Amber disembarked wearing a big silly grin. Olli was still gasping and giggling.

"Shush, you little fools!" hissed Almedon as he leapt from the last car and shook out his wings.

"Ohh," groaned Bohadea, as she peeled herself off the second red car. "That was awful!"

"Not as awful as being eaten by a Rumbler," warned Almedon. "Now everyone hush. Listen! There are Rumblers nearby."

Bohadea screwed up her nose. They certainly were nearby. The cavern reeked of their foul scent. And the pulsing hum they had heard at the top of the shaft had become the relentless drone of Rumblers on the march.

"What do we do now?" Amber was suddenly anxious again. She clasped her talisman and could feel its pulse urgent and skittish. "We need to get out of here," she blurted. "Right now!"

The tribe ducked into a side passage just as a Saroo patrol entered the cavern. They didn't wait to see what the Saroos wanted. They ran. Amber was in the lead, clutching her amethyst spider, moving with the pulse of the talisman.

11

Into the Pit

The Saroo mine was a maze of passageways. Some areas still sparkled with the few remaining crystals, but most places had been hacked and chopped to the bare black walls. There were no miners to be seen. The equipment stood unused and in disarray. It seemed that all the Saroo energies had been channeled into the service of the Rumblers. This was a stroke of good luck for the Tribe of Star Bear, for they had passed undetected through the twists and turns, arriving at a small access way that led directly into the Pit.

They scrunched themselves into a niche in the wall, disappearing from view just a second before a squad of Saroos bustled by. A zigzag crack that ran from floor-to-ceiling was pitted with chinks that made perfect peep holes into the main pit area. The tribe knotted themselves together and pressed their faces against the peep holes.

They watched as the squad of Saroos presented themselves at the gateway to the Pit of Darkness. It was a changing of the guard. The Saroos stomped and scrambled about in well-rehearsed patterns. The sentinels on duty raised and lowered their fire-sticks, then scuffled off in an orderly file. The newly arrived squad took up their positions, with weapons angled out like glowing red spikes. But no sooner had they settled into place, than there arose from the Pit a foul stench. The steady drone of Rumblers clawing their way upward grew louder and louder. The

Saroos hastily shifted aside, making way for the legion of Rumblers that erupted from the Pit. Out they rolled, six abreast, snarling and frothing at the mouth, a steamy trail of greenish slime bubbled in their wake.

The Saroos stood stiff as pokers, eyes propped wide open, jaws clamped tightly shut. Not one among them blinked, or as much as took a breath, until the Rumblers had passed. Then they sucked in the fetid air and slowly moved back into place.

"I don't think we can get in that way," whispered Amber, shaking her head. "It's way too dangerous."

Olli wrapped his tail tightly around himself and curled his front paws into two tight little balls.

"There's got to be a way," said Bohadea stubbornly.

"Indeed," declared the eagle. "There is always a way. We must simply discover what it is."

The Saroo guards abruptly shifted position again. Their arms coiled back and their shoulders hunched up. All weapons swung forward, aiming stiffly ahead. Something was scraping across the floors.

A ghostly wail echoed from the walls, and Bohadea felt an icy hand clench at her heart. Her nose shot up in the air.

Fear!

"Forest people!" she whispered. Her tawny brows knitted together in alarm.

A Rumbler of obvious high rank moved into view. He heaved himself toward the gateway. A cap of dead peacocks crowned his grey oily head and strings of dead rabbits hung like bunting from his torso. Two lines of Saroos moved behind him flanking a column of prisoners. They were *all* bears. Black bears, brown bears, white bears. They were clamped into leg irons and shackled together with chains that dragged heavily along the ground. Their heads hung low and their glazed eyes stared sightlessly ahead. Bohadea slapped one paw to her mouth to keep herself from shouting out, for she instantly recognized the third bear in line. It was Snowberry, her nephew.

Behind the bears was a mobile fire-web, a rectangular criss-cross of sharp red needles of light. It seemed to hum along on a base of swirling red fire that rolled like a single gigantic wheel. At each corner marched a Saroo wielding a heavy wand of red crystal. Limbs of trees were suspended inside it, and clinging to the wilted branches was a jumble of eagles. Bald eagles and golden eagles and even some large hawks. Some of the eagles who had lost their grip or had been jostled off the cracked tree limbs now lay as little hills of grey ash on the web's fiery bottom.

A second fire-web followed the first, this one crammed to overflowing with squirrels of every description. With wide shocked eyes, Olli searched the passing web for familiar faces. But all he could see were limp tails and clumps of fur blurred by the fine mesh of red light.

Suddenly the train of prisoners was halted by the lead Rumbler wearing the cloak of dead rabbits. "MAKE WAY!" he ordered the Saroo sentries, who scrambled as far back as they could from the span of his deadly claws.

"I don't get it," whispered Amber. "Why are they rounding up all the bears and the squirrels?"

As if in answer to her question, the Rumbler spun around to face the wretched column of prisoners. "This is your last opportunity to confess," he roared. "Once you have crossed this threshold, you will have entered the land of the damned. I ask you one final time: WHO AMONG YOU ARE THE ONES KNOWN AS THE TRIBE OF STAR BEAR? REVEAL YOURSELVES NOW, OR YOU WILL ALL DIE BY THE CUT OF A THOUSAND CLAWS!"

An eerie silence descended. Not one of the prisoners stirred, not one spoke a single word.

A horrible shiny-fanged grin spread across the Rumbler's face, then, like melting wax, it dripped away. A deep churning rumble welled up from his innards and exploded with a roar. Green spittle flew like shrapnel through the line of Saroos and prisoners. A sickening yellowish cloud of fumes rolled across the Pit. The Rumbler lashed out at the first bear in the chained row of prisoners. He swung one sword-like claw at her and the bear's body collapsed onto the ground in a lifeless heap. The forest people yowled with terror. The second bear, still chained to the body of the first bear, reared back in horror. The air was split by wails of grief. Snowberry clutched the second bear in his jaws and dragged her as far back from the Rumbler's claws as he could manage.

Amber's fist closed hard on a clump of Bohadea's fur. Bohadea's knees buckled and she went down. Almedon flapped unsteadily pitching to the ground. "NO!" shouted Amber. "NO FEAR! Remember?"

Bohadea scrambled back to her feet. Almedon righted himself.

"Tchip," said Olli.

They peered back out at the gateway, and froze.

The Rumbler had turned his great slobbering head and was looking straight at the place where the tribe had hidden themselves. But his kill had made such a commotion that he simply blinked and dismissed the noise as coming from one of the prisoners. He turned back to the matter at hand. He ripped the chains off the dead bear and stuffed her whole into his filthy gob. He gnashed and gobbled until there was nothing left but a trickle of blood running from one corner of his wet grey mouth.

"THAT," he said, addressing the prisoners with a sneer, "WAS THE LUCKY ONE AMONG YOU." Then he turned and led the column of prisoners into the Pit of Darkness.

The second fire-web rolled by them, and the next section of the prison train came into full view: it was a column of wolves, bound in steel collars and chained four across and twenty deep. As they slumped past, Amber gasped. She nudged Bohadea. "Diansha!" she whispered. "They've got Diansha."

"What do they want with wolves?" hissed Almedon. "There are no wolves among the Tribe of Star Bear."

"Or Saroos," murmured Amber. For at the end of the column came a double line of Saroo rebels. A dozen or so. Their spindly arms bent into an unnatural shape and chained behind their backs. They shambled from side to side, dragging heavy leg irons with them. Amber anxiously scanned their faces, relieved to see that Kog and Radg were not among them. The Saroos guarding these prisoners moved rigidly and silently with their eyes cast down.

"They're rounding up everyone who they suspect might have something to do with us," whispered Bohadea. "But I'll bet they don't actually know very much about us at all. They're going on rumor."

The last of the Saroos disappeared down into the Pit. Once again the sentries repositioned themselves at the gateway.

"Now what?" said Amber.

"Maybe we'd better just go home," whispered Olli.

"We fight!" growled Almedon. "We owe it to all those warriors who have been taken to die in our place."

"But how can we fight them?" asked Amber in a stricken voice.

"With Star Bear's magic," said Bohadea. "Put up your shields of light. Then we go in!"

It was no easy task to clear their minds and think light thoughts after what they had just witnessed. In fact, it took quite a while to raise the protective bubbles. But one by one the brilliant spheres began to glow, and as they pressed in closer to one another, the bubbles overlapped in a flowery play of light.

"Now we must trust in the magic of Star Bear," said Bohadea. "There can be no doubt! No fear!"

"NO FEAR!" Olli whispered fiercely. *No doubt! No fear! No doubt! No fear!*

Almedon clacked his beak twice. "A great warrior flies in the spirit world," he said. "He sees what is invisible to his enemy. He cloaks himself in the feathers of the spirit eagle. For he who is invisible is invincible. That is how we must be."

Bohadea nodded. "We go now," she said. The bear padded out of their hiding place, calm as can be, as if she was strolling from one berry patch to the next.

Almedon pulled himself up to his full height, riding on the bear's back. He opened his wings and held them aloft as a warrior eagle would do when approaching the enemy. His golden bubble blossomed inside Bohadea's ring of white light. Amber kept one hand trailing on Bohadea's back, her violet bubble bobbed half inside the white globe and half out. Olli, too, stood tall and strong and remembered that he was not just any old red squirrel, he was Ollidollinderi. OLLIDOLLINDERI from the Tribe of Star Bear!

The Saroos balked at the bold approach of the spheres of light. The brightness of it made them squint so they could not make out the forms within the bubbles. Some of the Saroos raised their weapons and pointed them straight at the Tribe of Star Bear. Others dropped their fire-sticks to their sides and just stared.

"We are the Tribe of Star Bear," Bohadea announced in a brave clear voice. "We have been summoned by Dreeg, King of the Rumblers. LET US PASS!"

The Saroos stared at them, speechless. They looked from one to the other for direction, and then, to the amazement of the tribe, one of the Saroos moved aside to let them pass. Then another stepped aside, and another, until the path was clear. Some of the fire-sticks were still trained on the spheres of light, but no Saroo made any attempt to block their way.

The Tribe of Star Bear entered the Pit of Darkness. They moved down into the Pit, along the beautiful red crystal stairway that belied the truth of what lay in wait beneath. *No fear!* whispered Bohadea. She did not say it in words, she thought it. And the others heard her speak to them inside their minds.

At the bottom of the grand staircase stood a line of Rumbler sentries. They stared up as the spheres of light glided down toward them. At first, they grunted in confusion. Then one began to snarl, a second raised a giant claw, ready to shear them in half.

The tribe froze in their tracks. "We are the Tribe of Star Bear," announced Bohadea again. Her voice soared across the immense dark cavern. The sentries snarled back. Bohadea continued: "King Dreeg has commanded that we present ourselves, and here we are. Take us to see your king!"

The red eyes of the Rumblers flashed dangerously, a greenish slather drooled from their grey lips as they gnashed their razor-sharp fangs. "KILL THEM!" snapped the sentry at the far left, a claw flashed out at the tribe.

"NO!" roared a deep voice from behind them. The sentries immediately broke formation, scuttling back to make way, bowing and scraping as they went. The towering form of the Mighty Toothed Poobah reared up out of the darkness, flanked by the V-formation of his personal Rumbler guard. There was a new addition to the horrible decaying ornament draped across his chest. Beside the dead bear hung the little figure of Ert, the Saroo bureaucrat formerly in charge of Logistics. Now deceased.

The sight and stink of the Poobah made Bohadea feel faint, but she gathered all her energies inside the bubble of light. *No fear,* whispered the bear, her words rippling inside the minds of the tribe. Their bubbles grew larger and brighter.

"WHAT SORT OF STUPID TRICK IS THIS?" boomed the Mighty Toothed Poobah. His greenish spittle flew at the tribe, fizzing like drops of water in a frying pan as each foul glob hit the spheres of light.

"We are the Tribe of Star Bear," declared Bohadea a third time, her voice rolling like thunder. "We are the Warriors of the Rainbow! We have come to do battle with Dreeg, King of the Rumblers!" As she spoke, Bohadea allowed the bubble of light to fade enough that her bear-shape could be clearly seen by the Mighty Toothed Poobah. The others, following Bohadea's lead, revealed themselves for a brief moment and then raised the light back up, even brighter and stronger than before.

The Mighty Toothed Poobah snorted, his jaws churned, his red eyes seemed to spin inside his monstrous head. He belched a great cloud of putrid fumes, then began to twitch as he unleashed a blood-curdling howl. It seemed infectious, for the other Rumblers began to twitch and howl alongside him. It took a while for the tribe to realize that the hideous creatures were laughing.

The Mighty Toothed Poobah snorted and sputtered and finally he bellowed: "YOU PUFFED UP MORONS! I would dearly love to rip your livers out right on the spot, but I think that King Dreeg will want that fun for himself.

It will make a delightful entertainment," he chortled. "But first, you must show him your little magic trick with the light bulbs. Very cute. Very cute." He shook his enormous head. "OH, and don't forget to give the speech about how you've come to do battle with him." The Mighty Toothed Poobah slathered and snorted and shook with spasms again. "Oh, my, yes! The Warriors of the ... What was it? ... The ah, rainstorm, rain something ..."

"Rainbow, sir," offered one of his personal guards.

"YES! That's it! Warriors of the Rainbow. Don't forget that bit," he snorted at the tribe. A dribble of green goo ran from his cavernous nostrils to the cleft above his fanged mouth. "Come along, then," he gestured expansively with one huge snapping claw. He spun around and led his entourage deeper into the Pit. The Tribe of Star Bear stepped forward and were immediately surrounded by Rumbler sentries.

Looming walls of black crystal glistened in the darkness; flecks of red light burned deep within and crackled like sparks from a midnight campfire. The space overhead was as wide and open as a starless night. The ground underfoot was worn flat from the eternal pacing of Rumblers. The stench was beyond the ordinary sense of smell—even the spirits would have shrunk back from such a strong scent of evil. The air hummed with the drone of countless Rumblers, and the distant cries of trapped forest people spun like dust in the thick, dank air.

The tribe's spheres of light had begun to waver, to thin out. *No fear,* chanted Bohadea. *No fear,* the others repeated, until the light began to shine brightly again.

The further they traveled into the Pit, the thicker and more frantic became the Rumbler traffic, the louder the cries of the captives. Bohadea did not allow herself to wonder what was being done to them. She did not let herself think about what might happen when they arrived at the throne of King Dreeg.

The tribe had to move very fast to keep up with the Rumblers, so they were almost relieved when the Mighty Toothed Poobah stopped short at a crystal gateway made of enormous slabs of black obsidian. The doors were flanked by a pair of Rumbler gargoyles, each sculpted with huge wings like those of airplanes rather than birds. Each sleek black door held a carved knob of red crystal cut in the shape of a Saroo skull. The Mighty Toothed Poobah grasped them in his deadly claws, and flung the doors open onto the throne room of King Dreeg. The Poobah turned back and sneered at the Tribe of Star Bear. Greenish slime bubbled up at the corners of his cracked grey lips. "Showtime!" he hissed.

The mountainous form of King Dreeg squatted on a massive throne cut from the finest black obsidian and studded with red crystals carved in the shape of Rumbler eyes, making the throne appear as if an army of Rumblers kept watch beneath their king. Shredded tree branches, discarded limbs, and the bones of forest people were littered around the throne and at the king's feet. At long trenches that radiated like wheel spokes out from the throne, the Mighty Poobahs feasted on the remains of the product that had been trekked back from the forest.

The dark crystal walls soared upward, pitted and ancient. Wide ramps led to cells that were sealed off with fire-webs where wolves, eagles, squirrels, and rebel Saroos were caged. Saroo guards lined the ramps, still as stones, and looking as oddly out of place as mushrooms on desert rock. Several other Saroos were leading a column of chained bears, including Snowberry, onto the platform that led to the throne of King Dreeg. But the sight of the beautiful colored spheres drifting in behind the Mighty Toothed Poobah stopped them in their tracks.

King Dreeg's head swung toward the Mighty Toothed Poobah. "WHAT IS THE MEANING OF THIS INTRUSION?" his voice boomed across the Pit, his red eyes pulsed with venom. "WE WERE ABOUT TO BEGIN THE INQUISITION!"

"Your Incredibly Awesome Immenseness," croaked the Mighty Toothed Poobah. He swept his monstrous claws to his sides as if in a bow, and then clacked them three times in the air. His personal guard and the sentries that surrounded the Tribe of Star Bear all did the same.

"I have delivered to Your Most Superb Immenseness," said the Mighty Toothed Poobah, "the Tribe of Star Bear!"

A shocked gasp swept through the cells. A lone wolf howled her despair, for if the Tribe of Star Bear had been captured, then all was lost. But when Snowberry looked into the spheres of colored light, his eyes widened and a small smile nipped at the corners of his mouth, as if he had understood something that the others had not.

"THIS HAD BETTER NOT BE ONE OF YOUR DUMB JOKES MIGHTY TOOTHED!" swore the King.

"Absolutely not, Your Immenseness!" The Poobah again clacked his claws three times in the air. A bubble of green snot popped from one of his nostrils and ran down his face. "They have already confessed, Your Immenseness. And I sincerely hope that Your Incredibly Superb Majesty will find a great amusement in the interrogation of these tricksters and terrorists." The Poobah scraped the ground once with his lower jaw and then sidled off to join the other Poobahs at the feeding trench directly to the right of the throne. The sentries and guards scuttled back against the walls, leaving the Tribe of Star Bear glowing brightly in full view of King Dreeg.

The king gestured at the Saroos who had led the procession of chained bears to the throne. "In that case," he said, "feed these things to the Poobah. It is his just reward."

"NO!" commanded Bohadea. She strode forward with her tribe, taking a stand right beside the armed Saroos and their chained prisoners. The Saroos began backing away, but the bears stood their ground.

"We are the Tribe of Star Bear, guardians of the forest," said Bohadea. "You have destroyed our homes and killed our people. You moved through our lands taking everything and leaving nothing behind. You have dishonored the spirits of the forest. You have angered Star Bear and Sun Eagle. You are not welcome in our world."

"Is that a fact!" snorted the king. He leaned his great bulk forward. A crown of obsidian spikes tottered on his head. His huge gnarled claws clutched at two globes of red crystal that sat at the tips of the armrests like enormous eyeballs on their stalks. "And this is your excuse for sabotaging my operations on the surface?" King Dreeg pointed one razor-like claw at the tribe in accusation.

"We make no excuses to the King of the Rumblers!" growled Almedon. "You are the one who stands accused."

"Yeah," squeaked Olli. "You're the nut worm."

King Dreeg leaned even further forward, his red eyes shot sparks of rage, a green froth bubbled around his fangs. "DO NOT PLAY GAMES WITH THE KING!" He twisted his outstretched claw in a deadly gesture, as if snapping the neck of some invisible prey. "UNMASK YOURSELVES, INFIDELS, OR I WILL TEAR OUT YOUR HEARTS AND SHOVE THEM DOWN YOUR THROATS."

"You see!" said Amber, her fists plunked down on her hips. "That's exactly the problem. You have one solution for everything: kill, kill, kill."

King Dreeg could see the violet sphere grow broader, and it seemed to emit a strange flowery fragrance as the girl spoke. The effect was irritating to the king, like a mosquito buzzing in his ear. He rose from his throne, a towering mass of grey flesh, shiny and fossilized like the body of some gigantic insect. The stink of the king's sudden movement washed across the length and breadth of the cavern. He wiped one huge claw across his face, splattering glops of green gunk from his nostrils across the row of Poobahs to his right.

"I SAID: UNMASK YOURSELVES!" roared the king.

Bohadea sent a thought-ball to the tribe: *Not here,* she said. *Fly up to where the king cannot reach you, then drop your shields.*

Three spheres floated up into the air like a fountain of coloured lights. The king's jaw hardened. He clenched and unclenched his claws, drawing an ooze of thick dark blood from his own grey flesh.

Near the ceiling were ledges and outcroppings of basalt, molten lava turned to rock. It was as if the cavern had once sat in the very heart of a volcano. Hot lava had bubbled through the cracks and crevices and then cooled. In some places it had dripped down the walls to form spires, or cones where it had dripped right to the floor. Almedon chose the highest ledge he could find, to the left of the king's throne. He folded his wings back, then lowered his golden shield. There was a chorus of ooohs and aaaws from the prisoners as his eagle shape was revealed.

Olli found a very tall spire at the opposite side of the cavern and perched himself on its very tip. When the tiny silvery pink light winked out, there were gasps of amazement from all who knew that squirrels could not fly.

Amber flew a full circuit of the cavern before choosing the top of a basalt cone stacked against the black crystal wall near the grand entrance to the throne room. It was not the highest or the safest place she might have chosen, but it was as near as she could get to Bohadea without being in striking range of the Rumblers. All eyes followed the violet bubble as it settled at the top of the cone. A moment later, there stood a young human in dreadlocks and war paint, legs solidly in place, arms akimbo. Even some of the Saroos were shocked enough to gasp at the sight of the small bold figure.

Bohadea allowed herself one proud glance at the girl. The sphere of white light faded from around the bear, and there she stood—a simple Medicine Bear—in front of the mighty King Dreeg.

Dreeg's face twisted with malice. "Very clever," he congratulated Bohadea. "So you think you can outsmart the King of the Rumblers?"

There was a clacking of claws and a rumble of snorts and snarls from the Poobah trenches. The Saroo guards nearest the throne who had been guarding the bears retreated further back toward the ramps. The chained bears shuffled bravely around Bohadea, forming a semi circle behind her.

Bohadea plucked a spike of pure white crystal from the willow bark strands of her Medicine Bear necklace. With a steady paw, she etched a circle in the ground in front of King Dreeg. Inside the circle she drew a six-pointed star. The symbol glowed on the smooth dark ground and Bohadea stepped into its center.

"In the name of Star Bear, I order the Rumblers back into the Pit of Darkness," she said, looking straight into the raging red eyes of the Rumbler king.

"All right, that's IT!" droned the king. "I'VE HAD ENOUGH OF THIS CRAP. YOU'RE DEAD MEAT! ALL OF YOU!" The Poobahs beat their claws against the

trenches in approval. King Dreeg cast his eyes from
Almedon to Amber to Olli, then lashed out with one deadly swipe, striking at Bohadea's middle. But the symbol
Bohadea had drawn in the earth sprang to life. The star
rose up and spun around her, its dazzling points whirling
like blades of light. And, the king took his deadly aim and
struck, his arm was sheared right off. Thick dark blood,
like tar, spurted from the wound and the king howled with
rage. He clutched at his wounded shoulder, staggered
back, and slumped onto his throne.

The Rumbler guards roared in fury and rushed to the
attack. The shackled bears turned bravely to face them,
but Bohadea could see that they would be shredded to
bits. "Bears can fly!" she cried out. She clutched at her
spike of white crystal, madly drawing spirals in the air.
Bears can fly!

The spirals of white light danced through the air winding around the bears. Chains and shackles sparked and
hissed, falling away like sparklers. Snowberry was first to
lift off the ground, and as soon as the others saw it was
possible, they followed. The Rumblers swiped and snarled
after them, but the bears were airborne, burly arms flapping, stocky legs paddling, up, up, and out of reach.

Too big to land on the ledges and spires, the bears
chose instead the ramps that snaked up the sides of the Pit
to the webbed cells. The Saroo guards, the very ones who
had delivered the prisoners to the Pit of Darkness, staggered back with wide shocked eyes as the bears plunked
down between them. Some trained their weapons on the
bears, while others dropped their weapons entirely and
raised their pink gangly arms in surrender. The prisoners
shrieked with delight. Wolves howled, and eagles and
squirrels filled the air with their war cries as the Poobahs
scuttled from the trenches.

King Dreeg raised his huge head and turned to the Saroo guards at the ramps. His face was slimed with green drool, his fangs were barred. "SHOOT THEM!" he roared. The Rumbler Poobahs halted in their tracks, their red eyes pulsed with the promise of vengeance as they hissed at the Saroos: "Shoot! Shoot!"

From the highest ledge, Almedon's voice soared across the cavern: "AGIDA!"

"Agida!" shouted the Saroo rebels from inside their cells.

"Shoot!" hissed the Poobahs.

"AGIDA!"

"SHOOT!"

The Saroo guards seemed frozen, eyes panicky, hands locked onto their weapons. One of the guards grimaced as though a tug-of-war was being played inside his head. He raised his red crystal wand. "Agida!" he screamed as he aimed straight at King Dreeg, and fired.

He missed!

The Poobahs roared in fury. Another Saroo guard raised his wand and fired back at the rebel Saroo, killing him on the spot.

Screams shattered the air. A red laser beam streaked toward the second Saroo guard; he clutched at this chest and toppled over. The Saroos fell upon each other, scrambling for control of the weapons. The bears fell into the fray, fighting with the rebels. One of the guards aimed her wand at the blazing criss-cross of a fire-web. It hissed and spit, then fizzled out. Prisoners spilled from the cell and pounced into combat using tooth and claw, talon and beak. Some formed a protective ring around the Saroo who had freed them, for she was moving rapidly from cell to cell, dismantling fire-webs. Diansha leapt free of the webbing and led the Quelicots into a final lethal assault against the pro-Rumbler forces.

At ground level, the Mighty Toothed Poobah was directing operations. None of the Saroos within reach of the Rumblers dared to desert so they were pressed into service, shooting up at the ramps at bears and wolves and rebel Saroos. They were ordered to shoot down Almedon and Olli, too, but both of them had chosen perches from which they could retreat back into the basalt outcropping. They were unscathed.

Amber was not as fortunate. She had selected an unprotected base. She was much too exposed at the tip of that basalt cone. And because she had been watching the action up on the ramps, she hadn't noticed the Rumblers and Saroos approaching from below. "I WANT IT ALIVE!" shouted the Mighty Toothed Poobah. One immense claw raked at the stones beneath Amber's feet. "GET IT DOWN!" he shrieked at the squad of trembling Saroos.

The protective star still spun around Bohadea, but she had kept one eye on King Dreeg and the other on the ramps. By the time she turned to check on Amber, the Saroos were already half way up the cone. "AMBURRR!" shouted the bear. "PUT UP YOUR BUBBLE! PUT UP YOUR SHIELD! FLY! FLY!"

Amber saw the Saroos crawling up toward her, weapons at the ready, Rumblers seething and snarling below. She could hear Bohadea's voice coaching her, but it seemed such a long way away, like in a dream. Her mind froze, knotted with terror. *No fear! No fear!* But she couldn't make the fear go away. She was caught firmly in its grip. Her heart thundered in her ears. Amber tried to raise the bubble of light, but it wouldn't come. The fear had solidified like a lump of cement in her gut, blocking the flow.

She yelped in terror as the Saroos surrounded her and roughly dragged her down the basalt cone, bumping and bruising her along the way. She was cuffed and whacked, then thrown like a sack of turnips at the feet of the Mighty Toothed Poobah. Six fire-sticks were aimed at her head. The Poobah threw back his head and yowled his victory, then hooked two claws into the squirming girl, careful not to damage the goods. He lifted her up high above his head and roared. Amber fell limp, like a mouse in the jaws of a cat.

"HMMMMEH," warbled the Mighty Toothed Poobah, holding his prize for everyone to see. He scraped over to the throne of King Dreeg, nodding at Bohadea as he passed, but giving her spinning star a wide berth. Its light was getting weaker, the Poobah noticed.

"Your Most Superb Immenseness," the oily-tongued Poobah said to the king. "I present to you one of the terrorists responsible for your terrible injury."

King Dreeg lifted his one blood-drenched claw from the gaping hole where his arm used to be and shifted forward in his throne. Slowly he plucked the girl from the Mighty Toothed Poobah's claws and held her up in front of his twisted face. "This one, I will savor," he said.

"LET HER GO!" demanded Bohadea. "IN THE NAME OF STAR BEAR, RELEASE HER!"

"Or what?" growled the king. "You'll slice off my other arm?"

Bohadea pointed her white crystal spike at Amber and drew frantic spirals in the air. But her mind was clogged with fear for the girl and nothing happened. Nothing at all.

A spasm shook the king's immense grey body. His red eyes rolled up into his head, his mouth snaked and squirmed as a sound rumbled up from his innards and exploded into a fearsome roar of laughter. A jet of black blood pulsed from the hole in his shoulder. It made him snarl with pain. "I guess not," he jeered at the bear. "I guess you'll just have to stand there and listen to your little friend here scream herself to death. I think I'll begin with the legs." King Dreeg lifted Amber up above his face and then began to lower her into the foul stinking pit that was his mouth.

Amber's scream sliced through the air.

"OH NO NO NO!" screeched Olli, standing out in full view at the top of his spire.

"Shoot it down," the Mighty Toothed Poobah hissed at the Saroo by his side.

"YOU PUNY LOUSY ITSY-BITSY ROTTEN STINKY SLIMY DIRTY OLD NUT WORM!" Olli cursed the king.

The Saroo raised his weapon and aimed.

Without thinking, Olli tore the silver amulet from his throat and hurled it straight at King Dreeg. The silver acorn streaked toward its target like a bullet, hitting the king right between the eyes in an explosion of white light. The acorn bounced off and rolled across the floor.

King Dreeg's eyes popped out, his jaw dropped to his chest. His claw snapped apart and Amber tumbled to the floor. Bohadea swiped at the girl and pulled her limp form inside the spinning star.

A shot of red fire streaked toward Olli.

The king's body began to wriggle and writhe as if possessed by a billion tiny squiggling worms. "NOOOOOO!" screamed the King of the Rumblers. His body slumped. It twisted and turned and pitched and heaved. It churned and boiled and gurgled. He was disintegrating in front of their eyes. Rotting apart. He was shrinking. Shrinking. Wasting away. Squirming into oblivion. Getting tinier and tinier and tinier.

The other Rumblers and Saroos backed away in horror.

Amber picked herself up off the ground and clung to Bohadea.

The king had become puny. Itsy-bitsy. Rotten. Slimy. Tinier and tinier until there was nothing left but one teenie weenie little nut worm squiggling by itself on the seat of the enormous throne of the Rumbler king.

Amber clutched at her talisman. The amethyst spider was pulsing, pounding, stronger than it had ever been before. She could feel it struggling to free itself from her grip. She opened her hand and the purple spider blinked up at her with shiny black eyes. She felt it scuttle in her hand. *I am Grandmother Spider,* it whispered in her mind. *Set me free!* With shaking fingers, Amber freed the amethyst spider from its silver chain and gently placed it on the ground.

Leaving a violet trail of light behind it, the spider scurried across the floor and up the throne of King Dreeg. They heard one tiny high pitched squeal as the spider devoured the nut worm who had been king. The spider scurried back down the throne, across the floor and stood toe to toe with Amber. She leaned over and lifted the spider back into her hand. It stood there unmoving, but for its soft gentle pulse—the same as before. Except for a tiny silvery squiggle embedded in its crystal violet belly. Amber strung the talisman back onto her silver chain.

"You Rumblers are ALL a bunch of puny little nut worms," came Olli's tiny voice from high atop the basalt spire. He was holding both little paws over a wound in his belly. "I've been shot," he said sleepily, then he pitched over sideways and fell through the air. Almedon swept off his ledge and dove sharply, catching Olli in mid-air.

A clear white light began to radiate from Olli's acorn as it lay on the ground by King Dreeg's throne. It carried a sound with it. A single note that set the air humming. The aura grew larger and larger. It reached out and touched the legs of the Mighty Toothed Poobah. He leapt back in disgust, but the light only grew larger. It enveloped the

Mighty Toothed Poobah and two of the Rumblers closest to him. Several Saroos were caught in the light as well, but it seemed to have no effect on them. The Rumblers, however, reacted just as King Dreeg had. They began to writhe and squirm. They screeched in horror as their bodies pitched and churned and boiled until there was nothing left but three puny little nut worms wriggling on the floor.

The light grew larger and larger, it hummed louder and louder, filling the entire throne room. All the Rumblers squiggled and squirmed. They frothed and bubbled and boiled. One after the other they disintegrated into teeny whitish worms. The loyal Saroos watched the demise of their masters with open-mouthed shock, then spun on their heels and raced for the great obsidian doors of the throne room. They forced the great slabs apart and rushed for the stairs, treading on the squishy little worms that wriggled underfoot.

The light filled the Pit of Darkness. It radiated out into Red City, across the redlands, into the Silver Desert. It followed the Rumbler highways across the Shadowlands, the hills, and the forests. And in every place that the white light sang, Rumblers fell. The earth became very still, and as the last Rumbler winked out of existence, it breathed a great sigh of relief.

Olli hung limply in Almedon's talons. Amber reached up her arms as the eagle coasted in. Tears streaked down her face. "Oh, Olli," she wept. "Please don't die." Her fingers strained toward the body of the little red squirrel. Almedon gently dropped him into Amber's waiting hands. She cradled him close to her heart, her dreadlocks falling like a curtain across his small lifeless body. Her tears splashed like raindrops onto his furry coat.

Bohadea tore the pouch of star dust from her Medicine Bear necklace. She sprinkled it on Olli's wound, and began to chant. The star around her spun a soft white light.

Almedon chanted with Bohadea, calling on the power of the Sun Eagle to return the light to the squirrel. Amber sang too. She copied the song of Olli's magical acorn, and as she sang, the light began to return, withdrawing from the earth, and sinking back into the silver talisman that lay on the floor. And as the last droplet of light winked from the acorn, a new light sparked inside of Olli.

The little squirrel stirred in Amber's hands. "He's alive!" cried Amber, tears of joy streaming down her face. She sniffed and blinked, watching through blurry eyes as Olli's wound knitted itself together.

The squirrel coughed and gasped, then propped himself up on his elbows. "I think I'm dead!" he crowed.

With prisoners freed and weapons discarded, the forest people and rebel Saroos streamed down from the ramps. They gathered around the Tribe of Star Bear and cheered Olli on. He blinked up in confusion.

"You're alive!" cried Amber happily, planting a big wet kiss on the top of Olli's head.

"But I saw angels!" he argued, flipping himself up on all fours. "I definitely saw angels!"

"Ollidollinderi," shouted a red squirrel from the crowd. It was Tullywanooli. Tully leapt straight at Olli, bowling him over with a hug. Both squirrels went tumbling to the floor, landing in two tangled puffs of fur.

"Tumbling Puffball," nodded Olli.

Amber scooped both squirrels up off the ground, boosting one up on each shoulder.

A golden cat with a white-tipped tail arched his back and rubbed up against Amber's leg. "Rum tum tiddle, no time to diddle," he purred.

Amber did not pause to marvel at Pudd Wudd's sudden appearance. "Something's up," she said.

"He's telling us that we'd better get out of here right now," said Almedon. And as he spoke, the walls of the Pit began to rumble.

"Look!" barked Diansha. She gestured to one of the basalt spires where red hot molten lava trickled over the grey stones. It was seeping in through all the faults that bore the basalt rock. It had even begun to creep in through the open obsidian slabs, blocking off the only avenue of escape.

"We're trapped!" cried one of the rebel Saroos.

"No," said Bohadea. "No, we're not! Everybody stay calm." Her eyes caught the feathery white tip of Pudd Wudd's tail as he disappeared into the crowd.

Rise ... on the wings ... of ...

Bohadea glanced down at the pearly white feather of the firebird that hung from her Medicine Bear necklace. Her nose pointed up to the dark yawning ceiling, and in her mind's eye she imagined the firebird's radiant wings, bright and beautiful and broad enough to take everyone up to the stars. She began to sing a bearsong, her voice rising upward.

A rumble shook at the very core of the earth, but still Bohadea sang, her eyes fixed on the ceiling. Others began to gather around her, eyes turned upward to see what mesmerized the bear. Amber clapped her hands together—to the beat of Istarna's drum. Almedon clacked his beak. Olli speedily retrieved two hazelnut shells and tapped out the rhythm of the spirit drums. The sacred music became visible as a thin spiral of white light that swirled upward. The star around Bohadea spun faster and its points reached out to enclose the tribe.

A wall at the back of the throne room shifted and crumbled. There were gasps of fright, but Diansha pressed in closer to the Tribe of Star Bear and raised her voice in song. Other wolves joined her, and as they did the spiral became a bright stream of light, swirling faster and faster. The light was reflected on the ceiling like sunshine playing on the water of a shallow pool. Suddenly, it broke into a rainbow kaleidoscope of patterns that flowed from one to the next. And the points of Bohadea's star stretched out further still.

Streams of molten lava crept in closer. Bohadea could feel the heat rising. The bodies of the warriors pressed in tighter and tighter. More and more voices were raised in song. The ground heaved and cracked around them. But still they made music, their eyes trained on the patterns of light that burned in the darkness above them.

The six points of the star reached out to embrace all the Warriors of the Rainbow. And when the last voice—the voice of one shy rebel Saroo—flowed into the spiral of light, the earth stood still. It seemed as if the whole of the universe had abruptly stopped. Time ceased to exist. Each individual warrior seemed to expand, to merge, to blend, one with the other.

Then the earth shifted. A great crack split the Pit of Darkness in two. The magical light of in-between time—when sun and moon and stars all shine at once—poured in from above.

The six-pointed star spun so fast that it no longer looked like a star. Instead, it looked like a flying saucer made of translucent white light. It began to lift off, carrying with it all the warriors. Up past the surface they went, into the air, higher and higher, until they were suspended so far above the earth that they could see it floating like a turquoise jewel in the indigo velvet of the universe.

Hovering high above the earth, they watched as hot molten lava spewed up from the Pit of Darkness. Rocks and fire showered the redlands of the Saroos, burying Red

City, burying the Silver Desert, even burying parts of the Shadowlands. It spewed and spewed until a mountain of molten rock, twelve thousand feet high, covered the place where the Pit had once been.

Then all was still again.

12

The Dawning

The saucer of light gently lowered the warriors, setting them down on the mountaintop. It slowed its spin, shrinking and fading until there was nothing left but a simple drawing of a six-pointed-star inscribed in a circle around the feet of a bear. Bohadea stepped out of the circle.

An icy wind kicked up and howled around the mountain. Fat snowflakes swirled at the top of the red peak. The Warriors of the Rainbow shivered in the cold.

"Our city has been destroyed," sighed one of the Saroos.

"You will come back to the forest and live with us," said Bohadea.

The Saroo nodded, but a silvery tear ran down her pink cheek. "It didn't have to be this way," she shook her head sadly. "If only they had listened."

"Can we go home now?" Olli asked, his ears pricked up.

"Home," sighed Bohadea. Her black nose wiggled happily at the thought of blueberries and honey, and a nice long mud bath in the dip at Hog's Hollow.

Home! Amber blinked at the strangeness of the word. At the strangeness of the world. From the top of Red Mountain she could see miles and miles of red volcanic rock edged by a wide ribbon of dark Shadowlands. Beyond that lay the rich greens and blues of the forest. But home? Home was someplace else. A million miles away. Her old life seemed almost like a dream now. "I wonder if I'll get home, too."

"Of course you will, Amburrr," said Bohadea. She nudged the girl affectionately. "Almedon will fly around and look for your homeplace when we get back to the forest. Won't you, Almedon?" She stared down the eagle.

"Huh," said Almedon. "Oh, yes, I can do that."

"It's freezing up here," complained one of the Saroos, his spindly arms wrapped around the thin cover of his pink fur.

"I guess we'd better get going then," said Bohadea. "It's a long way home."

It took them all morning to climb down the mountain, picking their way carefully around rock slides and loosely piled lava. In some places geysers of steam shot up into the air so the footing was hot and slippery. In other places, the cold had slicked the rocks with ice, or heavy drifts of snow. It was slow going. Many of the squirrels had taken to the backs of bears and wolves and Saroos to avoid the treacherous ground.

Eagles and hawks circled overhead, shadowing the downward passage of the tribes. By mid-day most of the birds had headed out across the Shadowlands and back to the forest. A few eagles still flew scouting missions across the debris-strewn fields that had once been the redlands, but by nightfall Almedon was alone.

They camped in a dark barren place where the last fingers of volcanic rock had reached into the ruined Shadowlands. It was soundless there, as if parts of the Silver Desert had lingered on. And although they slept peacefully, guarded by an unseen ring of forest spirits, they were glad to greet the soft pink light of another dawn.

As they set out across the bleak Shadowlands, a heavy stillness settled over the returning warrior tribes, for many of them had once lived in this dark lifeless desert. Now they were nomads who would wander the surviving forests, searching for lost loved ones and searching for a new place to call home.

As the morning shadows withdrew from the growing heat of the day, they marched on, hoping that over the next crest, or the one after that, would be a glimpse of green. But the endless grid of blackened stumps ran on and on across the dark pocked earth, broken only by the criss-cross of Rumbler trails.

Sun Eagle was already arcing toward the western horizon when Almedon sounded a loud trumpeting call from above. "Visitors!" he called excitedly. He dove into the band of weary travelers, then sharply raised his beak, clapped his wings against his sides, and bulleted back up into the sky. "Visitors from the forest!"

There was a milling about and the exchange of curious looks. Some of the warrior people began to lope toward the next crest of a hill, and soon they were all galloping, the wolves in the lead, Amber and the two-legged Saroos trailing at the rear.

"Look!" cried Diansha. "They've come to meet us!"

By the time the last of the stragglers made it to the top of the hill, Diansha was already halfway across the open space between the warriors and a great throng of approaching forest people. A welcoming party!

In the distance, a cool ribbon of green forest stretched across the horizon. Clouds of birds from every tribe winged toward them, led by the warrior hawks and eagles. On foot came forest people of every sort: deer and raccoons, coyotes and foxes, groundhogs and chipmunks, and bears and cats. They bore victory wreaths woven with laurel leaves and bunchberries. The birds carried sprays of wildflowers in their beaks.

Two little wolf pups raced toward Diansha, yapping and kicking up a spray of fine black dust. Diansha stopped short, forepaws stretched forward, rear end up in the air, tail wagging the whole of her back end. The pups jumped up on her, yelped with joy, and wrestled her to the ground. Quelicot wolves broke from both the welcoming party and the warrior group, racing toward one another, swirling around Diansha and her pups, dancing, sniffing, and licking.

Snowberry brushed up against Bohadea's side. They looked into each other's eyes, for they were the survivors, the only two left of their family. Bohadea nuzzled her nephew behind his ear. He nudged her with his nose. Amber pressed up against Bohadea's other side and the bear nuzzled the girl as if she were a cub.

The welcoming party surged into the joyful Quelicot reunion, sweeping them up and taking them back toward the crest of the blackened hill where many warriors still stood waiting. Bohadea watched them approach from her place in the center, flanked by Amber and Olli on the one side, Snowberry and Tullywanooli on the other. The warrior tribes stretched across the hilltop in both directions, ringed in a halo of coloured lights.

Clouds of birds began to circle the warriors. Wildflowers showered down on them, drifting from the sky like a riot of colorful snowflakes. The birds spiraled around the little hill and sang a song so enchanting that it reminded the tribe of the singing river of light in Istarna's cave. It was the music of angels.

Those on foot approached timidly, scattering themselves across the hillside. There was no leader or spokesperson, just one big hodgepodge of forest people that pressed up the hill and swirled around the warriors. Laurel wreaths were ceremonially laid on the warriors as crowns, although some were so big they had to be made into necklaces, and others so small they could only be bracelets.

The Saroos, too, were welcomed and greeted as kin-folk, for already their kind were numbered among the forest people. Kog and Radg stood together in front of the Tribe of Star Bear. Kog bowed before she laid a wreath on Bohadea's head, as did Radg, who reached with trembling arms to lay a wreath among the tangle of Amber's dreadlocks.

Olli was swamped by red squirrels who chittered and giggled and practically buried him under a huge heap of leaves and berries.

Almedon was respectfully approached by a beautiful golden eagle whose wreath was studded with dandelions, just like the ones that grew in his home valley. She fluffed up her feathers, then laid the wreath on his head with her beak. Almedon lowered his eyes, then blinked up at her. She was bright as a ray of sunshine, he thought.

It was a jolly, noisy celebration. A bearsong fête and a squirrel jamboree all jumbled together. And as they hugged and wagged and sniffed and sang, little bubbles of light began to wink on around each and every forest person. The lights grew and the colors merged with those of the warriors, radiating up into the sky and across the Shadowlands, creating a perfect gigantic rainbow.

Almedon was circling high above the tribes when the ribbons of bright colour swept by him. A current of golden light danced at Almedon's feet, then caught up the diamond teardrop. Before he realized what had happened, the talisman slipped from his talon and fell.

Almedon dived after it, distressed at the loss. *Let it go,* Ledonnia spoke inside his mind. *Let go of the past. Let go of your sorrow. Live in joy, and you shall set us both free.* Almedon lost his focus and the diamond talisman fell. Bohadea looked up just as the eagle pulled out of the dive. The diamond plunged earthward, leaving a trail of golden light. It fell into one of the gouges in the earth that had been a Rumbler trail, and when it touched the dead black soil it winked back into its liquid form—a single eagle tear.

The tear trickled across the earth and, as it did, it grew and grew from a trickle to a stream to a river. It was as if all the tears in the world had come to this withered dead place to bring it new life. The waters rolled and churned. They moved from one trench to the next, filling the Rumbler trails with clear blue water. They curved and flowed, creating lakes and rivers that sparkled like a jeweled lattice across the Shadowlands. The forest people watched with amazement as the dead lands suddenly ran with life.

Almedon coasted down to the tribe. "Did you see that?" he asked, his brown eyes wide with surprise.

"We sure did," said Bohadea, her voice bubbling with excitement. She tugged at her pouch of star dust, scooped a little onto one claw, then flicked it onto the ground. At once the earth began to shimmer with a lime-green light. Tiny shoots curled up from the place where the star dust had fallen, creating new plants that reached up to the Sun Eagle and unfurled their wee green leaves.

"Wow," said Amber. "You can even heal the earth with that stuff."

"Can I throw some? Can I throw some?" begged Olli, jumping up and down on Amber's shoulder.

Bohadea scooped a tiny heap of star dust into Olli's outstretched paws and the squirrel tossed it in a wide dramatic swirl. The star dust twinkled and danced in the air. As the tiny specs touched down, they shimmered with the lime-green light, then the earth sprang to life again.

"Almedon," said Bohadea, "gather all the birds. I will give a bit of star dust to each one of them. Then they must fly to every corner of the Shadowlands and drop it on the ground." She turned to Amber and Olli: "You two organize the ground people. Everyone must help."

Bohadea scooped and scooped. She filled every beak and every paw with star dust and still the pouch brimmed full. To each Saroo, she gave an extra measure, for their long spindly paws could be curled into long deep wells that were well-suited to carrying the healing dust a long distance away. Kog and Radg each touched the tip of their noses to Bohadea's before taking their leave, and though they did not speak of the future, it was understood that they would meet again.

Tullywanooli and Snowberry left together, as Tully had been invited to move into a beech tree that Snowberry knew of, not too far away from Blueberry Hill, where he denned each winter.

And so the forest people fanned out to every nook and cranny of the ruined lands. They spread the star dust and brought new life to every place they touched. Green things grew. Waters flowed. Bugs and butterflies played in the tender new shoots.

Sun Eagle was diving over the western horizon by the time the last of the forest folk wandered out into the green flecked Shadowlands with a pawful of star dust. And then there stood only the four. The Tribe of Star Bear. They camped right on that hillside for the night, chattering happily until the fires of Star Bear lit up the night sky, and then one by one, they fell into a deep dreamless sleep.

Amber was the first to awake the next morning. Olli mumbled something in his sleep and she nudged him closer to Bohadea, then she sat herself up on a lush green carpet of brand new grasses and wildflowers. She yawned and blinked up at a cloudless violet sky. The green meadows shimmered in the morning light. The dew sparkled like a billion tiny stars winking up from the grass tips.

But there was something very odd about it. It was the pattern of the sparkles. They radiated out in long straight lines from the place where they had slept. Like a spider's web! And at each place where the strands crossed there had sprung up a tiny sapling—the future oaks and beeches and pines of a brand new forest.

Amber caught the amethyst spider between her fingers. She felt it twitch in her hand and her fingers sprang open. There in the middle of her palm sat the large purple spider. A real live one! And the silver strand around her neck had turned into the fine gossamer thread of a spider's web. Part of the girl wanted to squeal in fright, but the purple spider was so vibrant and bright, that Amber merely stared at her, mesmerized.

Set me free, said Grandmother Spider. *I have much weaving to do.*

Amber gently placed the purple spider on the ground and watched as she scuttled off into the forest grasses and disappeared. Amber looked at the grass for a long time, hoping to catch one last glimpse of her beautiful amethyst talisman. But the spider was gone.

She gingerly picked her way down the hillside, careful not to tread on any of the fragile little saplings that had sprung up in Grandmother Spider's web. She made her way to a new stream that flowed in an old Rumbler track. Amber knelt at the stream's edge and scooped up the crystal clear water, then sipped it from her hands. It was the most delicious liquid she had ever drunk. She drank again and again, savoring the cool clean taste.

The surface of the water danced beneath her hands, and just beyond that she caught a reflected image of herself. It startled her. She looked like a Raggedy Ann. Her dreadlocks were stuck out in all directions, her face smudged with war paint and dirt. She splashed the water onto her

face and rubbed vigorously. She splashed and rubbed, until
her face was shiny and clean.

Then she removed her raggedy torn clothes, neatly laid
them out on the grass, and leapt into the water. She paddled
and splashed about. She took a deep breath and dived, then
shook out her dreadlocks, sending droplets of water career-
ing out in wild sprays. Joyfully she floated on the surface,
basking in the morning sun. Almedon's shadow sailed across
the water. Amber squinted up into the sky, then reluctantly
paddled back to shore. She was fastening the last strap of her
jumper as Bohadea and Olli padded over to the water's edge.

Bohadea drank her fill then flapped one paw around in
the water. "I don't suppose there are any fish in here yet,"
she said, more to herself than anyone else.

"I'm hungry," said Olli.

"Me, too," said Almedon, landing on the bank next to
Olli.

Olli scrambled up onto Amber's shoulder and frowned
suspiciously at the eagle.

"I think I'd better get back to my campsite now," said
Amber.

Bohadea looked at her, a glint of sadness in her eyes.
"Yes, we promised, didn't we?" She looked at the eagle.
"First things first, Almedon. We must find Amburrr's
homeplace."

"All right," said Almedon. "I'll head back for Lookout
Rock. She can't have come far from there." He turned to
Amber. "What does this homeplace look like?" he asked
the girl.

"A campsite," she said. "A big round tent."

Almedon looked at her blankly.

"You know, like a huge mushroom that three or four full-
size humans can fit into. And it's a sort of mushroom-colour,
too. Right on the shore by the lake. And there are stones set

in a ring for a fire. And a canoe." She paused. Almedon stared. "You know. A boat. A thing that floats in the water. It's made of bark and has pointy ends."

"All right. All right," said Almedon. "I'll go and scout it out. I'll meet you at Lookout Rock."

It was a full day's hike back to Lookout Rock, but they made good time considering all the side trips for nuts and berries and honey and the like. Almedon was waiting, as he had promised, at the very place Amber had first laid eyes on him. He was perched up on the splintered rim of the tall jagged tree trunk by the hazelnut patch, his head tucked under his wing.

"Almedon," called Bohadea, shaking the wobbly trunk.

"What?" snorted Almedon, snapping awake.

"Did you find it?" asked Amber eagerly.

"Find what?" grumbled Almedon.

"My campsite. My homeplace," said Amber, blinking anxiously up at the eagle.

"Oh, that." He shook out his feathers. "Of course, I found it. I'm an eagle. How could I miss it! It's right at the edge of the Cedar Snake Trail by Scitter Lake."

"Why, that's right around the corner from here," said Bohadea. "We could be there in no time at all."

"Now? Can we go there now?" asked Amber. Her eyes flashed wide and blue.

"If you like, Amburrr," said Bohadea. She blinked down at the forest floor as she spoke.

"I don't want you to go," said Olli quietly. "Can't you just stay here, with us?"

Amber looked around at her friends. Her chin dropped and she studied her fingers for a moment. "I think I'd better go," she said in a small voice. "My family will miss me. But you could come home with *me,*" she said, her eyebrows shooting up hopefully.

"What about my tree?" said Olli. "I need my tree."

"It's time," said Bohadea "It's time for all of us to return to our own places in the forest. I will show Amburrr to her lost home."

"I'm coming too," said Olli indignantly.

"So am I," said Almedon.

Amber sniffed, then smiled.

It was no more than a half hour's hike from Lookout Rock to Amber's campsite at Lake Wakimika. As they threaded their way along Cedar Snake Trail, Amber realized that she must have lost the path and then traveled round and round in circles. They traveled without speaking. Olli clung to Amber's dreadlocks, his tail wrapped affectionately around her neck.

The path came out onto a rocky overhang above the beach. From where they stood, Amber could see her tent pitched on the pebbled shore. It was clustered in among several larger ones. There were a number of boats as well. Mainly motorboats. And a seaplane. People bustled about on the beach. *So they were searching for her after all.*

Amber's heart leapt in her chest as she caught sight of a man in a blue plaid shirt crouched over a small cooking fire. His head was bent, his shoulders hunched over as he stirred something in a battered little pot. *Dad!* Amber clapped both hands to her mouth. "That's my father," she told Bohadea, pointing at the man by the fire.

Almedon landed with a flutter in the boughs of an overhanging pine. Bohadea craned her neck to catch a glimpse of the man to whom Amber pointed. She was surprised at the small stature of a full grown human. She'd expected them to be much bigger than that. Bohadea looked back at Amber with liquid brown eyes.

The girl leaned over and kissed the tip of her furry brown nose. "I love you, Bohadea," she told the bear. "I love you all!" she said. Her heart blossomed like a summer rose. She stroked Olli's back, then kissed the tip of his nose. "I'll never, ever, forget you!"

Olli rubbed her nose with his, then leapt into the limbs of a cedar tree. He sent her a thought-ball: *Never, never, never forget!*

Never forget the magic of Star Bear, Bohadea's voice echoed inside her mind. *We are One! Always!*

Go in the light of Sun Eagle, Almedon told her. *Walk the path of the Rainbow Warrior, and you will never be lost again.*

Amber nodded silently. Bohadea nudged her gently and Amber could feel the light of the Medicine Bear fill her up, making her feel strong and powerful. She turned and stepped out into the clearing. She didn't look back.

AGMV
MARQUIS
Québec, Canada
1998